Love of Money

L. A. Taylor

Walker and Company
New York

To Sallie Gouverneur, for her
faith and patience

First published in the United States of America in 1986 by the Walker Publishing Company, Inc.

Published simultaneously in Canada by John Wiley & Sons Canada, Limited, Rexdale, Ontario.

Library of Congress Cataloging-in-Publication Data

Taylor, L. A. (Laurie Aylma), 1939-
  Love of money.

  I. Title.
PS3570.A943L6   1986   813'.54   86-9194
ISBN 0-8027-5654-9

Printed in the United States of America

10 9 8 7 6 5 4 3 2 1

1 May 17

"THAT'S DONE." Clarice Klenk—known to her readers by a quite different name—shook the freshly typed manuscript straight in its box and pressed the lid down with firm, plump fingers. "I've already started my next book, can you believe it?" she exclaimed.

"I believe it." Miss Peck smiled faintly.

"What's the matter, Ethel?" Clarice asked, jerking her head to peer over her reading glasses. "Something wrong with this one, too?"

"No, not at all." Miss Peck looked down at her desk. She wasn't a romance reader, and she really had been out of line making even the few comments she had about her friend's last novel. She hadn't seen any serious flaws in the manuscript Clarice was now bundling into her worn canvas tote bag, really, but, if the previous four were any guide, the whole thing would come winging back for another run through Celie's, or Sharmille's, typewriter within the month, substantially altered. She sighed. "Just a bad day, I guess," she said. "I started out all wrong."

"On a gorgeous day like this? Not like you, Ethel." Clarice, a woman with short, wispy grey hair that gave her the look of a clematis gone to seed, resettled her freckled bulk in what Miss Peck liked to call the client's chair and gazed across the desk, her lips pursed. "It can't be the change. I haven't seen you have a hot flash in months. So what's wrong?"

Fifty years of friendship had long since accustomed Miss Peck to Clarice's sometimes startling directness, and she replied equally frankly, "Oh, I just had a bad dream." She shuddered. "One of those dreadful ones with nothing to see, only a feeling. Like suffocating. Let's not talk about it."

"I'm not surprised," Clarice remarked, leaning forward to rise, now that the problem had turned out to be nothing more exciting than a dream. "If I ran this dumb typing service, I'd feel suffocated, too. The only girl out there with half a brain in her head is Sharmille. That Babs is plain impossible, and as for Celie, I never in my life met anyone who reminded me more of a wet kitten."

"Celie's all right," Miss Peck said, surprised at feeling a kind of protective annoyance. "Just a little disorganized. And Barbra can at least type accurately"—Clarice sniffed; Barbra typed just what she saw on the page and never stopped to think how a word ought to be spelled—"which is more than some I've had could do." Miss Peck stopped and glanced at her office walls, schoolhouse-beige walls looking weary after more than twenty years of surrounding her. "Thank God for Sharmille, though," she murmured.

"There, you see?" Clarice sat back in triumph. "Bored, that's what you are. And no wonder! Who do you spend your days talking to? Wait, I've got it—let's go out for lunch. We'll go to the Nankin. That'll make a nice walk— you can't miss a day like this. I had my tramp around Lake Harriet before I came. It was glorious!" *Glorious* was spoken with the fervor and rounded tones of an evangelist, and was accompanied by an evangelist's gesture.

"The girls—"

"Oh, pooh, the girls. The girls are all grown up and can take care of themselves," Clarice declared, despite her earlier assessment. "So, come on."

Maybe Clarice was right. A little change of pace, a stroll in the bright May sunlight, might do wonders for her glum mood. Half an hour of girl-talk and some good Chinese food . . .

"Well, all right. You've talked me into it." Miss Peck

2

tapped stiffened fingers against the edge of her desk and stood up. "Maybe I'll stop at Dayton's on my way back and pick up a new pair of gloves. The ones I have are beyond mending."

"Oh, for heaven's sake! You and your efficiency," Clarice complained, pushing her fingers into her hair and rubbing her temples in exasperation. "This is just to be nice to ourselves." Miss Peck replied with a half-smile and went into the outer office to retrieve her spring jacket from the closet.

"I'll be back in an hour or so," she said over her shoulder to the three typists. Barbra, eyes half shut the better to hear the tape she was typing from, didn't respond. Celie glanced up and raised her hand in farewell, knocking a few pages of copy onto the floor, and Sharmille, bless her, flashed a wide, white-toothed smile and kept typing. Clarice picked up her walking stick. "Toodle-oo," she said, waggling her fingers at the room in general, and the two women stepped out of the suite into the dreary corridor.

Three hours' drive to the north, a less amiable pair of old acquaintances were entering a room. Michael Goodenough waited for Colin Frazier's only son to sit down before circling the end of the conference table and moving a chair to sit opposite the boy. Boy! Young man, and not so young at that. Must be—good God!—thirty-five. He had his father's angled face under well-cut hair as dark as Colin's had been when Goodenough first met him, though Colin had been much older even then. "Nice to see you again, Devin," Goodenough said.

"Come off it," the other man replied. "I know what you think of me, so let's just get this done with, okay?"

Jolted, Goodenough put his copy of Colin Frazier's will down on the smooth yellow oak table. Devin Frazier's dark eyes swiveled with the motion. Goodenough recoiled and looked out the window, where the elm that crowded up against the side of the building had just come into leaf,

3

spangled with clusters of oval green seeds someone had once told him were pretty good in salad, though he'd never tried them himself. . . .

Goodenough pulled his fleeing mind up short. Well, the old man had made it through to spring. Something everyone in these northern climes might hope for at the end, he thought, as he prepared for the charade of reading the will. Not that a will had to be formally read, but people expected it. Sometimes that could have its uses. . . . He put the moment off a fraction longer, fussing with the long sheets of thick paper a little more than necessary, tempted by the glow of the light through the window that sent leafy shadows dancing over the table, like the shadows on the surface of a shallow lake. . . . A man could be fishing. . . .

"Get on with it, can't you?" Devin snapped. "Or let me read it myself."

Goodenough sighed, glanced at the avid face across the table, and pushed his glasses up his nose. "I'd rather do it, if you don't mind," he said, and swallowed. "Here goes: I, Colin John Frazier, a resident of the City of Duluth, County of Saint Louis, State of Minnesota, do hereby make, publish, and declare this to be my last Will and Testament hereby revoking all Wills and Testaments by me heretofore made."

He'd expected an impatient outburst before getting this far and, when it didn't come, he found he had to stop and clear his throat. "Article One. I direct my Executor hereinafter named to pay—"

"That's you, I bet," Frazier interrupted.

"Er, yes." Goodenough met the dark eyes.

"Very nice for you." Frazier smiled a little crooked smile. Goodenough half-expected a narrow tongue to dart out, testing the air. "Personal attorney *and* executor of the estate. How'd you manage that?"

"*I* didn't draw up the will," Goodenough replied testily. "In fact, I refused to. I'm only the executor." He paused a moment, got no reaction, and started reading again.

4

"You can skip all that stuff."

Another deep breath. "It's all standard, paying debts and expenses and so on," Goodenough said, impelled by the conviction that everything ought to be set out as clearly as possible, under the circumstances. Frazier jerked his chin upward. Goodenough scurried into the next section of the will.

"Article Two." He read off a number of small bequests to charities and to a couple of servants.

"Chicken feed," Frazier commented. "What, sixty thou all together?"

"Er, about that much, yes." Goodenough groped for the mechanical pencil in his breast pocket and began to tot up the amounts on the margin of the will.

"Forget it." Frazier sighed as he tapped a cigarette into his hand and returned the pack to his pocket, a sigh that added, 'you fussy old man,' to the bleak command. "Keep going."

Goodenough hurried on, resisting the impulse to stare at the boy: he knew the rest by heart. "Article Three. Whereas my son, Devin John Frazier, has proven a disappointment to me in matters both practical and moral, I give and bequeath to him the sum of ten thousand dollars only."

Devin jumped up with a sharp hiss, knocking his chair backward. "Let me see that," he demanded.

Goodenough released the page, in preference to having it torn in two.

"Ten thousand bucks! The house alone must be worth half a million! I won't stand for it," Frazier said through his teeth, although he was standing for it already, if you wanted to take the technical view, Goodenough reflected. "Did you put the old tyrant up to that?"

"No. That was your father's own idea." Goodenough glanced away. "I did try to dissuade . . ."

"You sneaking weasel." Frazier bent over to pick up the chair. "You know you had him around your fingers."

Oh, dear Lord, and wait until he hears the rest of it! He'd seen this coming, of course; he'd stood in the outer office beside Betty Shannon's desk and warned Colin that the will as drawn wouldn't accomplish anything but a lot of extra time in court, extra legal fees, even if he himself were paid only as an executor and not at his regular attorney's fee. . . .

"Ten thousand," Devin said. He sounded almost woebegone. "I never thought he'd do that to me." He shook his dark head. "Ten lousy thousand!" he repeated, recovering his energy. "And I dropped everything and flew up from Cleveland for that!"

I feel it coming, Colin had said, just two weeks ago, when he'd delivered the copy of the will he'd had drawn up by the firm Goodenough had recommended. *That kid'll get me somehow. He needs the money.*

Colin had stood just inside the room, behind the spot where his son was now slowly reseating himself; had seemed already ghostly in a light grey topcoat, his sparse white hair blending with the white background of the panelled door. Even his deep brown eyes had seemed faded. "You don't mean—Devin wouldn't . . ." Goodenough had floundered, shocked.

"Oh, wouldn't he? You don't know my son very well, do you?" The old man had smiled, a tight smile with blue, freckled lips that suggested that Devin wouldn't have to do much to acquire "his" money. "Sometimes I think you're still the same innocent you were thirty years ago."

"Colin, do something," Goodenough had said, frightened at this unforeseen situation. He'd felt like murdering the old man often enough himself, but Devin? His own son?

"I've got time. He's living in Ohio," the ghost had said, somberly enough that the first thing Goodenough had done when Colin died was check. Devin really had been in Cleveland when his father tripped at the top of the stone stairs of his mansion and broke his skull. Witness: the woman Devin lived with, Colin's companion who had taken

6

the boy's collect call, the phone bill . . . so that was that. But Colin was no drunk, maybe a little bourbon from time to time, but not a *drunk*—Why had he been drunk when he fell? Blood alcohol, .18 percent, a lot for an old man. Misadventure. How could Devin possibly have arranged that? Poured half a bottle of Jack Daniels down the telephone line? Absurd.

". . . The rest of it?" Devin was asking.

Goodenough braced himself. "Article Four. The remainder of my estate, of whatever kind and nature, real, personal, or mixed, of which I may die seized or possessed"— now, there was a possibility: if anyone could possess the old man, he'd believe it of Devin—"I give, devise, and bequeath as follows: to my daughter Alexa Cecilia Frazier, born at Duluth, Minnesota, on March 3, 1959, and for whom I have provided sufficient identification deposited with my executor hereinafter named"—little black footprints from the hospital, bigger black handprints taken right in this office when the child was nearly three years old and the custody fight had just begun, a photograph of the birthmark on her right shoulder, all of them witnessed and notarized, a formal portrait of the toddler smiling out of a cloudy oval background, some of her pale ringlets drawn back with a velvet bow, a portrait that fortunately had shown her right ear—"the residue of the estate, less the sum of one thousand dollars plus whatever reasonable expenses may be incurred in the search for her, to be paid to my executor when she has been found.

"Should, however, my daughter, Alexa Cecilia Frazier, not be found within six months from the date of my death forward, the remainder of the estate as described above, less the reasonable expenses of my executor in searching for her, shall revert to my son, Devin John Frazier."

Just six months. A measure of hopelessness. Or, given Colin Frazier, a realistic estimate of how long the estate could go undistributed without much harm done. Goodenough risked a glance at the boy. Devin was handsome, like his father, with those nearly black eyes, the dark hair, and smoothly angled face. Some spark of the father, a brightness and honor, had been left out of the son, who now regarded him with something of his father's impassiveness.

"I guess that means whoever finds her first wins," Devin remarked.

A chill formed in Goodenough's stomach. He should have predicted that, when this whole harebrained scheme had first started to take shape. *Should have thought.* But men feeling the touch of mortality, trying to put all their wrongs right, often don't think. He'd seen that many times, even in this practice, neither large nor sophisticated as law practices go. "Devin, if anything happens to that girl, I go straight to the police," he warned. His light, not-grey-not-blue eyes could go cold, had frightened more than a few people with their stoniness in this very room. But now, with stoniness put on to cover his alarm, they seemed to have no effect upon the young man across the table.

"Maybe." Devin smiled for the first time, a broad grin that drew a little cleft into his chin. "Maybe."

"I don't know anyone else you've ever dealt with who can be so thoroughly disagreeable," Betty Shannon said when the door had closed behind Devin Frazier. "I'm glad he's not a client."

"Oh, come, come," Goodenough replied. His secretary tucked up one corner of her mouth, as if to say, *Oh, come, come, yourself,* and stood up.

"Lunch time," she announced. "You don't mind if I go?"

"No, no. Go ahead."

Damn the woman, so anxious all the time. Just because his heart had had a little twinge. Couldn't help it, he supposed, after working for him so many years, but still!

Out of sorts, Goodenough took the Frazier will into his office to return to its folder. Sunlight, sliced into bright bars by the venetian blind, fell across his desk, and he found the folder he had left there as warm as a living thing. *Stupid, doing it that way,* he thought. *If Alexa's still alive . . .*

But of course Alexa was still alive, walking around somewhere, twenty-four years old. She hadn't been kidnapped by some stranger and tossed into a gravel pit while her frantic parents negotiated an exorbitant, useless ransom. She'd been kidnapped by her own mother. Goodenough examined his hands, large-knuckled hands with pale freckles on their backs, thinking of Mary Frazier's desperation. Desperation caused largely by his own careless actions. Colin Frazier had been his client even then.

She hadn't taken the boy. Naturally not. The product of Colin's first marriage, a dark, brooding boy even at thirteen. Hard on him. Mary had been his stepmother seven years, and Goodenough supposed some kind of affection had sprung up, even in a withdrawn child like Devin. The maid had described how he had run after the car, shouting, "Mom! Mom, take me! Take me, too!"

Wrench your heart, it could—did—until you thought what the boy had grown into in the twenty-two years since. Yes, he'd better get a move on, find Alexa before Devin did. Six months, less, to find her in. Have to go into Mary Lewis Frazier's background, see where she might have gone to ground, talk to relatives, advertise—all done at the time, of course, but by now memory might have lost some of its sting. Someone might come forward. Maybe even Mary herself.

No line on the car, Goodenough remembered. The maid had had eyes only for the weeping boy; the thought of getting the license number had never entered her head. Color? Black, she'd thought, or dark blue, maybe even green. Useless woman. Well, useless as a witness, anyway.

To her credit, she'd taken on a sort of mothering of that boy—crazy kid who even then had called his own father *Tyrannosaurus rex*.

Goodenough muffled the start of a chuckle without even noticing that he'd done so. *What had Mary Lewis done, with no money?* he wondered. He assumed she'd use her maiden name; sticking to an entirely new name struck him as beyond the imagination of the woman he'd known. He laced his fingers behind his head and leaned back in his chair, remembering her. Young, decorative, a pretty thing, not at all bright and with no skills to speak of, but irrepressibly good-hearted and trusting; foolish beyond measure to be so careless meeting other lovers (a little discretion on her part and none of this need have happened) yet Goodenough, a man of passion in his time, could understand why she'd continued to cheat on old Colin Frazier, a cold man almost forty years older than she was . . . but, twenty-two years! Even the detective agency they'd used back then was defunct.

He drew the telephone book toward him and looked up the public library. He'd need names of a lot of newspapers, starting with the upper Midwest: Mary would have stayed close to home if she could. Appropriate that he'd have to do most of the work of finding her himself, considering that he couldn't pay Betty Shannon out of his executor's fee. . . .

As he started to dial, Goodenough was startled to discover that he was sweating heavily. He felt for the little bottle of pills in his jacket pocket, then decided that he wouldn't need one after all.

2 September 12

ONLY THE CAT?

The soft hair on Celie's neck still prickled. The skin of her forearms roughened and cooled. Feeling rather foolish, Celie laid the pack of cards on the kitchen table and turned around.

Nobody there, of course. Just the heavy cotton drape that covered the locked glass door to the screened porch: no way to get in. No feet sticking out from under the drape: Celie got up and checked, as if some paper-thin person could lurk behind the dull white folds. She went back to the table and put one hand on the deck of cards, but the funny feeling in her spine just wouldn't go away.

Honestly, Celie! Imagine if Miss Peck could see her acting this way, how the poor woman would choke trying not to laugh! Nevertheless, Celie returned to the drape and pulled it aside. The constant *hush-sh-sh* of the rain came through the glass. On the porch, dim in the filtered light from the kitchen, two yellow canvas chairs and a rickety wicker table. Period. She let the heavy folds fall back into place and told herself she should be calmed. But the feeling was worse than ever.

Willy-nilly, her search intensified. She found herself poised in the kitchen, breath held as she opened the coat closet door and peered into the dark beneath the hanging garments. Boots, her own and a pair Barb had left behind when she moved out. No extra feet.

The back door was locked and chained.

The cat curled loosely in one corner of the couch, asleep.

Nobody lurked behind the shabby blue wing chair or held his breath behind the drapes. The door into the front hall, steel, was bolted and chained. Celie paused on her way to the bedroom, ears crackling with the effort of listening.

Both her bed and the one that had been Barb's were fitted with drawers clear to the floor; the shades on the two windows were drawn.

Celie snatched open the closet door. She was expecting the pale woman in the strawberry-patterned duster who glanced at her out of the mirror hung inside the door, but not the white, staring eyes, the mouth slack with fear. She brushed her hair off her damp forehead and pressed her lips together. Nothing in the closet that didn't belong.

The shower curtain hung with a suggestive shadow across the end of the tub. If only she had pushed the thing all the way back when she'd taken her shower! Lungs filled for a scream, Celie peeked behind the curtain. The tub was empty.

Okay. Quit it. That's that.

Celie returned to the breakfast nook. She willed herself to breathe evenly, easily, still unable to shake the feeling of being closely watched. The third time this week the same thing had happened: *Am I going nuts?*

After a moment she picked up the deck of cards and slid onto the chair. With only one glance over her shoulder, she set one card aside, shuffled the rest of the deck; cut it and, with gritted teeth, began laying out the cards. First, the card she had saved, the Knight of Cups, to represent herself.

Rain tapped at the bare window over the sink, a rattle of fingernails against the glass. Celie glanced out: shadows of the two big maples, the street at the side of the old house glassy in the blue of the streetlight. Two parked cars hunkered beside the road. The streetlight itself was a little blurred by the thin, shifting curtain of rain and the endless repetition of its own image in the drops on the window. Celie turned back to her solitaire.

12

She lifted the next card from the deck and soberly placed it crosswise on the Knight of Cups. The Emperor, reversed. *Oh-oh.* The job must be going as badly as she feared, in spite of her extra effort this past week. Miss Peck's kindly mouth, compressed against rebuke, swam through her mind. A constriction came into her nose. Celie laid the Moon crisscross on the Emperor and murmured, "Oh, no!"

In the nearer of the two cars up the hill, the man with the binoculars let them drop into his lap and yawned. The girl wasn't going out. Should he take a chance, go home, get some sleep? The rain flicked at his nerves; he twitched at the *splot-splot* as the tree over him unloaded the water on its leaves onto the roof of the car. He raised the binoculars again. *What in hell kind of solitaire was she playing?* It didn't look like one he knew, and after twelve years in this business, he thought he knew them all.

Celie reached across the little stack of cards topped by the Moon to place another card. Sun, upside down, signifying stagnation. His curved mouth seemed to frown at her. She frowned herself, and floating through her worry was the hazy vision of herself stagnating week after week in the unemployment line. To the right of the Moon she carefully placed the next card she turned up: the Empress. Standing on her regal head, naturally. No surprise there! Celie didn't need the Tarot to tell her that her past hadn't been bountiful, all that moving around. Lucky to finish high school, for more reasons than just the moving. Even this crummy apartment, now that Barb had gotten married—Celie winced—and moved out, would be hard to keep without a roommate . . . and now that Tim had found another girl, a girl who had the knack of being free and warm. . . . *Oh, wouldn't anybody ever, ever understand?* Celie clenched her teeth.

Very deliberately, she breathed slowly in, slowly out, willed the cramped muscles to let go, felt her scalp loosen.

Might as well finish. She placed the next card close to

herself. The Fool. Upside down, again! Her own dumb mistakes, that would be . . . Luckily, Miss Peck had been more than patient . . . to the left, completing the cross, the Devil. Of all the cards to be rightside up! Meaning deviltry in her near future. *I'll get fired, for sure.*

The man up the hill yawned and rubbed his eyes. Girl must have something he couldn't see: a wispy, angular kind of kid, pallid, a hangdog way of sitting and moving. Nice legs, though. He reached for his fancy new airpot and pumped himself some hot coffee. Car coming. He scrunched down in his seat, too quickly, and got a lap full of hot liquid. "Damn," he said aloud. The car, not a patrol car after all, splashed past.

Celie pulled another card from the deck and slapped it onto the table. Strength, again upside down, signifying weakness. Vague fears, say. She didn't need the Tarot to tell her that, either! Above it, Chariot, also reversed. Celie, who tried to fight her fatalism most of the time, this time only sighed. What else would Chariot be? She already knew she had no control over what was going on around her. . . . Wouldn't *one* card do something to smooth the jagged edges of her mood?

"I should have turned the deck around," she said aloud. Again, the prickle of ancestral, invisible hair rising along her spine at the flat, silly sound of her own voice, the ghost of the crest of a spooked cat.

The man in the car up the hill finished stuffing all the napkins from his boxed supper down his trousers and lifted the binoculars in time to see Celie put down another card.

The Magician. Reversed: events doubly out of her control. Hands shaking, Celie fumbled the last card off the deck. She almost didn't have to look. Wheel of Fortune, right side up, as was the Devil.

She'd been thinking only about whether Miss Peck would fire her after they'd moved to the new suite. Now, as she stared at the cards, they seemed to shimmer and rearrange, little linkages falling into place. Now she could see only one reading.

"Nonsense, Celie," she said to test her voice. She was instantly sorry: all that did was remind her that no one would hear her even if she screamed. The old guy next door was visiting his daughter, the elderly woman upstairs had fallen and broken her hip and was now in the hospital. The other upstairs apartment was vacant. She was alone in the house, a vulnerable old house even if she did have a steel front door.

Serves me right for doing my own reading. Probably the cards trying to scare her off. *Nonsense.*

The refrigerator groaned and began to hum, startling her; she gathered up the cards and thrust them into their case any which way, then almost ran into the living room and turned on the television to let Howard Cosell soothe her with a football game. If she heard the car up the hill start, she didn't connect it with the car that stopped in front of her house a moment later. She was too busy wishing she'd left the dumb cards alone.

What Celie had seen, in eleven bits of brightly colored pasteboard lying quietly on her kitchen table, was death.

Her own.

3 September 12

THE GAME WAS over, the news was over, "Nightline" was over, and Celie could think of nothing to do but go to bed.

The creepy feeling was stronger since she'd read the Tarot. Dumb thing to do. People were always warning you not to do your own readings. Celie barely glanced into the mirror as she brushed her teeth, half-convinced that . . . something . . . might be looking into it with her, the red leering face of the Devil from her Tarot deck, the demented gaze of someone escaped from St. Peter's Security Hospital, the crazed demanding stare of an addict looking for money, or more.

She scuttled into bed to lie, breath held, listening. All kinds of creakings and cracklings; the old house was full of them. Barb used to tease her: *They're just ghosts, Celie. . . .*

Easy to laugh, with Barb in the other bed, the old man's TV blasting through the wall. Not so easy alone, not with the ceiling snapping as if someone were sneaking across the floor upstairs.

What is the matter with me?

She couldn't even call Tim, hang on the comfort of his voice, not anymore. Celie tried to distract herself from the sudden wave of loneliness with her favorite going-to-sleep fantasy: some long-lost relative would come, give her a home and a family, a real place for the first time in her life. Or maybe she, plain Celie Lewis, would inherit a whole lot of money, like that Alexa Frazier she'd read about in Saturday's paper. All out of the blue! Celie pushed away the twinge of sympathy for Alexa Frazier, who hadn't known her father either, and snuggled into her blankets, wishing for one fervent moment that she had a large, fearsome dog instead of the tortoiseshell cat that had just bounded onto the foot of her bed.

Real memories kept pushing fantasy aside, much to her distress. That uneasiness came back, like the fear she'd felt as a child, when voices were raised in the night: would somebody snatch her out of her bed, hustle her into the dark, never to see her friends again, to start again at yet another new school, be parked for weeks with people she didn't even know until her mother came back? Never a whole year in the same school, sometimes not a whole year in school, for that matter. She'd figured it out by her freshman year, fifteen years old. What she needed was something she could do to make money so she wouldn't have to have men come in . . . grunting noises filtering under the closet door to Celie waiting in the dark for the next morning's real breakfast, eggs and toast and milk, and her mother drooping over a cup of coffee, her head in her hands and her blondish hair straggling out between her fingers, *Celie, hurry up, you'll be late for school.*

And once . . . no, three times . . . Celie tightened into a fetal lump. Bit her lips to keep from screaming for her mother, the way she had then. Oh, he had been so angry when she screamed! She had learned *much* younger than fifteen not to ask if any of those men was her father.

She had learned to type. She had stayed after school to practice. The thought made her cringe, remembering that she might finally lose this job with Miss Peck. She had learned to type very, very fast and very, very accurately, and she had taken great pains to learn to spell. What she hadn't mastered was how to pay attention to what she was typing, that was the problem; the words flowed out of her fingers without her really noticing while she still half-listened for something to go wrong. . . .

Well, her mother was dead, four years now. Nobody was going to dump her under the plaid blanket in the back of some strange car to wake up with a new family, or—or do that other thing she *would not* think about. Never. No one would even give her a fortune, like they'd do for Alexa Frazier when they found her.

The man in the car in front of the house examined each of the cars parked nearby. None looked familiar. Either the other two men he kept running into, looking for this girl, had switched cars, or they hadn't been ordered to keep her under surveillance. Just possibly, they hadn't found her yet. He grinned. He'd had an advantage the other two didn't have. An ex-cop, nothing to do with old J. Edgar, he'd actually picked the kid's mother up for turning tricks a few times, recognized the photo, had a good idea where to start looking. Knew a name.

He glanced again at Celia Lewis's side of the house. He stretched and yawned. Dark. Waiting until he had gone halfway down the block to turn on his headlights, he drove away to find a telephone and call his client.

Then home, get out of those wet pants and into some dry pajamas, and catch a few hours of sleep. God, he was tired!

4 September 13

TOWARD MORNING, THE rain stopped. By dawn it had left behind one of those cool, blue September days that rewards one's suffering through the heat of August with the first intimation that winter is on its way. Miss Ethel Peck whistled cheerfully as she brushed her curly hair into a roll over her forehead and pinned it up at her temples and the nape of her neck, a style that had suited both her and Betty Grable in Miss Peck's junior year of high school, but which now revealed the white strands prominent in her dark hair. She continued to whistle as she pulled on the jacket of her navy-blue suit and fussed with the lace-edged jabot of her blouse.

The day promised to be perfect for packing up for the move to the new office. The new office? Well . . . the new office would do nicely, although it was on too high a floor for convenience and too low a floor to be chic.

Miss Peck smiled at herself in her dresser mirror, gave the jabot a last pat, clattered down the stairs in her black Enna Jettick pumps, picked up the books she would have to return to the library after work, sorted her car keys out of her enormous black leather handbag, and set out upon the day.

By the time she climbed the iron stairs to her present office, Miss Peck had stopped whistling, not because she felt less cheerful, but because it wasn't ladylike. Books tucked firmly under her arm and handbag slung from her shoulder, she *click-clacked* along the grey terrazzo floor of the third floor corridor to the familiar door with "Peck's

Typing Service" in gold letters across the pebbled glass. She raised her key and stopped.

The door was standing open.

Not wide open. Possibly no one but Miss Peck would even have noticed. But a space at least wide enough to accommodate the thickness of the key she had been about to use showed between varnished door and jamb, and Miss Peck knew that when the door was properly shut and locked it would be difficult to force an index card between the two.

She glanced at her narrow gold watch. One minute before eight.

Not likely that any intruder would still lurk in the suite, surely? She pressed the balls of her fingers against the door and pushed, a springy push that sent the door shuddering wide. Miss Peck stood on the threshold and listened. Nothing. No sounds of hasty concealment, no hiss of surprise. Nothing, that is, but someone coming up the steps from the lobby, the accountant who had the office at the end of the corridor, to judge by the slow, heavy tread.

"Something wrong, Miss Peck?" the accountant called, as he gained the top of the stairs and saw her poised in her doorway.

Miss Peck glanced over her shoulder into the hallway. "Not any longer, I think," she said.

The accountant regarded her for a moment. Miss Peck's salt-and-pepper curls were as perfectly combed as ever, her navy suit brushed, her white linen blouse a pristine statement of good sense beneath her rounded chin.

The suit was a classic, good blue wool cut to lie perfectly over Miss Peck's still-slim body, although vaguely out of style: Miss Peck, no failure in her own terms, was no success by the standards of the business pages or the glossier women's magazines. But the suit, like the blouse, carried its own message: *Miss Peck is a thoroughly capable woman,* the accountant thought. *She doesn't need me.* He continued down the hall to his own office, no longer even half-aware that what she had said had been phrased a trifle oddly.

Miss Peck waited until the door at the end of the hall closed before she moved a single step into her own office suite. The three typewriters were neatly hooded in grey plastic, the chairs pushed into the kneeholes of the desks: no one hiding under any of them. The daisies Celie had brought in last week and put on her desk were turning brown and trying to hide within themselves, shamed as they should be at dropping dead aphids all over the Formica surface. Miss Peck mentally shrugged; the offending flowers would be gone soon enough.

Still silence in the room. The steel cupboard to her right was full of office supplies. The copier, jammed inconveniently into a corner, had a space beside it hardly wide enough for a kitten. The moving cartons were still folded. They stood expectantly under the sign announcing the move, leaning against the varnished door of the coat closet where Sharmille had left them the day before. Nobody could draw them back up against the door from inside. No one in this room, then.

Wanting her hands free, she set the library books and her huge handbag down on the nearest desk, which happened to be Celie's, and crossed the worn carpet briskly but silently to the door that still said "Miss Ethel Peck" in gold letters edged with brown. She thrust the door open and stepped back.

Her desk chair was also pushed in. A square of sunlight escaped under the skirt of the desk; it held no shadows but those of the wheels of the chair. She sniffed.

Someone had smoked a cigarette in this room since yesterday afternoon at four-thirty, when she had closed the door to go home. The piles of papers she had left on her desk looked undisturbed. Besides the desk and the chair, the room held only one filing cabinet and a second chair for the customer (or, as Miss Peck preferred to say, the client). No one lurking here. That left the storage room.

Miss Peck wavered on the brim of her private office. The girls weren't due in until half-past eight. Miss Peck didn't expect to see them one moment sooner. Should she go get the accountant to accompany her, after all? But he was a busy man, a man who arrived early, as she did herself, and for the same reason: to get some work done before his job prevented it. No, she assured herself again, whoever had been in her office wasn't likely to be here still. She marched over to the door of the storage room, a large room that in any other building would have been an executive office, commanding as it did one corner of the third floor.

She wrenched the door open as suddenly as she had the others, although if anyone had heard her open those there was small chance of surprise. After a moment's close listening she looked in. As she had thought, nothing in the room but shelves full of boxed files, although the smell of the cigarette smoke had penetrated here, too.

A new cleaning person. That must be it. A more careless person than the old management of the building would have tolerated. Yes. That would explain the open door, the cigarette smoke, even its presence in the seldom-dusted storage room.

Nothing seemed to be missing. "Not worth complaining about," Miss Peck decided aloud. This was Tuesday. By Friday she hoped to have her typing service completely installed in her new office suite, a suite somewhat smaller— her storage room would have to shrink into the shelves concealed behind panels on one wall of her new private office—not at all lighter or airier, not nearly as much less expensive as she had hoped to find, but run by a wholly different management, thank the Lord! A management that didn't care about modern remodeling and passing off the cost to tenants whether they had objected to varnished oak woodwork or not.

Miss Peck closed the door of the storage room firmly and returned to the outer office for one of the moving cartons to pack the papers she had set aside on her desk the afternoon before. She packed briskly, efficiently, whistling snatches of a Strauss waltz between her teeth, sealed the top of the box, and began to label it in her square, legible printing with a black Magic Marker.

The door of the outer office opened and shut. Miss Peck froze over the label she was writing, shocked by a spurt of real fear.

"Good morning, Miss Peck," a young voice sang out. "What do you want me to do first?"

A short, wiggly line had appeared on the carton where Miss Peck had rested the marker in her wave of relief. "Hi, Barb," she called. Good, she sounded reasonably casual. "Perhaps you could start by putting some of those boxes together. The smaller ones first, I think, I've got the tape in here."

Barbra came into the inner office, one pale, plump hand out for the tape. It was on the tip of Miss Peck's tongue to ask, "Where's Celie?" but she caught herself in time. *Honestly,* she told herself, *your mind must be going.* Barb's been married over a month! She lived on the other side of town now, so, of course, Celie didn't ride to work with her.

The outer door opened again. Miss Peck looked up with a small lurch in her chest, only to see Sharmille slipping in, wearing a grin that made her brown face shine. Miss Peck grinned back, warmed as always by that flash of white teeth. *How different they are,* she thought. Pudgy Barbra, slow, docile, with that fair smooth skin like a baby's—a white baby's—and Sharmille, slender, almost skinny, sharp as a tack (as Miss Peck's grandmother would have put it).

"Should I help pack?" Sharmille asked as Barbra opened out another box. "Or should I finish up that job that came in yesterday first?"

"Oh, the job first, I guess," Miss Peck said. "Might as

23

well get it out of the way. What was the man's name again?''

"Somebody name of Johnson."

"New?"

"Yes." Sharmille sat down and opened her desk. "It's not very long. Not for a thesis, anyway. I should have it out of the way by the end of the morning." She grimaced. "Praise the Lord."

"Bad handwriting?"

"No, the handwriting's okay. It's just so dumb! Makes me want to write it over again, only better, you know?''

Miss Peck smiled briefly. She knew the feeling well. Johnson. Oh, yes. A man in a rush, just after lunch yesterday. Skinny, dark-haired man wearing jeans. "That's good, Barb," she said, trying to shake off a niggling unease as the girl stacked up the fourth empty box. "Empty the file drawers into them, hmm? Keep the files in order, and label the boxes." She went into the inner office and closed the door with her name on it.

"What's eating her?" Barb asked Sharmille.

"Dunno." Sharmille shrugged. "Maybe she's nervous about moving. She's had her office here ever since the place was built, I think."

In her office, Miss Peck smiled. She was nervous. Not about moving; over that she was almost joyous. But that open office door stuck in her mind, wouldn't let her go, ridiculous as it seemed.

Also ridiculous was the idea that she'd had *any* office since 1912! Youth!

Barbra finished the files in an hour or so, humming as she worked. She'd decided to type the labels, as more fitting to a typing service, and as she sealed the last box she straightened up, hands on her lower back, stretched, and plunked into her chair. She hit the return button of her typewriter a couple of times to roll the strip of labels up and typed one for the last box.

"Are those Miss Peck's books on Celie's desk?" she asked.

"I guess so." Sharmille looked over her shoulder as her fingers completed a sentence of Mr. Johnson's thesis. "That's her bag. What's she been reading now?"

Barb tilted her chair as far back as she dared and craned sideways until she could make out the titles of the books shadowed by Miss Peck's purse. "A couple of mysteries, of course. Something called *Flower Drying for Fun and Profit*," she reported. "Gee, she must really be losing money here. And *Gaelic Ghosts*? Can that be right?"

"Gaelic—" Sharmille giggled. "What next? Last week it was, what was that, early hominids, and Friday it was that book on karate—"

"Judo," Barb corrected. "They're different. My brother just got his green belt in judo."

"Well, whatever it was, and before that—"

"Shh, she's coming." Barbra stripped the label she had just typed off its slick backing and stuck it on the box as Miss Peck opened the door and glanced at each of the girls and then at the round clock. "Celie not in?" she asked.

Sharmille shrugged toward Celie's typewriter, still hooded beside the tarnished daisies.

"She didn't call?"

"Nope."

Miss Peck looked again at the clock and then at her watch. Nearly ten. "That's funny. You'd think she'd call if she weren't coming in."

"Didn't get around to it, I guess," Barbra remarked. "She's a little scatterbrained sometimes."

"On, no. Celie's very conscientious about calling when she's going to be late." Miss Peck retrieved her books and handbag. "I'm a little scatterbrained myself this morning," she commented.

Too bad. Packing cartons was just the job for Celie. Not that she wasn't a good typist. The trouble with Celie was

25

that in a way she was just *too* good. She rattled along with astonishing accuracy at an astounding speed. Alas, Celie never noticed *what* she was typing, it was so automatic, and she was forever knocking manuscripts to the floor and picking them up scrambled and going on blithely unaware that page thirty-two now followed page eighteen and what she was typing made no more sense than a hare in March. Miss Peck had tried to compensate by giving her the rare job that came in dictated onto tape, and otherwise the shortest jobs typed from copy—less chance for accident— but lately there had been a run of long manuscripts that scotched that strategem. Well, if the loan came through for the word processor, that would solve the problem. If.

Reminded, Miss Peck sat down at her desk and pulled out the center drawer. Celie's ring was still there. The child was forever leaving it in the ladies' room, and Miss Peck was forever finding it on the pink marble shelf above the sink and returning it to her. A lovely thing, delicate gold with a piece of irregular mother-of-pearl set into it, nothing very valuable, but pretty. On the back of the mount for the oval of pearl were engraved the initials A.F.C., twined together in the old-fashioned way with the F biggest, and a date, 3/3/59. Celie's birthdate, Miss Peck knew, but what were the letters?

Sometime she would ask. For now, mindful of the open door that had greeted her that morning, she dropped the ring into an inside pocket of her handbag and zipped it in. Safer that way.

She reached for the phone and dialed Celie's home number. The line rang and rang and rang, and at last Miss Peck hung up with a frown. Two mysteries in one morning were a bit much.

26

5 September 13

SHARMILLE FINISHED TYPING the new client's paper by a little after eleven o'clock. Puerile bit of work for a doctoral dissertation, Miss Peck thought, but then she wasn't the one awarding the degree. She gave the proofread paper back to Sharmille to run through the copier and then assessed the morning. The packing was about finished in the front rooms, and Celie had yet to come in. Miss Peck telephoned once more, and let the phone ring for a full two minutes. Still no Celie.

That left the storage room still to be packed up. Miss Peck took Barbra into the back room with her. "I suppose I really could throw some of this out," she sighed, looking at the rows of boxes. "Some of it's over fifteen years old, and we'll really need the space in the new place. I wonder if my contracts mean that I have to keep it forever?"

Barbra shrugged and said nothing, but then what would she know about the contracts? Looking at the stacked shelves, Miss Peck could picture every one of her steady clients, and some of the more *outré* one-timers, with no difficulty at all. She had what her mother had once called a "snapshot memory." Luckily, her memories weren't jumbled together in a box like her real snapshots, or she might have had to be put away.

By quarter to twelve the shelves to the left of the door, between it and the dusty window, were empty. Several cartons had been stacked, both women lifting, to the right of the door. The shelves on the wall opposite the door remained to be done, but the air was beginning to taste of

27

dust in a way that reminded Miss Peck of an old-fashioned elementary school, and her stomach had begun growling demurely. Lunch time.

"Tell you what, Barb, you go out for sandwiches and we'll take them down to the courtyard for lunch," Miss Peck suggested.

"Sounds super."

"See what Sharmille thinks."

Sharmille agreed, and after a bit of fussing with money and deciding what they wanted to eat, Barb left to pick up the sandwiches at a nearby deli. Miss Peck gave Sharmille some typing Celie had been working on the afternoon before to finish. She left the two inner doors open, in case Sharmille should want anything, and returned to the storage room to work on the dead files.

Sturdy brick inner walls in this building, that was one thing she'd be sorry to leave behind, Miss Peck reflected. Often, in the early days, she'd noticed how silent the office was when she was working alone. Would she miss the clanking radiators on a cold winter's day? she wondered.

The storeroom, too, had its silence, oddly sharpened by the faint notes of the radio in the outer office and by the whispered high-speed rattle of Sharmille's typing. As usual, Miss Peck worked steadily, removing each box from the steel shelf, dusting it, and placing it in order into one of the cartons Barbra had taped together. One more tier, she decided, then break for lunch. She and Sharmille could meet Barb downstairs and save her the climb to the office.

Miss Peck glanced at her dust-smudged hands and started to wipe the perspiration from her neck with her shoulders, then remembered just in time that she'd smear makeup all over her good linen blouse if she did. She picked up the dustcloth, wishing she had remembered to bring some cotton gloves to work in.

Someone had been at the next shelf, at eye-level on the far wall, already. Miss Peck frowned at the disturbed curds of white dust on the tops of the boxes. Nothing here anyone had needed lately and, instead of the neat stacks on every other shelf, these boxes were lined up badly: two of the top ones had been pulled so far forward they almost overbalanced; the box just below them was shoved all the way back. Miss Peck pulled the stack out. As she did so, something fell down behind it, a brown-paper parcel she didn't recognize . . . *odd, what could?* . . . She heard a distinct click and a couple of ticks.

A cold wave washed over her, as if she had been standing in green surf and bowled over, and she reacted as unthinkingly as she might to the prospect of drowning: dropped the boxes as she whirled and ran out of the storeroom and through her own office, snatched her handbag from her desk, tugged at Sharmille as she fled through the outer office, crying, "Move, move, get out, down the stairs, hurry!"

Sharmille stumbled after Miss Peck, off-balance. "What? What?" she protested. Miss Peck had her elbow so tight it hurt and kept pulling, and there she was down on the floor by the stairs, a *big* crumple thump crash and the office door slammed and cracked and pieces of the bumpy old glass skittered around her like cockroaches and the stairs, the iron stairs, rang one time solemn as the City Hall clock and Miss Peck said, "Sharmille, Sharmille, are you all right?"

Doors banged and people ran into the hall and down the stairs. Miss Peck pulled Sharmille to her feet and Sharmille ran, too. She'd lost her new highheel red slides and stumbled on the shredding soles of a new pair of pantyhose into the street. A hole had appeared in the corner of the building where the storeroom had been, and now the hole nibbled into the floor above and bricks came clunking down and Miss Peck pulled at her arm some more until she stood on the other side of the street staring at the dust and the thousand sheets of typing paper flying up into the sun and somewhere someone had called 911 already, Sharmille could hear the sirens and Miss Peck gasped, "Goodness! That was close!"

"What?" Sharmille coughed, the taste of grit acrid on her tongue.

"A bomb." Miss Peck sounded faintly surprised. "Somebody put a bomb in the storage room."

And then came Barbra along the street, her hands full of sandwiches in little waxed-paper bags and her mouth flapping down and those big brown cow-eyes just popping. Just popping.

Sharmille began to hiccup, and then to cry.

6 September 13

SOMEBODY TAPPED ON the open door of the cramped room where a policeman had been talking to Miss Peck for the past half hour. She looked up to see a large, sandy-haired man in a rumpled brown suit. "I'm Jim Clifford," he said, sticking out his hand. "From the bomb squad. Miss Peck?"

Miss Peck smiled uncertainly as the policeman who had been talking to her went in search of another chair. She had already answered more questions than she had dreamed could be asked, and she couldn't quite imagine what this Mr. Clifford could want of her.

"I'm a specialist," he explained when she inquired. "I get called in on bomb cases." He looked at her with concern. Miss Peck supposed she appeared as bewildered as she felt, and she didn't bother to protest her intact intelligence.

The first man came back with the extra chair, and Clifford took it with thanks. "Now," he said, frowning.

All her initial excitement at this stupendous break in her daily routine had faded. Weariness settled over Miss Peck like a heavy, fur-lined cloak. Would she have to answer all the same questions again? No, she had never contracted to type any manuscript on a sensitive topic. Mostly doctoral dissertations in the social sciences, a lot of amateur novels, and three times a year a historical romance for Amelita Terpsichore. Yes, *that* Amelita Terpsichore, only her name was really Clarice Klenk. Newsletters. Occasionally architectural specifications. No, she could think of no reason anyone would want to destroy anything that had been in the storage room. If they wanted their manuscripts back, all they had to do was ask; it was only because she offered the storage service that there was anything in the back room at all, really. Service? To people who were afraid of losing their work and thought an extra copy should be kept somewhere, in case of disaster. Miss Peck returned the bomb man's ironic smile. No, Clarice was an old friend, but she didn't use the storage service; she picked up her typescript at the end of every day and put a copy in a bank vault somewhere. . . .

The answers came slowly, even though they had been "rehearsed." Her mind kept swinging back to the office, to the jagged hole the storage room had become, to her desk, looking as if it had failed to survive a freeway accident, to the grit that covered everything like a thin, tumbled blanket.

"Was your whole staff at work this morning, Miss Peck?" Clifford asked. He had run his fingers through his short hair so that it stood up like windrows of hay. The gesture seemed familiar, but surely the man was too old to have been one of her fourth grade boys, so many years ago? Perhaps not.

"Miss Peck?"

"Oh." She realized that he had already asked the question twice and twitched her mouth in what was meant to be apology. "No." Miss Peck explained again about Celie.

"Did this woman have any reason to have a grudge against you, or against one of your other employees?"

The question didn't take her by surprise this time. She was able to answer quickly, "No, they got along well, my girls. I've had to deal with gripes and jealousies in the past, of course, but these three didn't go in for that kind of thing."

"And yourself?" Clifford prompted.

"A grudge against me? Oh, no, I don't think so." She

smiled and inwardly cursed her face for being so nervous. "I can't imagine what happened to Celie, but I'm quite sure it's only a coincidence that she didn't come in this morning."

Not possible that Celie had set the bomb, if that was what they were hinting at. Not only was Celie a dishwater blonde, there was something faintly dishwater about her whole personality. She could be sweet, she was thoughtful, and she certainly tried to be responsible, so the . . . dishwater . . . was something Miss Peck couldn't quite put her finger on. Almost as if something in Celie had been put on hold . . . and yet, the girl had that odd wariness. . . .

Miss Peck made a mental note to check the morning newspaper to see if by chance Pisces had had some utterly horrid horoscope for the day. That might make Celie think twice about coming in—not that she'd ever missed work because of a horoscope before—and wouldn't she just stay home? Answer her phone? Wouldn't she have called in, for that matter?

"You're looking thoughtful, Miss Peck," Clifford said. "Any ideas that might help us?"

"I'm worried about Celie," she said. "It's not like her just not to show up." The men didn't quite exchange glances. She could see they were taking Celie's absence the wrong way, but quite suddenly she didn't have the energy to put them right.

"Any idea when this bomb might have been set?"

Miss Peck started to explain again that she hadn't been into the storeroom for at least a week prior to this morning, and stopped. "Why yes!" she exclaimed, surprised at herself. "It must have been last night. When I came in this morning, the office door wasn't quite shut, and someone had been smoking a cigarette in my office. I can't think why I forgot—it bothered me all morning!"

"You noticed cigarette ashes, or what?"

"No, I smelled old smoke," she explained. Each man

looked at the cigarette burning in his hand. "It's a strong odor, you know. And it does linger. I thought at the time that the cleaning person must have been careless, but later I saw that the dust on the boxes this thing was hidden behind had been disturbed, and that must have been recent. The cleaning people only go into the storage room every couple of months."

"You actually saw the bomb?" Clifford exclaimed. "What did it look like?" The other policeman moved slightly behind the desk.

"Well, it was a boxy-looking package, a little smaller around than a shoebox and about as long, wrapped in lightweight brown paper—the kind that crinkles—with a string tied around it. Crisscross, you know. A thin white string, like bakers use." Miss Peck frowned. Incredible, that she could picture the thing in one piece, lying on shelves that had been in that room for eighty years or more, surrounded by boxes she herself had placed there over the last twenty years, and that, because of it, all of those things were gone forever.

"And how did you come to see this box?" Clifford sounded only mildly curious.

"It fell down behind the file boxes. They're boxes like the kind typing paper comes in. It had been balanced behind a couple of boxes at the top of a stack, with the one below pushed back to hold it, and when I pulled the stack out, it fell."

Clifford reached out and made a very thorough job of grinding out his cigarette in the stained metal ashtray on the desk. "Er, wouldn't your natural reaction have been to pick it up?" he asked.

Miss Peck shuddered. "Yes, I guess it would."

"Why didn't you?"

Miss Peck stopped to consider, fought down the remembered wave of fear. "It clicked when it fell," she said. "And then it sort of ticked, twice. And I was a little nervous, you see, about having found the office open this morning. So I ran, and I made Sharmille come along, too."

"Ah." Clifford sounded like a hungry man before whom a steak done precisely to his taste had just been set. "Now we are getting somewhere."

The remainder of the afternoon abruptly looked to Miss Peck like a long, dark tunnel through which she would have somehow to crawl. She could not think of one other single fact that might help these men figure out who had set that bomb, or why, even while Clifford asked a series of questions about the parcel, not one of which she could answer.

"I'm sorry," she said, feeling after all these years as if she had come to class unprepared. "I didn't stop to look at it, and I really can't judge the weight of something by the sound of it falling. I just ran." She sat and looked at her hands for a moment. "I would have felt the fool if nothing had happened, wouldn't I?"

"Better safe than sorry," murmured the policeman.

"Right," Clifford agreed. He leafed back through the notes he had been taking. "Does Miss Lewis smoke?"

"No. Never. It's one of the conditions of employment."

The policeman surreptitiously snuffed his cigarette as Clifford consulted his notes again. "You've got a lot of packed boxes standing in your office," he commented.

Miss Peck responded to the faint question. "Yes, we're supposed to be moving tomorrow."

"Mmm. How many people knew you were moving?"

"My whole clientele. We sent out a notice, and there was a sign up in the office."

"I see." Clifford stared at his notes some more, seemed about to ask another question, stopped. "I think we can let you get that stuff out of the front room, anyway. That building's pretty solid—most of the force of the explosion went outward. The second room is a little iffy—wait until somebody checks it before you go in. And stay out of that corner room entirely."

"Yes." Miss Peck looked again at her hands, folded over her big handbag, which had been sitting on her knees all this time, and wondered if she had perspired through her skirt. "Will that be all, then?"

"For now, anyway. I have your phone number, don't I?"

Miss Peck glanced at the policeman behind the desk, who nodded.

"Okay. Sure, you can go, as far as I'm concerned."

Miss Peck excused herself and set out to find her way out of the building.

"What do you think?" Clifford asked, after the door had closed behind her.

"She's pretty rattled, but she's observant. By tomorrow she'll be mad as hell, and any little thing she remembers, she'll call right up."

Clifford nodded.

"Make a pest of herself, probably," his colleague continued. "Reminds me of my mother." He pulled closer some papers on the desk, shook a cigarette out of a pack of Lucky Strikes, and lit up. "What did you find?"

"Dynamite residues. Gone to the lab. Sometime before Judgment Day we'll have an identification, if we're lucky. Then we can match it up with a manufacturer, purchaser, theft. The usual."

"What about that box?"

Clifford pinched his lower lip and frowned. "I don't recognize the description. I'll check, see if another one's been used somewhere else, but we haven't had anything like that in the upper Midwest."

"This Celia Lewis look good to you?"

"Best bet for now, anyway." Clifford snapped his notebook shut and stood up, grinning. "We'll have to get into her apartment, see if her thermostat still has the mercury switch." He yawned. "See you."

Miss Peck came out on the Fourth Street side of City

Hall, glanced enviously at the police cars parked at the curb, and began to walk toward her own car. She squinted up at the clock tower, but the angle was wrong and all she could see was a wall of pinkish granite lumps pierced by narrow shrunken windows, topped by a skinny oval of a clockface on which she saw the hands edge-on. She walked on, crossing Fourth by the Grain Exchange, thinking of the interview just over.

True, she had told Celie that she couldn't keep her if she kept screwing up manuscripts. But Celie's reaction hadn't been anger. She'd looked a little hopeless in that irritating way that made Miss Peck want to shake a little backbone into her and had promised to try to do better. And she had. Tried, that was.

Miss Peck had run her typing service for the better part of a quarter of a century, and in the course of all that time she had occasionally let an employee go. Some of them *had* been furious. On one memorable occasion a brand-new Royal typewriter had gone sailing out the closed window, fortunately injuring no one in the street below. Still, after knowing the girl for five years, she couldn't believe Celie would react that way. So she had said nothing about the shakiness of Celie's job to the police. How insistent they had been! Could Sharmille have mentioned it, or Barbra? Miss Peck tightened her mouth. *None of their business,* she thought, mistaking her perplexity for anger.

The afternoon had warmed into the high seventies, and by the time Miss Peck reached her car she was much too hot. She took her suit jacket off and folded it neatly into the back seat before she got into the car, and then she pointed the vehicle homeward, thinking almost obsessively about iced tea and her sleeveless seersucker shift.

She had just decided to stop at Lund's for lemons when she realized that she knew who had planted the bomb. More. For whom.

7 September 13

CELIE HAD PAUSED at her apartment door that morning just long enough to give the cat a gentle backward push and shut the beast in. After her semi-sleepless night, she was running a little late, but when she reached the top of the porch steps she came to a halt.

Across the street, where someone had put up a cedar stockade fence some time ago, the sun lit the cool tans, greys, and streaky greens of the vertical slats and glinted on the shrubs between the fence and the sidewalk, outlining them in sharp gold. Within the outline, bright and shadowed greens mixed with an air of mystery, from the dark impenetrability of the low-growing yews to the feathery, reddish leaves of false spirea. Celie took a deep breath of rain-washed air and smiled at the scene, to keep it in her mind to energize the day. Packing moving cartons! Ugh!

Up the street a car door slammed. A man in a light-grey suit strolled toward her and stopped on the sidewalk in front of the house. "Excuse me," he called. "Can you tell me where Miss Celia Lewis lives?"

Celie shaded her eyes. The grey suit fit perfectly. The tie, a sober stripe, was the right width and knotted under a shirt collar whose points were this year's length. The man's face had a pleasant look of inquiry, and he didn't look like a salesman. "I'm Celia Lewis," she said.

The man smiled and came up the walk as Celie went down the steps. "My name is Walter Morrison," he said. "I know you don't know me." He held out a business card.

Walter Morrison, it said. *Attorney at Law*. What could he want with her? "I'm a lawyer," he said, still faintly smiling.

"Yes, I see."

"You've read about the Frazier estate, haven't you?" Morrison asked, mentally crossing his fingers. The torn-out page from Saturday's paper was in the car, just in case she hadn't read it, but he always felt better if his proposed victim already knew about the situation he planned to use.

"Yes," Celie said, cautiously.

"Then you know that Alexa Cecilia Frazier will inherit a substantial amount of money—if she can be found in time. And time's running out." Morrison let the smile fade to just the right serious degree and watched the girl's expression.

"Alexa *Cecilia* Frazier?"

Something changed in the girl's face as she spoke, a good change, recognition, maybe, that put little prickles of excitement into Morrison's palms. Yes, this was the right girl, by God, and she knew it.

Celie was thinking of the initials inside her pearl ring. A.C.F. Her mother had promised to explain the initials when Celie reached twenty-one, but she'd died just a few weeks before Celie's birthday without saying a word. The birthdate beside the initials was her own, and her mother had promised to explain that, too, but never had. Celie licked her lips. "Uh, can you tell me what this Alexa Cecilia Frazier's birthday is?" she asked.

"March third."

The girl nodded.

March third. Same as her own. Celie felt a tide of anger wash over her, that her mother was dead and couldn't tell her what this was all about. After all the rest, she'd done this! *Celie, watch it,* she warned herself, willing her mind into that calm space she had found at the back of her skull. The anger left as quickly as it had come. Her thoughts started scrambling again.

"If you've got time, I'd appreciate your coming to my office with me," Morrison said. "I think you might be able to help me with this case."

"I don't know any Alexa Frazier," Celie said. Go with him? What the Tarot had said, what had kept her awake so long that even on a beautiful morning like this she felt grainy and dissatisfied . . . death? Or only deviltry. Her mother's deviltry?

"I thought the lawyer's name was different," she said.

"You're thinking of Michael Goodenough. But he can't leave his practice in Duluth, so I've agreed to help him in the Twin Cities. I've got a letter . . ." Morrison reached for the envelope in the inside breast pocket of his jacket.

Deviltry. Or just losing her job. You couldn't be sure, that was the problem, you couldn't really make your own reading. And then her horoscope, she hadn't cast it herself for several days but the morning newspaper had said, *Absurd requests are on the up-and-up. Be flexible in scheduling.* Yes. That might be, she thought again, trying without success to remember precisely where the moon should be.

Morrison slid the sheet of paper out of the envelope and handed it to her. Celie took it without enthusiasm. Miss Peck would need her today. Miss Peck had said yesterday that she'd be packing the dead files this morning, so that Sharmille could finish up that new man's typing and Barb could run errands. Celie unfolded the letter.

"It's just a Xerox, of course," Morrison said. "The original's back in my office." A beautiful Xerox, Longdel's work, getting a letter from that guy in Duluth and using the letterhead and the signature on a paste-up. Longdel thought of everything. "You could call your boss from my office, tell him you'll be late. I won't keep you more than an hour."

The files could be packed in a couple of hours. Celie raised her head from the letter, a simple request to contact one Celia Lewis with the information that she might be the heir to the Frazier estate, on what was surely the Duluth lawyer's own paper. She stared at Morrison, her face gone flaccid as her thoughts sparked here and there over the landscape of her dreams.

Good God, Morrison thought. *Is the kid a retard?* He was more than annoyed at the idea. It scared him. Ordinary greedy people he could play with the skill of an expert angler with a wily old trout on the line. Others—the insane, the indifferent, the street-wise, the stupid—were too unpredictable. He was on the point of suggesting that they meet some other time, of falling back on the alternate plan, when he saw the tip of her tongue dart across the edge of her upper teeth, and relaxed. Hooked.

"Where is your office?"

Morrison repeated the address on the business card, which the girl had barely glanced at. The building was a good one, full of lawyers, stock brokers, investment counselors, what have you. It was also only three blocks from her own job, a choice calculated to make her think of saving the bus fare. A master touch, if he said so himself, but it had almost backfired. They hadn't counted on this Peck woman moving into a new office—they'd only found out about the move when Longdel had talked to her yesterday—and that had hurried the plan. Today or tomorrow were the last possible days to use that little ploy, and Morrison wanted everything on his side he could get. He wanted this over with.

"Okay," Celie said slowly. "But not past nine-thirty. We're moving the office I work in, and I promised to help pack up this morning."

Morrison smiled his best attorney-type smile, imitated from his own lawyer, a good man to have on your side in court. "That gives us plenty of time," he assured the girl, lifting his arm slightly to suggest that he was offering it to her to cross the street.

She didn't take it, of course, nor had he expected her to.

They walked side by side across the street, past the mixed planting of yew and false spirea, to his car.

A nice car. Creamy white, a Lincoln Towncar with four doors. Celie looked it over as Morrison unlocked and opened the passenger-side door for her, comparing it with Barb's ancient Fiat, a creature of rust, dust, and crumpled Kleenex on the floor. This car was span-new and smelled of wax and leather. She glanced at Morrison. After that first business smile, he hadn't grinned at her, as a salesman might, and his eyes hadn't checked out her body; they'd stayed on her face, or looked past her. Not that round-eyed stare of the too-but-not-honest. She made up her mind and slid into the car and patted the upholstery, an action Morrison took note of with his almost gleeful smile sheltered by the solid roof of the car.

Careful, he warned himself. It wouldn't do to be too jubilant yet. He was nowhere near out of the woods.

He got into the car. His motions were smooth as he put the key into the ignition, put the car in neutral, and started it; his handling was casual as he pulled away from the curb and headed toward downtown. Nothing to show that the car was rented, nothing to show that he'd never sat in a car like this in his life until yesterday afternoon. *Practice makes perfect,* he thought, and was surprised when a little sour ball of fear gathered in the back of his throat. He was a con man. That was where he had the practice, not with this. He'd never kidnapped anybody before.

"Buckle up," he told the girl. He glanced at her as she found the seatbelt strap and fussed with the clasp. Dim-looking. Not stupid, as he'd feared for that one moment, just dim. Hair that wasn't quite brown, but wasn't blonde, washed-out blue eyes you could call grey if you wanted, thin, nervous-looking kid wearing a full-skirted navy print shirtwaist dress that showed more taste than money, but with feet in flat-heeled brown leather espadrilles and carrying a black leather purse that had seen better days. Maybe the only one she owned.

She should do something with that hair, he thought, as he followed the city bus route north: the route chosen as carefully as the rest of the scheme, calculated to get her to relax because it was familiar. *Bleach a few highlights,* he thought. *Get a better haircut, anyway.* The dress was okay, but somebody should tell her about those shoes and that bag. . . .

"I think I'll take 35W," he said casually. "It's a little faster."

"Fine," the girl said.

He couldn't believe he had her in the car. God, what if it was the wrong girl after all? Longdel would have that detective over the coals—if he could figure out how to do it without giving them all away.

"What was it you thought I could tell you?" she asked.

"Er—I have some documents—uh—I want to compare your fingerprints with someone's—"

"You think *I* could be Alexa Frazier?"

"It's possible." He was careful to sound like a man sure of himself, but intent on making no promises. "Now, don't get all excited. It's just barely possible."

"It would explain the ring," Celie mused. *Where was the ring?* She must have left it in the ladies' room at work again. With any luck . . . but the Tarot had just about guaranteed she wouldn't have any luck . . . with any luck, Miss Peck had picked it up and saved it for her, like she had other times. *How can I be so scatterbrained?* Celie asked herself. Wouldn't that be awful, if the ring was the only thing she could give them to show that she really was Alexa Frazier, and she'd lost it yesterday?

What ring? Morrison wondered, uneasy. He didn't like unknowns. Could he ask? Better not.

He slid into traffic on 35W and headed north. In front of him, the IDS building gleamed blue in the brilliant day, stealing the sky the way it always did. Pity the city was growing up around it, nice building like that. *Have to go up on the observation deck again sometime. . . .* Once, driving

43

along 35W, he'd even seen a flash of lightning blaze in all those windows. He occupied himself for a minute or two in trying to remember what his name had been on that day, what he'd been doing in town. Automatically, he kept to the right to get onto I-94.

"Where are you going?" the girl asked. "This isn't the way!" She sounded panicky; Morrison glanced at her, startled. So soon?

"Just going around the back way," he said soothingly. "A shortcut."

"There's no shortcut." Celie put her hand on the door handle, but the car had already straightened out of the slow curve and was speeding up as Morrison pulled into the left lane. She couldn't jump out. She'd be killed. She shrank, remembering the Tarot laid out on her table, the grinning Devil and the Wheel of Fortune turning there, all those reversed cards. "You pull over and let me out," she demanded. Her voice came out trembly and childish. "You let me out of this car, right now!"

"Now, now." He'd thought he'd be ready for this, but he hadn't expected it to soon. He speeded up to exactly fifty-five miles an hour, in the left lane still but already changing his plans. "I'm just going to my St. Paul office," he improvised. "I want to pick something up. We'll come straight back."

"You didn't say anything about any St. Paul office," Celie protested. "You said you were taking a shortcut."

"Just for a minute or two. You can wait in the car." Jesus, he was losing it already! What he got for daydreaming on the job. *Please, let there be no traffic tie-ups!* Let this settle her down until he could get his stomach under control, until he could get onto 35E! He glanced at her. She was sitting bolt upright, her hands clenched in her lap, and was staring out the windshield as if the hood ornament had turned into a ghost. He couldn't quite understand it, but for the moment it was good: maybe no one would notice her. Maybe he'd get clear of the city before she thought of signaling other drivers. Then everything should be okay.

Morrison began to regret the sleek Lincoln. What would have been wrong with a nice, anonymous Ford? A nice, anonymous little Chevvy?

Got to be an expensive car, he could hear Longdel saying, as if they were still planning all of this. *She's got to think you're a successful lawyer. We get you a good suit and shirt and good shoes, and we rent a big car, and she'll come right along. You try to get her into a clunker like that*—nodding at his rusted out '74 Pinto parked out in the street—*and she'll run screaming to the cops.*

Yeah. Right. Worked, too, hadn't it? Can't argue with success. Morrison suppressed an urge to tell Celia Lewis about the hole in the seat of his Jockey shorts, the transparent heels of his nylon socks. Nerves.

He glanced at her as he negotiated the junction with 35E. She still stared straight ahead, but tears had begun rolling down her cheeks and a drop hung from the end of her nose.

"Hey," he said, touched. "You don't need to do that. Nobody's going to hurt you."

She sobbed once.

"There's a box of tissues in the glove compartment," he told her. With a sudden qualm, he saw her reach forward out of the tail of his eye: what else was in that glove compartment? The gun was in a holster at his side, but Longdel had been sitting next to him when he checked the car out. . . .

Whatever else was in there, all she took out was the tissues. She wiped her nose. Morrison felt almost relieved.

My own fault, Celie was thinking. She sat in a kind of paralysis, guilty and shamed, scarcely breathing, like the numb, grieving state her mother had tried to cajole her out of, that time—*Oh, honey, I'm so sorry, I thought he was only going to sort of pet you, I didn't know* . . . Stupid woman! Anybody in the world could put anything at all over on her! *Celie, it's not such a terrible thing, grownups do it all the time. . . . Next time I'll say no. I promise, Celie, it won't ever happen again. . . .* But it had happened again, twice. *Look, he gave me a hundred dollars extra. We'll go buy you that Polly Flinders dress you liked, the green one in Dayton's. . . .* "Where are we going?" Celie asked, breathless with guilt.

"North." Back on top. Testing. If he got a sarcastic answer, he'd be doubly on guard.

All she did was nod and wipe her nose again.

The first rest area was just short of Rush City. Longdel and Baker had grumbled at that: Baker because he didn't want to get up early to make that drive, Longdel because he didn't want to leave his precious '58 Plymouth sitting there for the few hours that would be necessary. "Hell, we'll steal a car," Baker had said. "We can leave it there forever."

"And what if we get picked up before we get there?" Longdel had asked disgustedly. "Sure, that's a real good idea, Baker."

So that was how Hansen got into the act. Well, hope he'd be happy with his fifty bucks and not go poking into what they were doing. Drive them up and drive the car back and ask no questions, that was the deal. Morrison wiped the sweat off his left hand onto his thigh. Too many people. Too much money down the drain. Made him nervous.

"We're pulling in here," he said to the girl, as the blue sign for the rest area appeared on the right. "You sit tight, and nobody will hurt you. If you don't—I've got a gun. Understand?"

"I understand." Her voice was thin and wobbly. Good. He'd never used a gun, wasn't sure he could. The big car angled smoothly where the arrow pointed; he was getting the hang of the better handling now and scarcely over-steered at all.

Luck, oh, luck! Luck! Longdel's clunker was the only car in the lot! Once into the parking area Morrison slowed to just above stalling speed, gritting his teeth. Baker and Longdel popped out of the car and ran toward him. He barely braked, and they jumped into the back seat, one on each side. Baker gave a thumbs-up in the mirror, and Morrison floored it.

"Hey, watch it," Longdel said. "You damn near lost me."

"I just don't want to lose anybody else," Morrison said, jerking his head at the girl beside him.

"Who are they?" she asked.

"Just a couple of friends."

"You aren't really a lawyer, are you?" she asked. From the back seat came a hoot of laughter.

"Not really," Morrison admitted. He was already back on the highway, up to speed, heading north.

"That means I'm not Alexa Frazier, doesn't it?"

"Oh, no. It means we think you are."

"Then what's this all about?"

"He's got a thing about rich ladies," Baker growled. Morrison glanced again at the girl. Her mouth was open, her jaw stiff. "You wanna know what he likes to do to them?" Baker continued.

"Oh, shut up," Morrison snapped. "What do you want to do, scare her to death?"

"What's it to you?"

All of them shut up as a State Patrol car passed them, doing at least fifteen miles an hour over the speed limit. The girl lurched forward and began waving her hand close to the windshield.

"Do that and you get shot," Baker said. She sat back and glanced at Morrison.

He licked his lips. *Baker's all bluster,* he tried to assure himself. "You'd better do what he says," he said aloud. Beside him, the girl gripped the Kleenex box so hard he heard it crumple.

"What are you going to do with me?" she asked when the maroon patrol car had disappeared ahead.

"We're just going to keep you awhile," Longdel said, as if he were talking to a stray cat. Morrison flinched. Well, the whole thing had been Longdel's idea. He was just the point man.

"Until the six months are up," he explained.

"What good will that do?"

"We'll get paid for it."

"You talk too much," Longdel complained. "What does she have to know?"

"Nothing," Morrison admitted.

"You're working for my—my half brother, is that it?" the girl asked. "That Devin?"

"Forget I said anything," Morrison said. He held the car straight on the road; the road stretched straight ahead of him. Pine City came and went. He was stuck driving the damn car until they got where they were going, and he needed a john.

Suddenly, what had looked like such a great idea three months before looked like nothing but a whole lot of trouble.

8 September 13

CELIE SAT QUIETLY, mentally cataloging the contents of her purse. She wished, for once, that she carried a shoulder-busting handbag like Miss Peck's, a virtual survival kit—ruler, magnifying glass, penknife, folding scissors, thread and a couple of needles in a plastic case, safety pins, tweezers, emery boards, heaven only knew what else. Unfortunately, she wasn't Miss Peck, and all she had was a pocket pack of tissues, a comb, a pen, a lipstick, her checkbook and her wallet, in which she had exactly $8.93, her driver's license, a bus pass good for the month of September, and a couple of credit cards she didn't have the slightest idea how to use to spring a lock. She couldn't even write a note—on what, a piece of Kleenex?—and toss it out the window, not with this crew watching. So, all she could do was keep her wits about her and hope.

The car continued north along 35, carrying her somewhere in great physical comfort while her mind batted around like a fly caught between window and screen. Celie glanced at the man beside her, the one who had said he was Walter Morrison, Attorney at Law.

What did they want with her? He, at least, looked as if he had enough money. That suit—Celie knew good tailoring when she saw it, even if it was a seven-year-old suit like Miss Peck's, and this one was no seven years old. The shirt was cotton, fifty bucks at a guess. Silk tie. *We'll get paid,* he'd said.

Paid to keep her out of the way until the six months was over, she guessed. Hired by the son? He hadn't said so, but she didn't know who else would care. And how long before the six months ran out? She had the impression that this Frazier person—her *father?*—had died in the spring, so maybe only a few weeks were left. Must be that the son was paying them.

And *he* had money. He could have bought the suit . . . or maybe he *was* this guy? Celie studied the man beside her, looking for a resemblance to herself, and finding none. "You're not Devin Frazier, are you?" she asked. One of the jerks in the back seat started to giggle. "I guess not."

"Baker, you've got a head like a sieve," the man muttered.

Baker stopped laughing with a hiccup. "What d'you mean by that?" he asked. He sounded truculent. Truculent was a word that guy had liked, the one with the dumb novel she'd screwed up last month; everybody in the whole damn story was truculent this and truculently that until just typing the word felt funny under her speeding fingers, never mind beginning to wonder if it didn't have a *k* in it after all. . . . Celie shook her head, conscious that she was trying to run away in the only way she could.

The other guy in the back seat was cracking up, now. "Think about it," the man beside her—Morrison, she might as well call him—said.

He hadn't been talking to her, but Celie thought about it. Maybe he had been going to claim he was Frazier, for the reason she'd thought of, that Frazier had the most to gain by keeping her out of the way until the six months was up. Probably it wasn't even his suit—the other two were wearing scruffy jeans and T-shirts; one had a jeans jacket, the other a camouflage denim one. She wished she could see them, to memorize better descriptions.

Wait a minute. If it's not his suit, Celie reasoned, then mostly likely it's not his car. Is it rented?

Celie stared at the road unwinding under their wheels, the wheels of the fancy, possibly-rented car. Yes. Not one of them looked like a type who could borrow a car like this from a friend, not even Morrison all slicked up but lacking that indefinable sleekness her mother had taught her to look for. . . . *Celie, you dope,* she thought. *You absolute class-A dope!* Still . . . After a moment she sucked her lips inward to conceal her smile. "I've got to go to the bathroom," she said.

Morrison glanced at her. "Can't it wait?"

"Not long." She widened her grey-blue eyes at him. "Can we stop at the next rest area? I—uh—I have a little problem holding it sometimes."

"Where's the next rest area, Baker?" Morrison asked.

"How should I know?"

"Look at the map."

The map crackled as Baker unfolded it. Morrison kept his eyes on the road, exquisitely aware of the girl beside him. This far north, the goldenrod was in full bloom, past its prime in fact, and the grasses in the ditch beside the road had already lost their end-of-summer second green. Any day now, the leaves would be turning. He could already see an occasional flash of red or yellow in the trees beyond the fence that paralleled the road. He wondered if there was any heat in the playhouse.

"Maybe another ten miles," Baker said.

"What do you think?"

"If it's empty, sure, we can handle it," Longdel said.

The car hummed on. *Probably would be empty,* Morrison thought. Hardly any traffic on a Tuesday morning, getting on toward lunch time. At the thought of lunch, his stomach gurgled. Another problem: he still had a lot of driving to do. Well, maybe they could switch drivers when they stopped to let the kid pee, or maybe they could stop to eat some of the stuff in the cooler in the trunk a little sooner than they'd planned.

Signs for Askov and Findlayson appeared, and the brown sign for Banning State Park. "Not far, now," Baker said. "Couple of miles past the exit."

If the playhouse wasn't heated, Morrison figured, they

51

could get one of those kerosene heaters and put it in there. He wondered why Longdel hadn't mentioned that in all their planning. God, he hoped the kid didn't get hurt. He wanted no part of any hurting, just the money. The exit flashed past, and shortly afterward the blue sign for the rest area, one mile, came up. "This is it," Baker announced. Morrison felt a small scratching annoyance; just because it was a triumph for Baker to figure something out didn't mean nobody else could. He put the turn signal on.

"No, no!" Longdel shouted. "Keep going! Christ, look at that crowd!"

Morrison squinted toward the sunny rest area and saw what had alarmed Longdel: eight or nine cars pulled up close to the rounded brick building.

"Aren't we stopping?" the girl whined.

"Not with all those people around," Morrison explained.

"I'm going to wet my pants."

Explain that to the rental service, if you please. "Can't you hold it a little longer?"

"I don't know."

"Holy Christ," Longdel said. "Get off the road at the next exit, we'll drive out in the country a ways and she can pee in the ditch."

"I'd rather wet my pants." A bluff, but how were they to know? She did have to go, really, but wet her pants? Even if she tried, could she?

No.

"Get off at Willow River," Baker said, rustling the map. "She can pee in the ditch, like Steve said. Me, too."

Nerves, Morrison thought. All of them using some ditch for a urinal. "How far is it?"

"Ah, five miles?"

Morrison glanced at the girl. She stared straight ahead with the absorbed expression of a kid on a potty chair. "Hold it, can't you?" he pleaded.

"Watch it, Walt, you're speeding," Longdel said. Morrison glanced at the speedometer. Jeez, seventy-five! He eased back his right foot. Last thing they needed was a trooper on their tail.

Ten minutes later they slipped from the Interstate to a two-lane blacktop to find a quiet gravel turn-off where the girl could get out. Morrison glanced at her as the tires crunched on the shoulder. "Okay?" he asked. She was crying again, little drips sliding down her cheeks like rain on a window. This time it only irritated him. She already had the Kleenex.

The tears were tears of anger. Celie had found herself too well toilet-trained to wet the car seat, and much to her disgust found it difficult to go even when they all got out and let her crouch over a thin thread of scummy water in the ditch beside the road.

"Look the other way, can't you?" she demanded.

"Not a chance, lady." The one named Baker stood with his arms folded five feet away, staring insolently as she squatted.

She had pulled her skirt over her panties, to keep them from his eyes, and now she felt herself blush. "I can't go with you looking," she said. "Can't we stop at a gas station?"

Baker laughed. "Notes in lipstick on the mirror, kid? Forget it."

"Ah, turn your head, Baker, you're not deaf," Morrison said. "What's she going to do, run away from a great big hulk like you?" Morrison walked up to Baker and half-turned him away with a hand on his elbow. Celie almost cried again, with reief.

"Okay, that's taken care of, get back in the car," Baker said, hardly giving her time to get her clothes straight. "Come on, move it." He gestured with a hand in the pocket of his jacket, and Celie got meekly into the passenger side of the beautiful Lincoln. Baker slammed the door. While Morrison walked around the car and Baker and the other man, Steve, was it? argued about whether to tie her up and keep her on the floor in the back, she reached down beside the seat and felt her checkbook out of her purse. She slipped it into the pocket concealed in the side seam of her skirt and reached back for the pen.

"Hey, somebody's coming," Morrison exclaimed. Baker jumped in behind her; the other two got in on the other side and Morrison threw the car into reverse. Celie froze with the pen in her hand.

"I sure wish one of you two would take over the driving," Morrison complained, accelerating backward. Celie brought her hand up into her lap while he craned his neck to look out the back window.

"I told you, I don't want you in the back seat, all dressed up and us looking like this," said the man whose last name Celie still didn't know. "What if some nosey cop decided you were being kidnapped?"

Baker guffawed. Celie slipped the pen into her pocket. Morrison lurched onto the blacktop, shifted, and took off. The map crackled again.

In the mirror, Morrison saw a new red pickup turn the other way out of the gravel road they had just left. Close. Too close. He felt the carefully laid plan shredding around him, like bits of his own hide unraveling. "We can make a loop and get back onto 35," Baker reported, studying the map.

"Fine. Pilot me."

"You're gonna want a left in a couple of minutes." Two kids walking beside the road stopped to stare at the fancy car as it swept past. Morrison's stomach knotted.

"Get me back on the Interstate," he said. "We can't take her through Duluth."

"How come?" That was Baker, naturally.

"How far do you think we'd get before she tried to jump out, opened the window, and yelled, something like that?"

"I got a gun," Baker said.

"You crazy? We'd be picked up in ten minutes," Longdel pointed out. "And there goes our investment." *Stupid,* Morrison thought. *Both of them stupid.* Why not let the girl think she'd be shot, so she'd keep quiet?

"Go around town?" Baker suggested.

"Twisting around on Skyline Parkway, with five hundred thousand tourists up there gawking at the harbor with their high-powered binoculars?" Longdel asked. "You're even dumber than advertised. No way."

They drove on in silence, following the road that cut off to the left, just as Baker had said. The Lincoln passed through a small town, a row of stores and a firehouse ranged along the highway. Three young men drinking pop at a gas station gaped at it. *They'll remember us,* Morrison thought. Might as well paint a trail. Big red arrows.

Woods closed in on the road, birches and a few oaks. The blacktop began to undulate over real hills. A tractor crawled by on the opposite shoulder, the farmer staring.

"Get me back on the highway," Morrison demanded again.

"This is a highway."

"The Interstate, you jackass." He glanced at the girl. Her hand rested on the door handle. "Get your seatbelt on," he ordered. "Move it." She looked at him and slowly pulled the clasp down, slowly pushed it into the other end of the buckle. "That's better," he said when it clicked.

"We could put her in the trunk," Baker suggested.

"Crazier and crazier," Longdel commented. "Knock knock, who's there?"

A sign for a roadside rest reminded Morrison of the cooler. "Why don't we stop for lunch?" he asked, putting as much suggestion into his voice as he could.

"Now?"

"Got a better idea?"

Silence in the back seat. The lunch had been planned for much later, to lead the girl into thinking their trip was a lot longer than it really would be. Lacking objections, Morrison slowed down and pulled into the small lay-by, where a single fly-harassed picnic table sprawled under a skimpy tree. "Okay," said Longdel.

Morrison sat and looked without appetite at the picnic table. Slick green paint sticky with spilled pop. The trash can had lost its lid; garbage was scattered all over. Raccoons. Pick a lock, the damned animals could.

"You want to eat here?"

The girl sounded incredulous, and with reason, Morrison thought. "That's right. You wait with Baker."

Celie looked on, puzzled, as the other two men began to spread a picnic lunch on the cleaner end of the table. What was with these guys? One minute they were threatening to gun her down on the streets of Duluth or lock her into the trunk, where she'd surely die of heat exhaustion, and now they were calmly getting ready for lunch!

Starlings picking at the scattered trash caught her eye. What could she add to that trash to say she'd been here?

Her driver's license.

Cautiously, trying not to move the top half of her body, she reached for her purse and found the wallet inside. Staring out the window, keeping Baker in the tail of her eye, she fumbled in the card pocket. How could she tell her driver's license from her Visa card?

Her fingers encountered thin cardboard. Her library card. Perfect.

She palmed the card and let the wallet drop back into the purse as Baker opened the back door. "Get out," he ordered, grabbing her elbow as she emerged. He walked her toward the picnic table, making noises about how nice they were to give her a free lunch. Celie looked around.

A car appeared down the road, coming fast. Celie tensed. Baker's fingers dug into the soft flesh just above her elbow. By the time she had recovered from the impact of the sudden pain, the car was almost past. She had time only for a half-wave, which was returned by a small child in the back seat of the car. The driver hadn't even noticed, she was sure.

"Try that again, and I will shoot you," Baker growled. She could believe it. He was a coarse-featured man, with cool blue eyes and a mess of brown hair that hung in strings over a lumpy forehead; a catlike aura of energy seemed to surround him. *Absurd demands are on the up-and-up,* she remembered, as Baker pushed her down onto the end of the picnic bench. Trouble with sun-sign astrology; it wasn't precise enough. Now she'd taken it seriously and look where it got her. Maybe nothing was really that reliable, maybe there really wasn't any way to get an idea of what was going to happen to her. . . . If there was a slight echo of Miss Peck's voice in her throughts, Celie didn't notice.

"Have a sandwich," Morrison offered, pushing a square plastic container toward her. She flicked the library card under the table as she reached toward the sandwiches, hoping the motion seemed natural, almost holding her breath.

The men kept eating, standing around the end of the table. Celie tried not to sigh with relief, succeeded, looked through the plastic wrap at the middle of the sandwich.

Ham and cheese. Celie didn't care much for either, but she ate the sandwich, reasoning that she might need the energy. The soft white bread seemed extra-sticky on her tongue.

The lay-by was fenced off from the nearby patch of woods; gleaming through the tree trunks Celie could see a field of something still green. Tangled in the fence were a lot of blue and yellow flowers, but more important, three strands of rusty barbed wire ran along the top of it. The fence stretched far enough in both directions that she'd never outrun any of these men to whatever farm that was. Not even Morrison, who looked the softest of them.

"Pickle?" Morrison offered.

Celie took the pickle. Bitter, but she ate it anyway. She ate the potato salad, too, and half of another sandwich.

"Coffee?" asked the third man, the tall one with the big brown eyes and the brow line like a shallow V, whose last name she hadn't heard yet.

"No thanks."

The men looked at one another, and somehow the mood changed. Celie noticed the noise of grasshoppers, suddenly, grinding away in the weeds near the road, and the warble of some small bird, and over the trees on the other side of the road and very high up, she saw a hawk lounging on the wind.

"Have some coffee," the same man said.

"No, thanks. I really don't like coffee."

The man poured a lot of coffee into a Styrofoam cup and held it out. "Drink up," he ordered.

"No, really—"

"Drink it," said Baker. He yanked her to her feet, gun in hand. She took a step back. "Drink it, I said."

Celie took the cup and sipped. Whatever it was, it wasn't pure coffee. It was bitter, like the pickle. And hot.

"Get it down."

"I can't. It's too hot."

They all stood back from her, the gun in Baker's hand perfectly steady, and watched. Celie sipped at the coffee. The sun was broiling, the weeds white with dust. No cars came along. She thought she heard a crow, somewhere far away, four short calls like barks. The little bird nearby still sang and the grasshoppers still fiddled and the breeze was very still, the day very yellow.

"Come on, come on," Baker urged. "I want to see you tilt that cup right back."

It almost scalded her, but she did as she was told.

"Back in the car now," Morrison ordered. He held the door for her, and Celie remembered sliding into this same seat early that morning, the air cool and the sun golden on the bushes against the fence, and she had actually patted the leather upholstery, she could remember the feel of it under her hand, she had actually thought that maybe one day she'd have a car like this of her own. She closed her eyes and plunked into the seat. "Get your feet in," Morrison said. "And this time, get your seat belt on right away."

Celie pulled in her feet and reached for the belt as Morrison slammed the door. She folded her hands in her lap and waited for them to grow heavy, as they surely would. Morrison got in beside her. She heard the tires go over a stick, *pop!* and the gravel turning under them, felt the sway as the car lurched back onto the pavement.

Long before they reached the Interstate, she was asleep.

Celie woke in an unfamiliar room. A small room with a low, peaked, bare-raftered ceiling, somewhat chilly. No inner wall, just bare studs. The windows had been covered from the outside with plywood, so she couldn't tell if it was day or night, but someone had left a light on, a low-wattage bulb in a stick of a table lamp. Desperate enough, she could break the bulb and use the lamp as a weapon, frail as it would be. For now, she'd rather have the light.

She was lying on a thin mattress on the floor of this place. The floor had been roughly swept, at least, and there was the table with the lamp and an old-fashioned, fat, upholstered chair.

Celie started to pull her knees up and found her legs so heavy she could hardly lift them. Propped on her elbows, she stared at her ankles. Someone had encased them in a narrow plaster cast, with about a four-inch neck of plaster between her legs and some kind of padding sticking out of the top end around each calf.

With an effort, Celie got herself to her feet and baby-shuffled over to the chair and sat down in it. At least the chair was comfortable. She wouldn't be going anywhere very far or very fast, not with this contraption around her ankles. Someone would have to come looking for her, but who?

Not Tim, she thought, biting her lips. No knight, with or without armor, shining or dull. Barb, or Miss Peck. Who else would miss her?

No one. At least, not soon enough. Shivering, Celie wrapped her arms tightly against her chest and dropped back off to sleep.

9 September 14

"YOU GOT YOUR shoes back, I see," Miss Peck remarked.

Sharmille looked down at the red slides she was wearing. They weren't too badly scuffed, just one little scar she hadn't been able to polish out on the left one. "Oh, nice carpet," she exclaimed. "Did they put that in for us?"

"No, they just cleaned it." The carpet, a tight bluegreen twist, looked pretty good. "Where do you want your desk?"

She must have had as much dust and grit in her hair as I did, Miss Peck thought. Yesterday's precise narrow braids were gone and Sharmille had pulled her hair into a fluffy brown puff on top of her elegant head.

"Oh, anywhere." She strolled across the carpet and put her head in at what would soon be Miss Peck's own office. "This is nice, too," she approved. Her voice shook just a trifle.

"I think so."

"What will you do for a desk?"

"I went down to Podany's last night and bought a used one," Miss Peck said. "It should be here almost any minute."

The outer office door opened as if on cue, but it was only Barbra. "I guess I got the right place," she said, surveying the empty, white-walled room. "When is the furniture coming? Gee, do you think it will all fit?"

Miss Peck glanced about vaguely. "I measured . . . the movers were supposed to pick everything up this morning." She perched on the single windowsill, her slender legs crossed at the ankle. "I hope they do. We've got nothing to sit on, otherwise."

"What do we do in the meantime?"

"Talk about yesterday."

Sharmille winced. Barbra glanced swiftly from her to Miss Peck. "What about yesterday?"

Miss Peck clasped her hands and let them fall onto her thighs. "I mean the day before. You remember that new client, Mr. Johnson?"

Barbra nodded. Sharmille took a deep, quiet breath.

"Just what exactly did he say when he came in? Did he ask about anyone in particular?"

"No," Barbra said, after a moment. "He just said he had this thing he needed typed and he'd seen your card on a bulletin board at the U, and he wondered how much it would cost. So I told him, and I told him about the storage service, and so on. Just like anybody."

"Nothing at all unusual about him?"

Both young women shook their heads. Barbra said, "Not unless you count him wearing new jeans instead of faded ones."

"Or writing even worse than my sister," Sharmille added.

Miss Peck sighed and shifted against the windowsill. "I thought he might have asked about Celie," she said.

"Have you heard from Celie?"

Miss Peck shook her head.

"Me neither," Barbra said. "I tried calling her this morning before I left, but no answer."

"The police seem to think she set that bomb," Miss Peck said.

"Celie?" the other two exclaimed in unison. "Never," Barbra said. "No way," said Sharmille, at the same moment.

"That's what I thought," Miss Peck sighed. "But she didn't come in, and she didn't call, and she isn't home. It does look a little suspicious, I guess."

"They think she ran away?" Sharmille asked.

Miss Peck nodded, watching their familiar faces, wondering what went on in the brains behind them. *How to do this?* She wanted to see if they'd come to the same conclusion she had, but without asking too many leading questions.

The windowsill was beginning to cut into her buttocks; she lowered herself to the floor and tucked the wide skirt of her grey linen dress around her legs. The two girls plopped down with her. "I forget," Miss Peck said, only a small lie. "What was I doing when this man came in?"

"You were, uh, talking to Celie," Sharmille said. "About the, uh, history paper?"

"Dr. Eaton's paper, yes, poor man," Miss Peck agreed briskly. "It's too bad about that. I guess it got blown up with the rest of the stuff. That is what you were working on, isn't it, Sharmille?"

Sharmille nodded, opened her purse and took out a pack of gum, looked at Miss Peck and put the gum back.

"Maybe it can be retrieved," Miss Peck mused. "But how did you know that's what I was talking to Celie about?"

Barbra and Sharmille traded glances. "Well, just after this guy came in, this client, you came out of the office with Celie," Barbra said. "And you were saying, oh, something like it wasn't too bad this time, she could retype it in the afternoon and tomorrow morning—yesterday, you meant—she could pack up the stuff in the storage room."

"I said that? About the storage room?"

"Yeah, because then this guy said, 'What's this storage room?' and I told him about the storage service."

"You told him *where* we keep the manuscripts?"

"Yeah, sure, I told him all about the back room."

"Why?"

"He asked. No big deal, they all want to know that. Some people think they need atmosphere control, you know, like what they write has to last forever."

Miss Peck looked from one to the other. Something was going on behind Sharmille's face, but she'd never come out with the suggestion she wanted, not unless **Barbra** did first. A stray thought: *like Celie, somehow.* Miss Peck brushed it away. "That's all he asked about? He didn't ask who'd type his stuff, not even to give instructions?"

"He didn't ask for anybody by name, if that's what you mean," Barbra said. Miss Peck sighed. She was going to have to come right out with it.

"But he did hear you call Celie by name," Sharmille said quietly. "And it sure brought his head up."

"So he knew her name, and that she'd be in the storage room yesterday morning, packing up the boxes," Miss Peck summarized. Barbra shifted uncomfortably. She was beginning to get it.

"What department was that dissertation for?" Miss Peck asked.

"Sociology," Sharmille said. "At the U of M."

"We'd better check that out, don't you think?"

"Miss Peck, what are you saying?" Barbra asked, her voice edged with panic. "That this guy set that bomb? To kill Celie?"

"The thought crossed my mind."

"But *why?*"

"I don't have the faintest idea."

Barb's mouth sagged, but Sharmille was nodding and Miss Peck was well satisfied. Not her imagination. As she'd come out of her office with Celie, that lean dark man had given Celie a stare of such intensity that Miss Peck had had an impulse to pull the girl back into the office and shut the door to protect her. And then the man had turned to Barbra and asked about the storage room, his hands twisting together behind his back as if he had a plump young pullet by the neck and fricasseed chicken on his mind.

While Miss Peck sat thinking, Sharmille reached for the telephone's snaking cord and pulled it close so she could dial information. "I know that number's in my directory," she said. "But my directory happens to be six blocks away, so could you just give me the number?" She scribbled seven digits on the margin of her checkbook calendar and pushed the disconnect button. "I'm calling the U," she told Miss Peck.

Miss Peck nodded.

"But, Miss Peck—I mean, Celie never harmed anybody in her whole life," Barbra protested. "She had a rotten childhood, but she never hurt anybody. Why would this guy want to kill her? And Celie didn't know him, I'm sure, she didn't say word one about him all the rest of the afternoon, just went on like usual."

Exactly as usual: she'd dropped Dr. Eaton's paper again, but this time only three pages were out of order.

Sharmille spoke sweetly into the phone, pressed the disconnect, and dialed again.

"You're sure you never saw him before."

"Swear." Barbra started to cross her heart and thought better of it.

"He couldn't have been an old boyfriend, somebody she jilted, someone like that?"

Barbra's mouth sagged a moment and shut with a little snap. "Well, I don't know her whole life, of course, but I lived with her almost four years. The only guy she ever really dated dropped her."

"When was that?" Miss Peck asked.

"Just last month." Barbra almost squirmed. "Celie's—well, she's kind of a—a prude, you know? And Tim, he wanted, uh—"

"I understand," Miss Peck interrupted crisply. "Nobody from further back?"

"Gee, I don't think so. And I mean, wouldn't she have been a little nervous, if it had been, you know, like that?"

Miss Peck nodded thoughtfully. Sharmille murmured into the telephone. Barbra flicked a glance at her. "And I mean, why a bomb? Why not just shoot her, or something, if he was that mad, you know?"

"Maybe to hide who was supposed to be the victim," Miss Peck suggested. "In order to make it harder to trace. If it had gone off as planned, Celie, if she had knocked it down, and maybe me, if I'd been in my office, I would have been badly injured or killed. Since it's my office, the police would look for somebody with a grudge against me, you see? That's what they're doing right now. That's why they think it might be Celie."

Sharmille hung up. "No John Johnson is getting a degree in sociology this year," she said flatly, her voice echoing in the empty room. "Or any other Johnson, either. Nobody named Johnson is even close to having a thesis ready to type."

"You see?" Miss Peck said to Barbra.

"Then why bring this thing to us?"

"To get a look at the office, I suppose." Miss Peck absently watched Sharmille line up her kicked-off shoes heel to toe. "Say he found out where she worked, and he wanted her dead."

Barbra shuddered. Miss Peck felt her own back tremble. "He came to see if he'd have a chance to get at her where she worked," she continued. "And almost the minute he walked in, I told him Celie'd be in the storage room, packing—he can't have missed that sign we had up about moving—and I even told him when. So, night before last, he set up his bomb."

"Well, but you couldn't have known." Barbra smiled at Miss Peck, a single wan twitch of the corners of her mouth.

"I wonder what he's doing now?" Sharmille speculated.

"Reading the papers and finding out no one got hurt."

"Miss Peck"—Barbra licked her lips—"you think Celie ran away and she's hiding someplace?"

"Why?"

"Well, because of the bomb."

"How would she have known about it?"

"Well, but if he called . . ."

"Why warn her?"

Barbra licked her lips again. "Maybe he decided it wasn't such a great idea, after all. . . ."

"But in that case, Celie would have called us, to warn us, wouldn't she?"

"Yeah."

"It's the timing that's off, see?" Sharmille explained to Barbra. "She was gone before the bomb."

Barbra nodded slowly. "I've still got a key to Celie's place," she said. "You want to go over and check it out?"

"Excellent idea," Miss Peck agreed. "Let's go."

"Hunh-unh," Sharmille said. "Not me. Can't I do something here?" She surveyed the empty room. "Take delivery on that desk, something?" Her eye fell on the telephone. "Answer the phone?"

"Good idea," Miss Peck said. "The movers are supposed to be over at the old office, getting out what they can, and somebody should be here to let them in. I thought of the superintendent, but you'd do a better job."

"Thanks."

"Wait, here's a better idea. Run over to the old place, will you, and see if you can rescue Dr. Eaton's paper? And while you're there, see if you can find the original of that thesis of Johnson's. And check up on the movers. We've got their tags on everything, but—" Miss Peck grimaced.

Sharmille rolled her eyes and nodded.

Miss Peck climbed to her feet. "Well, Barb? Shall we get a move on?"

Miss Peck reached out, turned off the ignition, and sat staring at the incongruous Victorian corbels and aluminum siding of the house Celie lived in. "Well," she said, after a moment. "We won't accomplish anything by sitting here."

"No." Barbra fumbled with the seat belt. The house

where she had lived for four years, in the right-hand downstairs apartment, looked strange somehow. Ah—the orange curtains in the upstairs windows were gone. The bare glass looked dusty in the sunlight. "That's right. Celie said the Kowalskys moved," she told herself aloud.

Miss Peck was already on the sidewalk. Barbra forced herself to put her feet on the ground beside the car. The rumbling in her stomach couldn't be hunger. It must be plain fear. No wonder Sharmille would rather answer the phone. *Damn Miss Peck!* Whenever the woman saw something she thought should be done, she just went ahead and did it. *I'd have called the cops,* Barbra told herself, forgetting that the idea of using her key had been her own.

By the time Barbra started up the weedy front walk, Miss Peck had her hands up to peer through the oval glass of the outside front door. Barbra unlocked the outer door as Miss Peck stood aside. "Straight ahead," she directed, listening to her heels hit the scarred parquet of the foyer. Lord, the house was quiet! Where was everybody?

The old guy with the TV was on vacation, she remembered Celie saying. The Kowalskys were gone, and the old lady upstairs was sick or something. She could hear Melange meowing even before she turned the key in the inner door; as she pushed it open the cat skinned out and twined around her ankles, almost tripping her.

"Looks hungry," Miss Peck commented, bending down to give the cat a scratch under the chin. "Oh, aren't you a pretty beast! I do like a tortoiseshell."

As they started into the living room, the cat ran to the kitchen, returned, meowing loudly, twined around their feet some more. "She's saying something," Barbra said. Foreboding filled her sinuses; she bit her lip and forced herself to follow the cat, her mind busy with visions of Celie strangled on the kitchen floor, shot at the table near the uncurtained window, stabbed with her own kitchen knife . . .

Melange waited at her empty dish, meowing. The chewed corner of a carton of Tender Vittles lying nearby showed that she'd tried to feed herself. Barbra looked at Miss Peck and opened and shut her mouth a couple of times before she got any words to come out. "Celie wouldn't leave her to starve," she managed finally. The words seemed to balloon into the empty room.

"We'll have a look around then," Miss Peck said. "What's that, the back door?"

Miss Peck crossed the room and opened the door. As she stepped outside, Barbra examined the kitchen. A dish and spoon, licked clean, stood in the sink. Celie's cereal bowl, Barbra was sure. She picked up the cat food box, tore it open, and emptied one of the foil pouches into the cat's dish. Melange settled down, purring, to eat. Miss Peck came back in and leaned the door shut, as if her knees were a little trembly, too. Barbra made herself smile.

"Have you looked at the rest of the apartment?" Miss Peck asked.

"Not really."

"Well." Miss Peck took a deep breath. "We'd better do it." She went back into the living room and looked behind the wing chair while Barbra waited in the doorway.

"Miss Peck? That's Celie's Tarot deck on the coffee table. She, uh, she wouldn't go away without it."

Miss Peck picked up the box and opened it and looked at the top few cards, then pushed them back into the box in the same order she'd found them in and dropped the box into her handbag.

"Oh, Miss Peck, you really shouldn't do that," Barbra protested. "Celie says you can't let anybody touch the cards but the person who owns them, or it spoils them! She'll be mad when she . . . if she . . ."

"Finds out? Nonsense. Besides, I know somebody who might be able to tell us what Celie was thinking if she can have a look at the cards," Miss Peck said.

Shocked—she thought of Miss Peck as having only the most rational of friends, if she had friends at all—Barbra watched her employer peer into the bathroom and bedroom from the little stub of a hall. "Nobody here," Miss Peck announced.

Barbra went into the bedroom, both timid and annoyed with herself. Miss Peck checked the closet and walked around to the other side of Celie's bed. The bed was unmade, Celie's faded seersucker nightgown flung across the end of it. A teacup with a dry stained teabag in the saucer stood on the night table and the morning newspaper lay in a heap on the floor. Normal morning bedroom, otherwise tidy.

"Wherever she went, she had breakfast first." Barbra cleared her throat, surprised at how strained she sounded. "The dishes are in the sink. I think she was going to work."

"So do I."

Bolder now that no body had been discovered, Barbra opened the drawer of Celie's night table. Sure enough, there was the tattered ephemeris. "And she left her planet book, Miss Peck. You know she likes to cast her horoscope when she's going to do something important." *Miss Peck's gonna think Celie's a total nut case,* Barbra thought. She didn't entirely understand herself why Celie always clutched at anything that might tell her what was going to happen next, though she knew it had something to do with moving around a lot as a kid.

Miss Peck gave her what Sharmille called her "bright bird look." "Well, she's surely not here," she said, resting her hands on her hips and tapping one foot, something Barbra had seen often enough that she reacted by wiping her hands down the sides of her skirt. "And we can't leave the cat. Could you take her?"

"I'm not allowed pets in the new place," Barbra said. "That's why Celie kept her."

"I'll take her then. She can sit in the kitchen window and terrorize the neighborhood wildlife. Is there a carrier?"

70

"No."

"We'll use a pillowcase. First, though, let's go see if any of your neighbors noticed anything odd yesterday morning."

"Nobody's home."

"In the whole neighborhood?" Miss Peck asked, with raised eyebrows.

"Well, in the house."

"Oh. Who in the neighborhood snoops?"

Barbra shrugged. She didn't know. She'd never paid much attention to other people who lived on the street, just to the ones she met in the front hall or out in the alley while she was trying to extract her car from a garage barely big enough even for it. Miss Peck seemed undismayed. She went out onto the front porch and teetered from toe to heel on the top step, looking at the houses on the other side of the street.

"What I need is a nice, nosey old lady," she said.

"I don't think—"

"Ah! There's just the one I want!" Miss Peck interrupted. She clattered down the wooden steps and marched diagonally across the mown dandelion patch that fronted the house.

Barbra followed in greater confusion than ever. Not a soul in sight. Just the quiet street in the shade of the boulevard elms, quieter lawns catching a bit of sunlight. To Barbra's surprise, the front door Miss Peck had aimed for opened as they approached. An old lady Barbra remembered seeing trundling one of those folding grocery carts down the sidewalk pushed open the screen door and stood in the opening with her arms folded.

Miss Peck introduced herself. "A young lady who lives across the street works for me," she explained. "And this is one of my other employees. The young lady hasn't shown up at work for two days—"

"Wispy sort of girl? Walks like somebody's going to take a slap at her?"

Exactly, Miss Peck realized, shocked. "That's her."

"Wants to practice with a book on her head, that one does," the woman said. "In my day, we played eraser tag at school. Taught good posture."

"Yes, it did," Miss Peck agreed, holding herself erect. "Have you seen the girl since yesterday morning?"

"Nope. Foolish young woman, in my opinion. Going off with a stranger like that."

At Barbra's age, Miss Peck might have had the same impulse to flee, but with the advantage of thirty-odd years she knew the woman's snappishness was nothing personal. "Going off with a stranger?" she repeated.

"Taken in by that fancy car, I imagine." The old woman sniffed. "I don't know what the younger generation is coming to, truly, I don't. Youngsters like you—"

Barbra was so astounded at hearing Miss Peck described as a youngster that her jaw dropped.

"How did you know it was a stranger?" Miss Peck asked, before the threatened tirade could get underway.

"Why, because he sat in the car for such a long time. Waiting for someone pretty to come along, I think. I almost called the police! And then when she came out of the house, out he popped like a jack-in-the-box to talk to her, and she comes and gets in the car blithe as you please. Now, I've heard of that happening other places, but this here is a decent neighborhood, we don't get that kind here as a rule. No, if he'd known her, he'd have gone to the door and rung the bell like a gentleman."

"Very probably," Miss Peck agreed, although she herself thought it might depend upon his age—and even then, she'd expect a few blasts on the car horn. "You said it was a fancy car. You don't happen to know what kind?"

"I do indeed. A Lincoln, just like my son-in-law had repossessed on him last month. I don't know what the world is coming to, people buying such expensive things without so much as blinking, whether or not they—"

"What color car?" Miss Peck demanded, reckless of manners.

"That one yesterday? Cream. Just the color good summer cream ought to be. You're young, but you're old enough to know what I mean by that."

Miss Peck nodded. She did indeed. She remembered her grandmother standing just inside the front door, complaining about the paleness of the cream that rose to the top of the round milk bottles left in the box on the step. *June,* she could almost hear her grandmother sniff, *and the cream's still white. I declare, I don't know what George Himmelmacher can be feeding those cows!*

"What did the man look like, did you notice?" she asked.

"Good grey suit, white shirt, black shoes, nice-looking man, medium size, maybe in his forties, just sort of smooth and nothing particular about him. Light brown hair. Couldn't tell you about his eyes, although I did have the binoculars on him."

"I rather thought you had," Miss Peck said, smiling approval. "Well, you've been very helpful."

"Four doors on the car," the woman said. The screen door closed and Barbra heard the hook snap shut.

"Thank you very much," Miss Peck said. Barbra grimaced a sort of a smile, but for some reason the woman had her mouth set for censure and wasn't about to change it.

"Took you long enough to miss her," the woman shouted after them as they went down her front walk, and the house door slammed. Miss Peck chuckled, a dry little sound Barbra identified with a shock.

"Now, that's what I call pure blind luck," Miss Peck said as their feet crunched on the street. "Though I do say one has to help manufacture one's own. Still, imagine finding her right off the bat!"

"She was awfully grumpy," Barbra commented.

"That's just because she's mad at herself for not calling the police when she thought she should. Come on, let's go pick up Melinda, or whatever her name is, and drop her off at my house on the way back."

"Melange," Barbra corrected, as they climbed to the porch of Celie's house again. "Miss Peck, how did you know that old lady would know about the car?"

"I didn't. I saw her curtains move, and then I saw the ends of the binoculars, and I thought, there's just the nosey old biddy I need. If anyone saw something strange going on, she did."

"What if you hadn't seen her?"

"I'd have gone knocking on doors."

Barbra fell silent. She'd lived in this house for nearly four years. A shiver went down her back at the thought of being spied on all that time without ever noticing. Once more, she put her key into the front door lock and turned it, glad that it wasn't her home anymore.

10 September 14

MISS PECK RETURNED to her new office flushed and irritable, after a frustrating interview with a police officer who seemed to know little about yesterday's bombing and to care less. He hadn't appeared much interested in Mr. Johnson of the incompetent thesis, or the unknown driver of the Lincoln, or even in Celie, not even with the information gleaned from Celie's closet by Barbra, that Celie had been wearing a navy-blue shirtwaist dress with a small yellow and white print, and no coat.

She found Sharmille perched on the end of a desk, a clipboard on her knee, snapping a good-sized wad of gum and checking off the boxes as each arrived, while Barbra tried a framed poster against the wall—three fluffy kittens in a basket with a ball of yarn that had seen better days.

"Hi, Ms. Peck," Sharmille said distractedly. "Your new desk came. It's in your office."

"What's that picture?" Miss Peck asked Barbra on her way into her office to check that it was the right, beautiful desk.

"Oh, these walls looked awful bare. I had this thing left over when I moved my stuff in with Bill, and I thought maybe it would look nice here."

"Very thoughtful of you, Barb," Miss Peck said with an inner sigh. She poked her head into her office and gazed with satisfaction at the desk, an almost-unused teak-grain Formica slab with elegant "floating" drawers and a typewriter extension so that she wouldn't have to keep hauling the machine out on the rising shelf. When she got a new typewriter. Thinking of the insurance claims to be filed, she put a hand to her forehead.

"How'd you make out with the cops?" Sharmille asked.

"Not too well. They didn't pay much attention, I'm afraid. Barb, surely we could hang the picture later, if we must. Why don't you unpack some of the stuff into the supply cabinet? Here, I'll help you push it closer to the wall."

"How come?" Sharmille grunted, as she kicked off her shoes and helped lean on the heavy steel cupboard. "Didn't they believe you, or what?"

"Oh, they believed me." Miss Peck stood back and tilted her head. The cabinet didn't look quite straight. "They just didn't seem interested."

Two men in coveralls came into the room carrying another desk and demanded to know where to set it down. Sharmille waved an arm at a remaining space and slid back into her shoes. "Where are those plastic things?" she asked. "You know, that go under the desk to save the carpet?"

"Ah, they're in the back of the truck," said the fatter of the men.

"Christ, Harry, can't you do nothing right?" asked the other as they left. "Now we got to pick that sucker up again, and my back already aches."

"I guess if anybody follows up on that Lincoln it's going to have to be us." Sharmille picked up her clipboard to check off the desk.

"I wouldn't begin to know how," Miss Peck remarked. "We haven't even got its license number."

"I bet that old lady could give it to you," Barb said.

"I don't think so, Barb. Remember where she pointed? The plate would have been out of her line of vision. She didn't know what color the driver's eyes were, and those were pretty powerful-looking binoculars."

Barbra located a box of supplies and shoved it toward the cupboard. "Not that it would do us any good," she said.

"The police could look it up."

"You just said they weren't interested."

"True." Miss Peck paused unhappily in her quest for another of the boxes. The case of a file cabinet came in the door, assisted by the men.

"Where you want it, lady?" asked the one with the bad back.

"Oh, that goes in the other room, against the far wall. Thanks."

"What if he rented the car?" Sharmille asked.

"Even worse." Miss Peck wished again that she had remembered to bring work gloves. She found a box that belonged in her own office and carried it in. Nothing to put its contents in yet, she saw. She parked the box on her new desk, struck by an idea. "Maybe not," she called into the other room. "How many places rent cars? Avis and Hertz and Budget, I know. There can't be many others, can there?"

"I saw the Yellow Pages around here a minute ago," Sharmille said. She slid off the desk and rummaged through a nearby box. "Here we go."

"You think they'll tell us if somebody rented it?" Miss Peck sucked in her lower lip. "We can ask, anyway, I suppose. Couldn't hurt."

Sharmille dredged up the telephone. "I wish they'd get the chairs up here," she grumbled. "Oh, my lord! Ten pages of car rentals! Can I skip A. McFrugal?"

"Yes, and Rent-a-Wreck," Miss Peck said, laughing as another possibility occurred to her. *Take it easy,* she told herself. You've built a nonsensical structure on a shaky foundation. Don't make it seem too solid.

Sharmille pulled the pencil out of her hair and used the eraser end to dial. "No Lincolns?" she asked a moment later, sounding disappointed.

"This should help," said Miss Peck, who had paged through the listings while Sharmille talked. "Lincoln-Mercury Daily Rental. Lots of places."

"Can't hurt to try." Sharmille took the phone book back. Miss Peck stacked several boxes of soft-lead pencils on the supply cabinet shelf while she waited for her to complete the first call. No luck. Next to the pens, cellophane tape . . .

"Hey, now, that's interesting," Sharmille said. "What was that party's name? . . . Oh, gee, thanks . . . No, no accident. Did I say something to make you think I'd had an accident? . . . Hunh-unh, I didn't hit him, no sir." She hung up.

"What did you get?"

"The car is not cream-colored, first of all," Sharmille announced hautily. "The car is *champagne* in color. I think maybe this guy says *color* with a *u* in it. A Lincoln Town-car, *champagne* in color, was rented Monday to a Mr. Walter Morrison, Attorney at Law. Mr. Morrison has an office near our old place. The car has not yet been returned."

"Call his office," Miss Peck said. "Find out when he's expected back—or if he's there, let me talk to him. Or no, I'll do it myself, you take care of them," she said with a flap of her hand at the two movers. She took the Yellow Pages from Sharmille and flipped backwards from the middle to *Attorneys*. "I don't see him listed," she said slowly. "Walter Morrison, is that what they said? You're sure?"

"The guy even spelled it."

"Why wouldn't a lawyer be listed in the Yellow Pages?" Miss Peck wondered aloud. "Did you find the directory while you were looking?"

Sharmille silently reached into the box and handed her the fatter White Pages.

"Well, I don't see him here, either," Miss Peck said, a few minutes later. "I guess he could live too far out, or in St. Paul."

"Call up the Bar Association," Sharmille suggested. "I bet they never heard of him, either."

Miss Peck zipped the pages backward past her thumb

and made the call. Five minutes later, she hung up thought-fully and stared out the window she had been sitting against that morning.

"Well?"

"No."

"It doesn't look too good for Celie, does it?" Sharmille commented.

"What do you think happened to her?"

"I don't know, Barb," Miss Peck said. "I can't figure it out. Why would somebody pick her up in a fancy car and at the same time set a bomb for her? Or was the bomb for us, so that we couldn't try to find her?"

Barbra hunched her shoulders and let her hands drop. "You know, Miss Peck, this is getting a little scary."

"It is, indeed. Sharmille, you say the car hasn't been returned?"

"That's what the guy said."

"I think I'll go see what I can find out about it. How late is the place open?"

"Gee, I didn't ask." Sharmille looked so stricken that Miss Peck reached out and touched her shoulder.

"What are you doing tonight?" she asked.

"I was going to have my sister do my hair."

"It looks lovely just the way it is," Miss Peck said, gaining enthusiasm. "I'm going to play detective, and I need you to help."

Sharmille checked off the plastic floor guards as they were propelled through the door by the movers. "I dunno, Miss Peck. I kind of want to stay out of trouble. After yesterday."

"I don't think there should be any trouble," Miss Peck said. "Just asking a few questions?"

"For Celie's sake," Barb put in, with hands clasped for high drama, as Sharmille scratched thoughtfully at her jawline. "Only, Miss Peck, I have to go home and get dinner first."

"Don't worry about your dinner; I need you here. I just want to be sure I can call on someone if I need help. What do you say, Sharmille, curiosity got the cat?"

"Yeah, I guess. What do we do first?"

"First," Miss Peck said firmly, "we get this stuff straightened out. I'll leave you two to do that while I go over to that rental agency and see what I can find out about that car." She surveyed the room, which seemed to have shrunk since morning. "When the copier comes, Sharmille, it will have to go in my office. Just make sure they don't block those doors on the right-hand wall, okay?"

Miss Peck parked near the rental agency and fed the parking meter a quarter. *Butterflies in the tummy,* she thought, crossing the street. Like the day she'd signed the lease on the first office. She put one hand on the aluminum door handle and took a deep breath. *Here goes.*

The interior was a cool relief after the hot street and the hotter car. Miss Peck, playing flighty female, fanned herself with one hand and smiled at the clerk behind the desk.

"May I help you?"

"I hope so." Miss Peck produced what she hoped was a winsome smile; she was a little out of practice when it came to men. "I was interested in a Lincoln Towncar you rented to a friend of mine on Monday."

"Oh?" the clerk said, in a voice that seemed to have emerged via the air conditioner. "You the lady I talked to on the phone?"

"Phone?" Miss Peck widened her eyes. "Oh, no. I didn't call." She hoped she had sounded as if she thought calling was slightly distasteful.

"Well?"

"Well, that is, I think you rented it to a friend of mine," Miss Peck continued, feeling as flustered as her act demanded. "That is, I saw my friend, Mr. Morrison, driving this car, and I'm sure he rented it."

"What car is that?"

"Why, it was an off-white Lincoln, four doors, I believe you call it a Towncar? My, it was shiny."

The clerk shot her a disbelieving glance. *Back off, Ethel,* Miss Peck thought. *You're hamming it up.*

"We did rent one of those a couple of days ago," the clerk said grudgingly.

"Could you—" Miss Peck leaned over the counter and almost whispered. "Could you tell me when it's due back? That is, he couldn't have driven it to"—clutching a city at random out of the air—"Des Moines and just left it there, could he?" Reckless of Walter Morrison's reputation and her own, she put some extra pleading into her voice. "I've just got to see him. It's so important."

"It'll come back here," the clerk said gruffly. "It's due now." He glanced at the clock. Two-fifteen.

"Oh, thank you so much," Miss Peck fluttered. *Oh, dear!* she thought, as she saw that she had boxed herself in. *Now what can I ask him?* Nothing. "I'll just run along now. Thanks so very much."

She flurried out the door and reached for her usual staid aplomb. That little performance had gained practically zip. How was it all those fictional detectives got people to unburden themselves at the drop of a hat? At most, she knew that the car would be back soon, maybe any minute. Anyone who had planned carefully enough to rent that particular car to entice Celie into getting into it would be careful not to commit any unnecessary crimes, like car theft, wouldn't he? To lessen the chance of getting caught?

A convenience store stood on the next corner. Miss Peck hurried toward it, hoping for a telephone. None there, but a blue and aluminum booth beckoned her on one more block. She dropped a quarter into the slot and dialed the office number.

"Peck's Typing Service," Sharmille said.

"Sharmille, it's Miss Peck. I'm over by the car rental

place. That man is supposed to bring the car in this afternoon, and I need you to help me. I'm parked just around the corner. Could you come? Right away?"

"Sure." The telephone made a small rubbing noise as Sharmille palmed the transmitter. "Okay," she said, a moment later. "Just let me get my flats on, and I'm on my way."

"Thanks."

Miss Peck hung up. She had passed the convenience store when she thought, too late, that she should have told Sharmille to take a cab. Shrugging, she hurried to her car and stood beside it, reconnoitering. She had parked in the end space of the block, more by luck than by plan, and the building the car rental agency occupied was set back from the curb far enough that she could see both sides of the street for the whole block it stood on. So, while she couldn't actually see the entrance to the lot from where she was, she might as well stay put. She slipped into the driver's seat and rolled the window all the way down, wishing she had the air conditioning the luxurious Lincoln undoubtedly enjoyed. Sighing, she folded her arms on the hot steering wheel and leaned forward to be sure she could catch a glimpse of any light-colored Lincoln—she assumed it would have a boxy rear end like others she had seen in the parking lot—as it came down the street.

A Blue and White cab pulled to the curb ahead of her, and Sharmille got out. Miss Peck leaned across the front seat and pulled up the lock button as Sharmille paid off the cab.

"He come yet?" Sharmille asked, sliding into the car.

"Not yet."

"What you want me to do?"

"When he does come, you go into the office and just listen for any information you can get, especially how far the car was driven. We don't want to scare him off now, we don't know where Celie is or if anybody else knows.

Pretend to want to rent one of their cars yourself, if you think it will help. What did that cab cost?"

"Three bucks."

"Let me pay you back, it's my show." Miss Peck thought a moment. "Did you bring your other shoes?"

Sharmille lifted the tote bag she held in her left hand.

"Put them on. You'll look more like somebody wanting to rent one of their fancy cars."

"I get it," Sharmille said with one of her good-humored smiles. "You want me to play nigger."

"Sharmille!" Miss Peck gasped. "No such thing!"

"That's not why you wanted me, and not Barb?"

"Oh, really." Miss Peck drew in her chin. "I can't go in there and put on another act. The last one I did was ridiculous enough. Besides," she confessed, "I flubbed it." She winced. "And Barb would do exactly what she was told and not one thing more. She's got no imagination."

Sharmille grinned. "Miss Peck, don't you know when you're being teased?" she drawled.

"Oh." Miss Peck pressed her lips together. "Sorry."

"That's okay."

Miss Peck eyed the young woman beside her for a moment. "Naturally, if you want, you can act any way you think would get you any more information."

The grin faded. "Who's behind the counter?"

"A twenty-five-year-old good-looking white snot."

Sharmille giggled. "Miss Peck, I love you. Right, I'll do whatever."

"I hope he comes soon," Miss Peck worried. "I can't stay parked here much longer, to say nothing of melting."

"He's gonna want to get out of town before the rush," Sharmille said confidently. "If he comes. Say, Miss Peck, I'm thirsty, aren't you? What say I go into the Tom Thumb and get us each a can of pop?"

Miss Peck leaned forward and looked down the cross street as far as she could in each direction. No light cars of any description. "Thanks, that sounds good. Get me some iced tea, if they have it—but be quick!"

Sharmille was out of the car before Miss Peck could hoist her handbag into her lap and find fifty cents for the drink. She checked the street again. The white car down the block turned out to be something else, something Miss Peck didn't recognize and which drove right on past.

Sharmille popped back into the car and handed Miss Peck a cold can of iced tea. "Find a five in my wallet, will you?" Miss Peck said. "That'll cover the cab and the drink and give you a little extra in case something else comes up."

"Fine." Sharmille located the legendary handbag and lifted it onto her knees. She'd hefted lighter suitcases. The wallet was right on top, but beneath it she glimpsed a paperback mystery novel, a steel tape ruler, a checkbook, a glasses case, the sewing kit that so often came to the rescue of one or another of them in the office, and enough shadowy other things to fill her with a ludicrous awe. She took a five dollar bill, the only one, from the wallet and tucked it into the outside pocket of her own purse. "That leaves you a little short," she said.

"I know, it's okay. Where is he?" Miss Peck beat a rhythm on the steering wheel with her fingers.

Sharmille popped the top of her Coke. She took four long, long, cold swallows and sighed. The car felt hot enough to whip up a batch of shirred eggs; she'd already rolled the window down as far as it would go and kicked off her shoes. Beside her, Miss Peck peeled the cover back on the top of the can of iced tea and sipped at it. "Let's take turns watching," she suggested. "My eyes are beginning to burn."

"Okay." Sharmille took another quick sip of the Coke and set the can down between the seats.

Half an hour passed. The iced tea and the Coke were long gone; Sharmille had fumbled her feet into her shoes and taken the cans to the trash basket on the corner and returned to the warm seat of the car, wishing she were almost anywhere else. Preferably in the health club swimming pool, diving open-eyed into its blue depths. Then home, so her sister could plait her hot hair. While Miss Peck had taken one of her turns watching, Sharmille had switched to the high-heeled red slides, and now, Miss Peck watching again, she leaned back and crossed her long, sweaty legs at the ankle and wondered if she could go back to the store and get a pack of Chiclets.

"There he is!" Miss Peck crowed. "There, see? Turning into the lot?"

Sharmille gazed dully at the long-awaited car. Now that it was time to do her stuff, her mouth went dry. "See you," she said. She opened the car door and got out. Even the warm air of the street was a relief after the car. She crossed the street pulling her knit shirt down on her shoulders and strutted past the glass windows of the rental agency and pushed the door open into the icy pleasure of the air conditioning.

A man in grey pants and a white shirt, with a grey suit jacket slung over his shoulder, came in from the parking lot, followed by the clerk. *Grey suit!* Sharmille perked up. She took in the dude's clothes: ex-pen-sive, and super conservative, but that didn't stop him having a little tear in his T-shirt down by his waist, on the left, that showed through the fine cotton shirt. Sharmille smiled a small, tight smile and moved up to the counter as the man in grey and the clerk sorted themselves onto opposite sides of it. The clerk—Sharmille would have classed him as thirty, and only not bad, but most assuredly a snot—had a bunch of papers in his hand and was running a little adding machine that spat the numbers onto the tape with a sound like an old wind-up toy. "I get three hundred eighty-four," he said to the guy in the grey suit. "You agree?"

"Sounds about right."

"So, at forty a day and forty a mile, we get"—the little adding machine rachetted out some more numbers—"two hundred seventy-three dollars and sixty cents, and the tax on that will come to, mmm, sixteen dollars and twelve cents, making two hundred eighty-nine dollars and seventy-two cents all together." The clerk presented his figures to the man with a little flourish of his pen. "Will you put that on your American Express?"

"No." The man unslung his jacket and pulled a new-looking wallet out of the inside pocket and peeled three hundred-dollar bills off a fat wad and handed them across the counter. Sharmille de-focussed her eyes to keep her eyebrows from jumping. Nobody she knew would be dumb enough to carry that much cash around, even if they had it to carry. Not unless they were dealing something, and those dudes were no friends of hers.

She studied the man to make sure she'd know him if she saw him again: about her own height; in these heels, make that five-eleven. A medium build. Might weigh, say a hundred-fifty-five, a hundred-sixty, somewhere in there. Dark brown hair, by which Sharmille, a Minnesotan by birth and by eye, meant something roughly the shade known as fruitwood when applied to furniture. Blue eyes, as his glance slid over to see who was staring at him. Sharmille looked away, out the front window of the agency, leaning on her elbow on the tall counter with her hands clasped over her purse in front of her. Yeah, this guy fit the description Miss Peck had repeated.

The man put his wallet away and headed for the door. "Thank you, Mr. Morrison," the clerk said and turned to Sharmille. "May I help you?" he said, projecting his doubt.

Sharmille laid it on thick. "Why, Ah was thinkin' 'bout rentin' one o' yo' ca's but, mah land, when Ah seen what that dude pay fo' such a little bitty trip, Ah think maybe Ah gonna think some mo'." She smiled at him—her full, brilliant, friendly smile that made him smile back in spite of the arrogant sneer he was all set to put on—chuckled gently, and sashayed out the door.

"You do that," the hapless clerk called after her. She turned and gave him another couple hundred watts as the door closed behind her. The corners of his mouth twitched and she chuckled again. She strutted past the window despite the wilting heat that hit her, waggled her fingers in farewell to the clerk still staring out at her, hurried across the street, and made for Miss Peck's car, triumphant.

Miss Peck wasn't there.

11 September 14

THE INTERCOM BUZZED. Goodenough picked up the phone and said, "Yes, Betty?" his eyes still traveling over the brief he was reading.

"That detective is on line two," Miss Shannon said.

"Oh. Thanks." Goodenough shoved the brief away and pushed the blinking square button on his telephone. He pictured the detective, a small man with straw-colored hair cut short and a large nose in the lead of a face that seemed to recede, as if in childhood his mother had once put a handkerchief to his nose and said, 'Now, blow,' and the man had sneezed instead, driving the rest of his features back from that motherly grasp. A former FBI agent, the man kept his shoes polished and his nails trimmed against the remote possibility of appearing on TV, or maybe the ghost of J. Edgar hovering behind his shoulder disapproved of any sloppiness.

"I think I've found your girl," the man said.

"Really!" Shocked out of his physiognomical speculations, Goodenough grinned at the leather-bound books on the opposite wall. "Where is she? What's she calling herself?"

"She's going by the name of Celia Lewis."

"Her mother's name was Lewis, and her middle name is Cecilia."

"Yes," the detective said. Goodenough remembered that he'd briefed him on all of this long ago. "Actually, there's been a legal name change."

"Where is she?"

"Well." The man's embarrassment came clearly over the line. "That's kind of a problem. I know where she lives, but I'm not sure where she works. And she's not home. She could be on vacation—there's no mail accumulating, just a couple of morning papers. Nobody else in the house seems to be home, either."

"House?"

"One of these old places divided up. I got onto it yesterday. But her name is on the mailbox, and the landlord says the girl matches the description I've got."

"What is the description?" Goodenough asked, aware of an old stirring. He listened to the colorless list. "Sounds something like her mother, except for the hair. Her mother's hair was blonde—at least, I think it was really blonde. And the mother was more vivacious."

"I know," the man said patiently. Goodenough flushed. What was the matter with him? He'd given the man that old photo himself: Mary in a sleek strapless gown at some function or other, Colin blinking into the flash, handsomer than Goodenough had remembered him.

"When's she due back?" he asked, mostly to cover his confusion.

"See, I don't *know* she's on vacation," the man said, again embarrassed. "That's just my surmise. If I knew for sure where she worked, I could find out for sure."

"Doesn't the landlord know?" Goodenough asked. "Surely she couldn't have moved in without references!"

"Er, he says she works at a place called Peck's Typing Service. I went there, but the office is closed—they were moving things out. There was some kind of explosion in the building yesterday morning."

Goodenough's stomach cramped. "Explosion! Anyone hurt?"

"The paper says no. I went around to the address the movers gave me, but there was nobody there but some other kid who refused even to say whether she'd ever heard of Celia Lewis. I think she thought I was a reporter. And the police think your girl is the one who set the bomb."

"Bomb?"

"For the explosion," the detective said, very patiently indeed.

"Listen," Goodenough said. "That girl didn't set any bomb. She's in danger. We've got to protect her."

"Got to find her first," the voice on the telephone pointed out.

"Isn't there anything you can do?" The urgency in his own voice startled him. He thought of Alexa as he'd last seen her, a chubby blonde three-year-old with a quick, heart-lightening smile, and turned away from his desk to look out his window.

"I got a man camped on her doorstep. The minute she comes home we'll talk to her, give her your letter, and so on. She'll be all right then."

"Yes, she'll be all right then," Goodenough echoed, not believing it for a moment. "Isn't there anything else you can do?"

"Well, I can try the office again, see if the woman who owns it will talk to me."

"Do that," Goodenough agreed. "Do whatever you can think of—within reason. I have to account for all of this to the court. Where's Devin?"

"Frazier? He's in Duluth."

"Oh? When did he come out?"

"Flew up last night. He hasn't contacted you?"

"No." No real reason why he should. But with Devin in Duluth, the danger to Alexa—Celia Lewis—was surely less? "Have you run into any of those other people your contacts told you had been asking about her?"

"Not yet."

The money was pouring down this investigation like a tide down a sinkhole. Goodenough tapped his fingers on the desk. "Well, all I can say is, keep your eye on her," he said finally.

"Got to find her first," the detective repeated and hung up. Goodenough sat with the receiver in his hand for a few seconds before replacing it. He opened his center desk drawer and pulled out a pocket notebook. *Celia Lewis,* he added to a list, just under the entry of a collect telephone call from Cleveland to Colin Frazier's business phone, late on the night the old man had died. He stared at the list for a few minutes and buzzed his secretary.

Her too-bright what-can-I-do-for-you told him she'd been listening on the line again, probably holding her damn breath to make sure the detective didn't upset him. He bit back his annoyance and said, "See if you can get hold of Jack Carrera for me, will you, Betty?"

"That would be Colin Frazier's companion?"

"That's right. Make an appointment for the first opening I've got—a long one, a couple of hours. I've got to talk to him."

I keep running into other people asking questions, the detective had once remarked. Goodenough firmly quelled the fizz of pain he began to feel.

He'd had a lot of practice at that since Colin Frazier's death.

12 September 14

"HE'S ON A bus," Miss Peck gasped as she jumped into the car and slammed the door. "Oh, my, am I out of shape!" She pulled into traffic with brakes shrieking behind her, careened left without signaling and stomped on the accelerator. Sharmille grabbed the armrest and hung on.

"Where are we going?"

"After the bus." Miss Peck, still panting, glanced over her shoulder, changed lanes, and raced through the tail end of a yellow light. "Oh, my goodness. I hope we haven't lost it! I'm not the runner I used to be."

Sharmille tried to picture Miss Peck sprinting down the sidewalk in the sensible shoes and the dignified dress, and failed. "Is that it?" she asked, pointing to a red MTC bus half a block ahead.

"What number is it? Can you see?"

Sharmille squinted at the number dimly visible through the smoked-up back window of the bus. "Looks like a twenty-two," she said.

"Then that's it, I hope, I hope." Miss Peck maneuvered her car behind the bus. "You didn't see him on the sidewalk, did you?"

Sharmille hadn't been looking. "No," she said.

"Then he must still be on the bus."

Sharmille didn't have the heart to point out that even if she had been looking she might have missed the man on the crowded late-afternoon sidewalk, or that they might have the wrong bus after all. She relaxed her grip as Miss Peck slowed to the sedate pace of public transportation, and rolled up her window against the bus fumes.

"Ick, he would take a bus," Miss Peck commented.

The bus halted at the next corner. Miss Peck stopped a couple of car lengths back to avoid the worst of the exhaust. The bus pulled out; Sharmille checked the people who had gotten off. "Not there," she reported.

"I hope he gets off soon," Miss Peck said. "Between the heat and the running and that smelly bus, I'm getting a little sick to my stomach."

"Want me to drive?" Sharmille offered.

"No thanks." Miss Peck stifled the deep inhalation that tried to come as she finally caught her breath. "That's sweet of you, but I don't think we have time to trade places."

"What will you do when he gets off?"

"Follow him," Miss Peck said, surprised. "I'm sure it's the man that woman told me about—right kind of car and the right color suit, and he's the right size and hair color. So we'll see if he leads us to Celie."

Sharmille shook her head. "I don't think so, Miss Peck." She slipped her feet out of the high-heeled shoes and into the flat ones. "He drove that car almost four hundred miles. He wouldn't do that just around the Twin Cities, not in three days, would he?"

"He could have," Miss Peck said stubbornly.

"Well, yeah, he could've," Sharmille allowed. "But c'mon, do you really think he did?"

The bus slowed and stopped. Miss Peck stopped, too. Several people got off the bus, but the man in the grey suit wasn't among them.

"I guess not," Miss Peck agreed, having thought it over. "But he's still our only chance. Where does this bus go, do you know?"

"Sorry, no." Sharmille ran her long fingers through her hair, trying to let some air through to her scalp. Dumb. She could've bought some rubber bands at the Tom Thumb, put her hair in a few pigtails, at least. Like a little kid, but cool.

"Looks like it might go down Cedar," Miss Peck said. "Maybe there'll be more space between stops, once it gets moving."

No such luck. "I don't know why I thought playing detective would be fun," Sharmille complained, after ten minutes of following in the smelly wake of the bus.

"It's the intellectual challenge."

"Say what?"

"The intellectual challenge," Miss Peck repeated firmly. "Hold that in mind. It helps to settle your stomach."

"It's my lungs I'm worried about."

The bus slowed and stopped. The car stopped behind it. People got off. People got on. The bus ground into motion, spewing thick, black, oily smoke. Miss Peck stepped lightly on the gas. The bus racketed along another long block, slowed and stopped. Miss Peck stopped behind it. People got off. People got on. The bus ground into motion. Miss Peck stepped on the gas. The bus traveled two hundred yards and stopped. Miss Peck stopped behind it. People got off, people got on. The bus ground into motion. Miss Peck stepped on the gas.

"Hey, hold on," Sharmille exclaimed. "Isn't that him?"

"Oh, good heavens, so it is! I must have been getting mesmerized." Miss Peck turned onto a side street after their quarry and pulled down the visor against the sun. "I guess it's my turn," she said, leaning forward and trying to see around the next corner, where the man had just turned. "He got too good a look at you in the car agency, I expect."

"Yeah, right. What do you want me to do?"

"See if you can follow me with the car, about a block behind." Miss Peck released her seat belt and opened the car door. She half-ran to the corner and looked after the man with the jacket slung over his arm. *There he is,* she congratulated herself, and waved back at Sharmille.

Sharmille, rather than try to maneuver her legs over the gearshift, got out and went around to the driver's side and got back into the car. She fumbled for the seat release, her knees almost knocking at the dashboard, and finally located it at the side of the seat. The seat scooted backwards, too far, and jammed.

Sharmille murmured a word never before heard in Miss Peck's car.

She rocked the seat loose and got it adjusted, moved the inside mirror until she could see out the back window instead of only the faded padding of the back seat, and started after Miss Peck.

There she was, coming back. Sharmille pulled to the curb and waited.

"He's gone into a house," Miss Peck said through the open passenger-side window.

Sharmille caught herself before the word came out of her mouth again. "He probably lives there," she said bleakly.

"We ought to watch anyway, don't you think?"

"Well, for a while, maybe."

Miss Peck got into the car and glanced at her watch. "You're still on my time," she said. "Sure you don't want to wait for him to come out?"

"Maybe. For a while. Where's this house?"

"About halfway along this next block." Miss Peck pointed west.

The block was a short one. Sharmille reparked just around the corner and looked. Three houses, the kind divided into rooms to let, furnished out of the Salvation Army store, with the bathroom down the hall and the kitchen shared with a lot of other people, each with a different nonnegotiable idea of the way things are done. The exact reasons Sharmille had moved back in with her parents. "Which one?" she asked.

"The white one."

The white house, covered with asbestos shingles streaked with dirt, had red-painted window trim that had started to peel. A scrap of lawn composed chiefly of dandelions separated the house from the sidewalk. The lawn had been mowed, but no one had made the effort of the people next door, who had set an old tire on each side of the front walk, painted them a sort of sea-green and planted them with orange and yellow marigolds.

"He could stay here all night, y'know?" Sharmille said. "I'm sorry, Miss Peck, but I'm not gonna stay here all night."

"Won't he have to go out to eat?"

"Not if he's got kitchen privileges, or a hot plate."

"You think he's got Celie in there?"

"No way. Not with all that driving he did." Sharmille imagined the man leaving Celie tied up in a room with fading cabbage roses on the walls and an overhead light with a string hanging into the center of the room. "Besides, there's no privacy in a place like that. Not enough, anyway."

Someone came out of the house door onto the glassed-in front porch, and then the porch door swung and the man in the grey suit—except that he was now wearing a short-sleeved plaid shirt and green slacks and carrying a denim jacket and a small suitcase—came down the steps.

Morrison, the name was supposed to be. Morrison stood on the bottom step looking around for a moment, and then he went down the short walk and up to an old clunker of a car. He unlocked the trunk and tossed in the suitcase and jacket.

A dude walking a fuzzy German shepherd puppy on a long piece of clothesline stopped and said something to Morrison. Morrison shook his head. The puppy ran under the car and the dude hauled it back yipping. Morrison said something and the dude laughed. Sharmille felt exposed, as if eyes everywhere were turning to stare at her. Two Hmong children playing in a yard across the street had stopped to try to entice the puppy. They hung over a ragged picket fence, snapping their fingers and calling to the dog until a window opened in the second floor of the house behind them and an old woman with a creased moon of a face called out. The children stopped snapping their fingers, and the woman gave Sharmille a hard stare and slammed the window.

Morrison opened the door of the car, a red one with one blue fender on the off-side front and some repaired rust spots that had started to rust through again. The puppy came and checked out Miss Peck's car and the owner gaped at them while the puppy piddled on one of Miss Peck's tires. *Come on, come on,* Sharmille thought. *Get it moving!* Either the dog or the car would do.

The puppy spotted a flock of sparrows on the sidewalk and lunged after them, tongue flapping, and dragged his master away. Morrison—a name most likely just as real as John Johnson's, Sharmille reflected—finally started his car. A whoosh of blue smoke came out of the exhaust pipe. The car didn't move. A man came out of the house across the street and said something to the two children, who went into the house ahead of him.

Now Morrison got his show on the road! Sharmille let him get halfway down the next block before she started the car, despite Miss Peck twittering in the seat beside her.

"We don't want him to know we're after him," she explained.

"Don't lose him," Miss Peck pleaded. "Not after all this trouble."

"Don't worry." Sharmille eased the car into gear. She kept two short blocks behind the red car. "You've got his license number, haven't you?"

"Oh, yes." Miss Peck reached for her handbag. "I'd better write it down before I forget, though I don't know what we can do with it."

"Go to the cops," Sharmille said. "You're not planning to do this all by yourself, are you?"

"Well, no." Miss Peck didn't sound too certain. Sharmille glanced at her and saw that she was biting her lips. "They weren't very interested this morning, though."

"They'll be more interested now," Sharmille predicted. The car ahead turned right onto Park Avenue, and Sharmille stepped on the gas. It crossed her mind to try to stay parallel to him, one block away, as he headed north, but that might just be trouble. And what would she say to Miss Peck? The poor woman would have a heart attack.

"What do you bet he gets back on a bus?" Sharmille mused.

She was wrong. Morrison parked by a hardware store with a bus stop bench in front of it, but he went in. "You want to go in and see what he's doing?" she asked, slowing down only to find the curb parked solid.

"No. He'd get suspicious, don't you think? If he happened to glimpse me when I followed him before?" Miss Peck reached into her handbag and came up with a tissue, with which she blotted her face and neck.

"What should I do? I can't double-park."

Miss Peck craned her neck to look behind her as far as she could see. "I don't see a bus coming," she reported. "You'll just have to go around the block, I guess."

Sharmille made a right past the hardware store, moved slowly down a short block in which some kids were playing kickball, accelerated down the long block the next right turn brought her to, and made two quick rights to complete the circuit.

"He's still there," Miss Peck sighed. "You'll have to go around again."

Sharmile repeated the right-hand circle, amid a lot of flack from the kids. When she got back to the hardware store, the red car was gone.

"Oh, no!" Miss Peck groaned. "We've lost him!"

"No, there he is!" The glee of the hunt seized Sharmille; she stepped on the gas and closed the gap between herself and the red car, which was still heading downtown. The man was in a hurry, taking lights on the yellow and getting up near forty-five sometimes. Sharmille went nervously after him, almost losing him twice at traffic lights, then picking up that blue fender again.

"Why, Sharmille, you're really good at this," Miss Peck marveled. "A talent I never suspected." She sat forward as Sharmille once again closed the gap, straining forward like a hound on the leash.

"Just lucky," Sharmille admitted. "If he didn't have that blue fender, he'd have been lo-o-o-ng gone."

The red car continued north. Sharmille settled back against the seat with a grin. She felt *good*. Never mind the unseasonable heat, never mind the sweat. This was better than sitting in an air-conditioned room at a typewriter any day. Maybe she should apply to the cops for a job, see if she could get on their list. She'd have to take a few courses, maybe, at the community college, maybe, show she really could hack it in spite of those grades in high school. . . . A frown crossed her forehead. Had she read something about cops having to be college grads? . . . The red car turned left onto Seventh Street, just on the tail of a light. Sharmille abandoned her plans for her future and braked.

"Go, go," Miss Peck urged.

"There's a cop over there!"

"This is an emergency!"

"Miss Peck!" Cars began streaming by on Seventh, a better argument for staying put than mere legality. Sharmille tried to keep the red car in sight as it went up toward the bend Seventh took, past Goverment Center. "I think I lost him," she said, so disappointed she could feel the beginning of tears inside her lower eyelids.

"Go after him anyway." The light changed; Sharmille turned left and stayed in the middle of the one-way street, ready to move to either side.

"You drive, I'll check side streets," Miss Peck said. Sharmille gave her attention to trying to get through downtown Minneapolis at rush hour without running down a pedestrian or altering Miss Peck's car. She made what progress she could, weaving ahead as chances presented themselves, and with disbelief saw, two short blocks ahead, the red car with the telltale blue fender.

"It's him!" she squealed. "It's him, it's him!"

"Go get 'im, Sharmille," Miss Peck cheered, pounding the dashboard with both fists. "I knew we could do it!"

13 September 14

ONE MOMENT THE car was right there ahead of them, caught in the same traffic, and the next it wasn't. Presto change-o.

"How could he just vanish in the middle of a block?" Miss Peck's voice skittered upward. "He was there when we crossed that last intersection, wasn't he?"

"He sure ain't there now."

"Could he have crossed the next street already?"

"Not unless he ran the light, and in this traffic we'd have heard the crunch." Sharmille sighed and poked her fingers up through her hair. "Unless . . . is that a parking garage?"

"Yes! That's it! Sharmille, you're a genius!" Miss Peck bounced in her seat again. "Let me off. I'll watch the entrance. You go around the block and get into the garage and find the car."

Sharmille pulled to the curb as traffic started moving again, and Miss Peck hopped out and slammed the door.

Outsmarted myself, Sharmille thought with profound disgust, as she twisted to look for a space to slide into. Keeping over to the right like that, to keep an eye out for the blue fender. The guy had just turned left into the garage and disappeared, just like that. On the left side, the car was all red, and without the mental tag she'd hung on it visible, Sharmille just hadn't noticed. She sighed, figuring out how to run the maze of one-way streets to come back on the left side to get into the garage herself.

Miss Peck waited for the light to change, her eyes on the pedestrian entrance to the parking ramp, now all too obvious in the middle of the block. Surely Morrison hadn't had time to park and get away? She couldn't see the plaid shirt and green slacks anywhere, not waiting to cross any of the streets, not walking along the opposite sidewalk.

The light changed, and Miss Peck darted across the street. Reckless, she took up a post right next to the pedestrian entrance and waited. No one came out for a minute or two. Then a man pushed open the door. She almost accosted him, but it was someone quite different, in jeans and a blue T-shirt with a gigantic mosquito printed on it, blond hair. Miss Peck let her hand drop.

Five minutes went by. Miss Peck waited, tapping her foot and twisting cold fingers together, while a good many cars came down the ramp, paused at the attendant's booth, and eased onto the street. Only a few cars entered. Her own turned in, Sharmille looking harassed and tired at the wheel. Miss Peck waved and got a half-hearted flash of white teeth in return. Sharmille took a ticket from the dispenser and drove on.

Miss Peck waited. Four more minutes crawled past. Where could that man be? Where was Sharmille?

Another man came through the glass door and stared briefly at her as he went by.

"Miss Peck."

She jumped and turned around. "Sharmille! How did . . . ? Oh."

Sharmille nodded. "Yeah, there's another exit. I saw the car. It's locked. I guess our man went out the other side, huh?"

"Must be." Miss Peck sagged. "Well," she sighed, "so much for our detecting. I guess we ought to stick to typing."

"Right now I just want to go home."

Miss Peck glanced at her thin, gold watch, blinking back disappointment. She felt as weary as Sharmille sounded, and the watch hands stood at ten past four. "It's past time, isn't it?" she said. "Well, thanks for being such a good sport, Sharmille."

Sharmille shrugged. "That's okay. My bus goes right past the end of this block, so if you don't mind?"

"No, sure. Go on. Oh! You'd better give me the ticket for the garage. What do I owe you?"

"Nothing. You pay when you leave." Sharmille handed over the slip of blue cardboard and the keys and vanished into the crowd, like the Cheshire cat leaving only the warmth of her grin. Miss Peck pulled open the door and wearily climbed the concrete steps inside. She had forgotten to ask Sharmille which level she'd parked on, so she'd have to search for her car. Start at the top and work down, since the ramp was still crowded.

The staircase seemed to stretch into eternity over her head. Miss Peck looked up and kept climbing.

Morrison relaxed into the seat as the four-thirty Greyhound for Duluth left the terminal a few blocks away. He smiled, satisfied with his day's work. The parking garage ticket was in a trash basket on Hennepin Avenue: no sense keeping the car, he'd never gotten around to getting the title transferred and he'd get a better one when Frazier came through with his half million. Doubly useful: he wondered about those women. Such an unlikely pair, both classy ladies but in such different ways—and why had they taken such an interest in him?

Well, forget it. They'd lost him at the garage, and they sure couldn't trace him onto the bus!

"Look, Miss Peck," said the police officer. He visibly summoned his reserves of patience. "I can understand that you're concerned about this employee of yours. And I know it's a lot of fun to run around town playing detective, though I might point out that it's a good way to get yourself into a lot of trouble. But I can't just go arrest some guy on your say-so, not in a case like this."

"But he kidnapped her!"

Stubborn old dame. Right on the edge of her seat, little

fists white-knuckled on her knees, ready to go out and take on the world. He sighed. "No, you *suspect* he kidnapped her. That's different. You might be satisfied, but we'd need a lot more evidence than you've given me before we could make an arrest. I mean, turn it around. What would you think if you were arrested for kidnapping, just because you'd rented a car of a certain make and color?"

"Why would he rent a car when he already had one?"

Women didn't understand about cars. Oh, they could be impressed, all right, but when you got right down to it, cars for women were just boxes on wheels. The policeman sighed again. He knew an impossible explanation when he saw one coming. "Any number of reasons, Miss Peck. Some important occasion to attend, say. A play or a concert—"

"Monday night? Tuesday?"

He nodded, to keep her happy. "Not big date nights. I see your point. Maybe he went to a wedding. Business conference, with an important client. Who knows?"

She set her mouth in that tight little line he'd seen so many times on so many other faces.

"Did you check all the rental agencies, Miss Peck?" he asked gently. "Or did you stop with the first one you found that had rented out the kind of car you were looking for?"

Miss Peck slumped. "We stopped when we found one," she admitted.

"See, we couldn't do that. We'd have to check them all. Several cars of that description might have been rented out over that period, and if we thought one of them had been used in a kidnapping, we'd have to go over every single one of them, see?"

"What about the false name?"

She had something there. "Could be a real name and a wrong address. Could even be the clerk wrote it down wrong. Who knows?" She shook her head slowly, chin lowered, reminding him of a pint-size bull thinking of charging. "See, Miss Peck, the girl seems to have entered the car willingly. You can't even be sure it was a kidnapping. It could have been something else altogether—her dad in town for the day—"

"Celie has no father."

"Or somebody else she knows. You don't know."

"I still think you should go after this man," the woman said. "I feel it in my bones."

"Well, sometimes that means something, and sometimes no. I can't take your bones to a judge and get a warrant, now, can I?"

She didn't laugh. He had bones of his own, of course, and from time to time they told him a thing or two. This time they told him to check all this out and check back with them.

"Maybe I should take this up with the Chief of Police!"

Threats, now. "Sure. His door's open. He's always happy to hear what the citizens have to say. Call him at home if you want, he's in the book. But he'll tell you the same thing, we can't arrest people when all we've got for evidence is a—a thin tissue of supposition. Like this one." He picked up a pencil. "Unless you've got more to tell me?"

"No." The woman sagged as she gathered up her valise of a handbag and got to her feet. He felt for her, he really did, as she left with slumping shoulders, but—!

Celie Lewis. Possible bomber. He couldn't see how that linked up with a man who rented an expensive car and drove her away the morning her office blew, but it was possible. He drew circles around the two license numbers in his notes and went to talk to Jim Clifford.

Miss Peck, on the steps beneath the clock tower, paused to make up her mind. Above her head, the deep voice of the clock declared seven.

Home. Bath. Think. Oh, and feed that fool cat.

14 September 14

CELIE LUNGED FOR the big chair as someone tapped on the door and the padlock rattled. She had barely hauled herself straight when Morrison came in, carrying a Styrofoam tray with a hot TV dinner on it.

"Hello," Celie ventured.

"Hi." A friendly smile. "Dinner time."

"Thanks."

About time!

They were treating her okay, considering. She had awakened the afternoon before, still in the chair, but covered by a scratchy blanket smelling of moth crystals, chilled by the thought that they—Baker, especially—had been back while she was sleeping and defenseless. But the blanket was welcome, as was the chemical toilet now in one corner of the room. The man who called himself Morrison had looked in on her when only a little twilight had come through the open door with him; he'd been carrying a flashlight, so it must have been nearly eight o'clock. He'd brought her a thermos of soup and a stale roast beef sandwich and a second blanket.

She had spent this day exploring her prison. At first, she'd tried getting around with a kind of inchworm crawl, but with her legs locked together she had had to rise on her stockinged toes and lever herself forward, with all the extra weight of the cast around her ankles. The process was hard on her toes, hard on her knees and, above all, hell on the arches of her feet. After a few minutes she gave up and lay on the cold, stained wooden floor, looking at the dust in the cracks between the boards. Cigarettes had been stubbed out on this floor, leaving little blackish areas of ground-in ash. By the lingering, sweet smell, Celie suspected that the cigarettes had not been composed of tobacco.

A centipede, enlarged by its long, furry shadow, had skittered across the floor and brought her back up to her knees with a muffled shriek.

For a while after the inchworming failed, she'd gone back to her baby-shuffle, a kind of hobbled step that might have been specified by some sadist directing a game of "Giant Steps." It was nice to be upright (the centipede wouldn't climb her legs, would it?), but blisters rose on her heels and the balls of her feet, so that way of getting around was out, too. She had removed one of the diamond-paned windows and pushed at the plywood covering the opening. It didn't seem solid, but she didn't know which way the little house faced, or what to do if she did get a window open—she surely couldn't climb out—so she simply re-placed the sash and tried to push the rusted pins that held it back in place.

The rest of the morning she spent in the chair, holding the lamp in her lap in the hope that any self-respecting leggy creature would keep to the dark corners.

By the time someone—the man she knew only as Steve—brought breakfast, near noon to judge by the angle of the sunlight pouring through the open door, she had settled on a fairly rapid means of locomotion: with her skirt tucked up, she sat down, stretched her legs as far as they would go, raised herself on her hands, and scooted forward until her rear end hit the plaster. She was startled that she had had so much trouble thinking of the simple expedient of facing the ceiling in order to move around, but by breakfast, she was pretty good at it.

"Anything else I can get for you?" Morrison asked now, setting the TV dinner on the lamp table.

It wouldn't do any good to ask for a radio. They'd been through that: too much noise, people would ask questions. Enough of a hint to give Celie hope that others were near, enough that last night she'd pounded and yelled until they threatened to gag her. Now she wasn't sure she even wanted the radio; she wanted to be able to hear if anyone did come. One of the people who had come here once to smoke a few joints, maybe.

"I'm out of water." The water had come that afternoon, warm and tasteless, in a plastic pitcher. "And I'm dying for something to read."

"I'll look around," Morrison promised. She heard the padlock slide into the hasp after he closed the door. Beyond its iron-bound planks the crickets and katydids were going at it with an intensity that suggested they knew their time was short. Celie blinked back tears.

One other thing she had done, when she'd thought about people using this place: she'd taken her checkbook out of her pocket and torn out a deposit slip. She had stopped to listen. The man whose last name she didn't know knocked. Morrison knocked. Baker didn't bother, but she had discovered that she could hear one of them coming on what seemed to be a gravel path. She had listened for several seconds. No one.

Across the space provided for totaling an inconceivable number of checks, she had written, "Help. I am being held here against my will. Please call police." She'd sat and stared at the message for a few seconds and then added, "Also please notify Miss Ethel Peck," and had written down the new address of the typing service.

Checkbook and pen she hid in the depths of the chair; the note she folded and tucked into her bra. Now she was ready. If anyone came.

No one did come until Morrison brought dinner, long after dark. After that, no one came until Morrison brought her a stack of *Reader's Digest* magazines a couple of years old. After that, the slim silver crack of moonlight under the door faded and went out, and no one came. Celie sat in the fat old chair next to the lamp, reading.

15 September 15

THURSDAY DAWNED COOLER than Wednesday, without haze or threat of rain—none of which, surprisingly, did anything to lift Miss Peck's spirits. She breakfasted, did the upper right-hand corner of the daily crossword puzzle, and, reminded by a miaow, fed Celie's cat. She dressed without enthusiasm and, also without enthusiasm, got into her car and drove into town. Early, as usual, she surveyed her new office.

Barbra had accomplished about what she expected. Perhaps half of the files had been unpacked and presumably replaced in the cabinets. The steel cabinet was again full of supplies. No typing had been done, but on the other hand, she had put off customers until next week because of moving.

Miss Peck went into her own office, conscious of a lack of excitement. She ran her hand over the surface of her elegant almost-new desk and felt herself deprived of the glow of ownership. On the desk were the handwritten pages John Johnson had left to be typed, rubber-banded to the finished manuscript—not that Miss Peck expected the job to be picked up, or to be paid anything more than the usual deposit, which she hoped Barbra had had the presence of mind to collect. Clipped to the manuscript was a note in Barbra's neat, round handwriting:

Clarice Klenk called and said she has another book ready will you be free to type it right away I said yes. Also some man has been coming around while you and

Sharmille were gone this, I mean yesterday afternoon and he asked a bunch of questions about Celie I didn't tell him anything what should I say. (If he comes around again.) (He was NOT police!!!) Here is that Mr. Johnson's stuff you wanted.

Miss Peck cast an eye over "Mr. Johnson's stuff" and found it to be not nearly so badly written as Barbra's note, but surely not the work of a graduate student. In hindsight, Miss Peck felt that she had been uncommonly stupid. But there was no use crying over spilt milk, as her mother would have said, so she shrugged and put the manuscript into her desk drawer and locked it. Later it might be useful.

Sharmille, her hair braided into a single gleaming spiral that began over her right ear and wound to the crown of her head, where it ended in a pouf tied with a piece of yellow yarn, came in, yawning.

"Good morning, Sharmille," Miss Peck said. "Could you mind the store for a bit? I have to go out."

Sharmille gave her a glance in which curiosity struggled with fatigue. Fatigue won. "Sure," she said, plopping into her chair.

"Clarice Klenk may bring in a manuscript," Miss Peck said. "You and Barbra can divide it up any way you like and we'll paginate later."

"Oh, whoopee," Sharmille commented. Miss Peck paid no attention. She hoisted her handbag strap onto her shoulder and left the office.

Back down Fourth Street, past the police cruisers parked outside City Hall, past the big clock tower and the Grain Exchange, Miss Peck mingled with the crowds, her eyes and mind focused in the middle distance. Never-Fail Employment Service had supplied her faithfully with typists for several years, and so it was several years since she had last placed a classified ad: she pushed through the revolving door at the *Star and Tribune* and ascended the inside steps only to be directed by the young man at the guard desk to the new building, across Fourth on Portland Avenue. She thanked him and went back out, feeling disoriented.

The woman walking beside her, reflected in the polished black granite of the building facade, seemed more gaunt than slender. Miss Peck stopped beside the "1947" inscribed in newspaper gothic in the wall, and examined her reflection. Yes. Definitely more haggard than usual.

She crossed Fourth with a lively enough step, however, and went up the diagonal walk to the new building. The Want Ad desk was straight ahead.

Miss Peck hesitated, unsure exactly what to put into her ads. She dropped down on one of the mulberry-colored chairs to think, staring at the tapestry that showed the checkmark of the *Tribune* in glowing flamelike colors instead of the familiar black on white, as if it could stimulate her imagination. Instead, for some reason it reminded her of the cheap print—of kittens about to strangle themselves in a skein of yarn—that Barbra had hung beside her desk. A wave of depression passed over her: what, after all, had she accomplished in her life? Hundreds of thousands, millions, easily a hundred million words, not one her own, typed for hire, a little house and a car getting crochety, some good, and perhaps not too much evil.

She forced her mind back to the reason she was here. The name in caps, yes. Extra for that. Miss Peck sighed, thinking of the balance showing in her precisely-kept check register, and got a note pad out of her purse to compose the ads.

"Celia Lewis," she wrote. Next line, small print: "Or anyone knowing her whereabouts." No. "Where she is" took less space than "her whereabouts"; that might save one line. . . . She'd have them call the office number and put an announcement on the answering machine with her home number, much as she hated to. Customers could be difficult at times. Clients.

Miss Peck ran her tongue over her teeth and added "Right Away" after the telephone number.

The other ad was longer. "Off-White Lincoln," she printed. "Seen in odd circumstances within 175 mi. Twin Cities. REWARD for right info." She added the office phone number, reread what she had written, and walked up to the desk.

Ten minutes later, astounded that her handbag didn't feel any lighter with nearly two hundred and fifty dollars removed from her checking account, she walked out of the door having contracted for six days of ads in all editions of the newspaper. Well, she argued with herself, Celie's life might be in danger, and didn't that warrant every conceivable effort to save her? The police seemed inclined to do nothing, and she had already invested so much time and effort, so much emotion. . . .

Accomplishing good. Not much evil. Good and evil, what was that? Oh, yes, Saint Paul . . . so she shouldn't be worrying about the money, should she? Even if it did leave her short? Miss Peck walked on, puzzling over her own motives. Really, what was Celie to her?

Five years was it, now? Sharmille three, and Barbra seven. Wouldn't she have done the same for either of them?

Maybe not just the same for Sharmille, without Sharmille to help, but she'd have tried something, she knew she would have. . . .

"I put a couple of ads in the paper," she told Sharmille and Barbra. "They start tomorrow. If anybody calls, just transfer the call to me."

"Ads? Already?" Barbra stared at her, mouth dropped. "For somebody to replace Celie?"

"Of course not. To try to find Celie," Miss Peck said,

biting her lower lip. "They'll run a week. I hope somebody reads them."

Sharmille rested her hands on the chassis of the typewriter and stared at her. "A week! That must have cost you a bundle. Can you afford it?"

"Can I afford not to?"

"I don't get you."

Miss Peck plopped down in Celie's empty chair and rested her handbag on her knees. "I got to thinking. Saint Paul said that the love of money is the root of all evil," she said, repeating the thoughts that had occupied her all the long walk back from the newspaper building. "But I think he was wrong. The roots of evil are greed and fear. Any kind of greed, not just for money. And any kind of fear. That's why we all have it in us to be evil, whether we love money or not. I don't want to be evil."

She rose stiffly after this unaccustomed sort of speech, leaving the two younger women gaping at her. In her office she slumped into her own new, unpaid-for chair. There. That was it. That was why. Not to respond to Celie's need because she'd rather spend her money on other things, wouldn't that be evil?

Well, maybe not. No, of course not. All the same—Miss Peck sighed deeply—if she backed out now, she wouldn't be very happy with herself.

Greed and fear. What kind of greed, what kind of fear, had led to the bomb, to all those dreams her clients had committed to paper blowing away like so much trash, down the streets of Minneapolis with last week's newspaper? Miss Peck put the handbag into her bottom desk drawer and tried to concentrate on the work that would replenish the money she had just spent. Fear Celie Lewis? The idea of it! A likeable girl, but sometimes such an exasperating wimp! *Like you at that age, Ethel,* she thought. On the outside, at least.

Could it be that she got to see only a small part of Celie Lewis, working in the office? Miss Peck prided herself on her ability to "read" people, but she'd been wrong before . . . sometimes spectacularly so, often enough that she was in no danger of confusing herself with, say, Jane Marple of St. Mary's Mead . . . and she had to admit, she had a prejudice against people so insecure that they felt the need of fortune-telling to get through the day, as Celie sometimes seemed to do. Courage was a thing Miss Peck valued, along with loyalty (which Celie had shown), and attention to duty, to doing what ought to be done, not just what was required . . . and truly, wasn't part of her exasperation with Celie the feeling that there was more to the girl than met the eye, that she was capable of . . . something more . . . not like Barbra, who sometimes gave her the impression that although she'd heard people talk about something called 'living,' most of what she knew about it she'd learned from her TV screen.

"Well, Ethel!" Clarice Klenk sailed into the private office without even bothering to knock, clutching to her large, freckled bosom an even larger bundle of hand-scribbled notebook paper. "Daydreaming, you! What is it, a new beau?"

"Hello, Clarice." Miss Peck managed a wan smile. "I was thinking about a mystery, to tell the truth."

"A mystery! I always thought that was right up your alley, Ethel, the way you gulp the things down," Clarice Klenk declared, settling into the client's chair as thoroughly as a hen into a dustbath. Miss Peck, as usual, had the impression that little scraps of manuscript were being shed onto the floor, but that was only an illusion; the ragged sheets of paper were firmly disciplined by several thick rubber bands. "They say you ought to write what you like to read, and you know I've always wanted to write mysteries," Clarice continued. "But it's the plotting, you

114

know. Such a drag! Also they don't make nearly as much money as romances."

"I wasn't thinking of writing one, Clarice," Miss Peck said. "I've got one."

Clarice started back in her chair, one hand pressed to her heaving bosom, Miss Peck thought, as her friend did precisely that—although the heaving bosom was undoubtedly the result of running up the stairs: Clarice hated elevators. "You jest," she cried, *her hazel eyes flying open.*

Miss Peck smiled at herself. Clarice's style tended to become infectious. "No, alas," she said. "One of my girls has disappeared."

"The timid one?"

Miss Peck nodded.

"She always looked like she'd rather be invisible, anyway," Clarice remarked. "Did she do it on her own?"

"Not likely," Miss Peck sighed. "The police think she set a bomb in my old place—you heard about that?—and took off on her own, but I think she was kidnapped."

"Tell more," Clarice commanded, after a second's silence.

"For fifteen percent of the royalties?"

"Now you are joking." Clarice wriggled her shoulders. "You can have it, if you can pry it out of my agent, but I'll tell you this very minute, that's not bloody likely. Besides, I just said, I can't write mysteries."

Miss Peck grinned. Clarice hadn't changed, not in essence, since grade school. She cheerfully put up with the woman's affectations—a walking stick for tramping the wilds of Lake Harriet, where the paved path was marked with directional arrows, for instance, or the huge, flopping, reddish tweed cap (worn over a Gore-Tex jacket in winter) that Clarice had adopted as fitting apparel for a romance writer, but which reminded Miss Peck irresistibly of a tough old chicken with her beady eye on freedom—for the sake of her shrewd, caring (although not always gentle) candor as much as for the easy comfort of long acquaintance. "It's quite a story," she said with a rueful smile, and recounted all of it.

"So now you're rushing off in all directions to save her." Clarice nodded. "You always did have an impulse to ride to the rescue. Remember that kitten you fished out of the storm sewer that time?"

"We, Clarice," Miss Peck corrected. "*We* fished the kitten out of the storm sewer. You were skinnier then."

"That's right. You held the lid up and I climbed down and handed the beast out," Clarice acknowledged. "I can still see your lip sticking out, and your mother standing there tapping her foot and a big wet mark on her apron where she'd wiped her hands. Whatever did happen to that cat?"

"My mother gave it to a neighbor."

"No good out of all that pouting, just like *my* mother used to tell me. Ah, well. But still, you're a rescue addict, admit it."

"What about you?"

"I've matured," Clarice declared loftily.

"Put on weight, you mean," Miss Peck said, not unkindly.

"Keeps me out of sewers," Clarice commented. "But you, you've had a busy three days. I don't think I've ever run one of my heroines through anything like that, poor, put-upon little things. But then, you didn't have to take time out for romance—terrible nuisance, always getting in the way of their doing anything, but some man has to be there, poor dears. Rule of the genre. What's next?"

Miss Peck sighed. "Wait and see if somebody answers the ads, I guess. I can't think of anything else, can you?"

"Sure. Hire a private detective."

"Clarice, I don't know anything about private detectives."

"Neither do I, but presumably they know all about

themselves." Clarice tilted her head with momentary victory. "How long will these ads run?"

"A week."

Clarice opened her mouth, with a perceptible delay before any words came out: "My God, Ethel, did you come into a fortune?"

"They did cost a lot," Miss Peck murmured. "But they're necessary."

"Why?"

Slowly, redly, Miss Peck presented Clarice with her theories of greed, fear, and evil. They sounded rather silly on second telling.

"Oh, pooh!" Clarice said, more or less as feared. "Saint Paul as pop psychologist. Really and truly, Ethel!" She leaned over the desk and patted Miss Peck's arm. "You're bored, that's why you won't hire a detective. You want all the fun for yourself—not that I blame you; I would, too."

Was that it? Miss Peck stared at her hands, clasped on the desk in front of her. Was she making a game out of Celie's misfortune, money or no money? *Pretending* to be noble, courageous, all that . . . crap? Just to relieve her own boredom? Boredom didn't sound like a respectable motive, somehow . . . "I don't think I'm bored," she said.

"Sure you are. And sick to death of being the proper Miss Peck, I bet. Your mother should have named you Eileen, then you wouldn't be stuck being stodgy."

"Eileen!" Miss Peck exclaimed. "Stodgy! Well, thanks a bunch."

"Simmer down," Clarice advised. "There's no use fighting over your mother's eccentricities. Think about what to do next, like I said."

"My *mother's* eccen—oh, I don't know, Clarice, really I don't."

"Think detective."

Miss Peck pressed her lips together and glared at her friend and found herself, after a few seconds in which her mind simply sputtered, thinking detective. "How would I go about finding a reliable one?" she objected.

"Oh, I don't know." Clarice could afford to be airy; it wasn't her typist. "You're the one that's good at that kind of thing. You know *I* can't do anything practical."

"You can't?"

"Haven't you read my press releases? I'm a tender reed, dear heart. But that's what to do, I'm sure of it. Hire a detective, there're probably dozens in the Yellow Pages. Now, about this new book—if you'll forgive me. Oh, you're going to love this one! Yum!" Clarice made smacking noises. "It's set in Spain."

"Not during the Inquisition, I hope," Miss Peck said, her mind apparently still running along theological lines.

"Of course not, silly. It's more a kind of a *Carmen*, only with different characters and a different story, of course." Clarice unwrapped a number of the rubber bands, revealing that the pages had been bundled into chapters.

Miss Peck reached into the center drawer of her new desk—*Clarice could have admired it, just for a second*, she thought—for a receipt book and filled the top slip out. She handed it across the desk and took charge of the scribbled pages. "Oh, Clarice, I almost forgot!" she said. "I've got something you can help me with."

"For your mystery?"

Miss Peck nodded as she rummaged through her bottom desk drawer.

"Ooo, exciting! What?"

"This." Miss Peck handed Celie's boxed Tarot cards to Clarice. "I thought Celie might have told her own fortune before she disappeared—it would be just like her, if she were worried about something—and you'd be able to figure out what it was."

"Told her own fortune? That's a no-no, the naughty child." Clarice pulled the deck out of the box and started counting off cards. "So's this, you know. One doesn't handle other people's Tarot cards."

"I'd heard."

"But what she doesn't know won't hurt her. Let's see." Clarice stared at the cards for a while, quite soberly. Miss Peck missed the guileful twist of the mouth with which Clarice had once done readings at school bazaars.

"Well, I can't help you, Ethel. This card"—she picked up the Knight of Cups—"is the eleventh one down in the deck. She'd have used it to represent herself, so I think she was doing one of the shorter readings, probably a Celtic cross. That would take eleven cards, see?"

"Not really."

"You can take my word for it. The problem is, I don't know where to go from there. The two on top of it might have been there when she laid them out, but I don't know which way they lay. And I've got no idea where the others were."

"Can't you even tell what *kind* of fortune it was?"

Clarice pulled her chin back, pressing a soft pillow of freckled flesh onto her collar. "It was either very, very good or very, very bad," she said. A ghost of the guileful smile passed over her mouth. "Then again, it could have been somewhere in between."

"Thanks," Miss Peck said.

Clarice shrugged. "Sorry." She heaved herself out of the chair. "Well, must run. I'll see you later, to pick up whatever gets typed today."

"Okay." Miss Peck watched her friend leave, wondering how she would get through the twenty-four hours before her personal ads appeared, and the wait for a reply that might not even come.

By having no choice, of course. The same way she had made it through every other major wait of her life. But the conversation must have done some good, after all. As

119

Clarice tootle-ooed her way through the outer office, Miss Peck realized that she did know something she could do. She could go talk to the woman who lived across the street from Celie and find out for certain whether she had noticed a license number on the Lincoln. If she had, and it turned out to be the same as the one on yesterday's car, the police could hardly ignore that!

16 September 15

THE OLD LADY wasn't home.

Miss Peck walked slowly down the cracked concrete walk and slumped into the driver's seat of her car. What now? Arms folded across the steering wheel, chin on her arms, she idly watched a robin prospecting at the edges of the shrubs for several minutes. Absurd to be so disappointed: she could hardly have counted on her luck holding out. Still, she didn't want to go back to the office without accomplishing something to raise her girls' morale. Or maybe just her own.

So. She knew what the woman looked like. She could go look in the most likely places for an old woman to go during the day—the grocery store, the Laundromat—looking for company.

But a quick tour of the neighborhood provided nothing to satisfy Miss Peck's need for action. She tried the old woman's house again. No one came to the door. She was forced to return to her car, no further ahead than she had been before.

Mulling over what she knew, she started the car and headed for 35W, the quickest way downtown. What did she know? Not much. Two license numbers, one for the Lincoln and one for the red car with the blue front fender. *Could a private citizen find out who owned that car?* Miss Peck wondered. Why not?

Worth a try. She edged into the far right lane, to take the turn-off for St. Paul.

Over an hour later, but only two dollars poorer, Miss Peck left the Transportation Building possessed of the name of a young woman who purportedly owned the red car with the blue fender, and who lived on Park Avenue in south Minneapolis, suggestively close to the house where the man Morrison had changed his clothes. It wouldn't take very long to swing past there, Miss Peck convinced herself.

But this stop, too, was fruitless. "Jeannine? Oh, she sold that car before she moved," said the thick-waisted woman who had answered the bell beside the peeling front door of the house.

"Where did she move to?"

"California," the woman said. "Seattle, I think."

Miss Peck smiled and thanked her for the information, such as it was, and retreated to her car. Now, she really had better get back to the office. She'd spent entirely too much time away from it as it was. What luck that this problem had come up this week, when the work load was low and she could rearrange her time so easily!

"Or is it luck?" she wondered, about to turn the ignition key. Could someone's hand have been forced by her move? But whose hand, and why?

Miss Peck sat back to think. If someone had bribed the super in the old building to let him in . . . or a cleaning lady? Not unlikely, considering how small office supplies had been disappearing of late. Bribes there might go down more easily than in the new place, she hoped. So that the bomb had been set on the last possible day. But why Celie? How to fit the bomb in with the kidnapping? Or were the police right, after all, had Celie just run off with someone— someone wealthy—but then she couldn't need to revenge herself for losing the job, could she? Especially when she hadn't lost it? Just a last explosion—Miss Peck's lips twisted wryly—of built-up rage? The girl would have to be insane!

No. Not Celie. Odd, but not insane. Shaking her head, Miss Peck started the car and drove away.

"Here she is," Barb said as Miss Peck entered the outer office.

The man who stood up as Miss Peck closed the door behind her was lean, with polished dark hair that matched his polished brown shoes. Despite his angular frame, his face rounded through somewhat plump cheeks to an indeterminate chin, a chin with a metallic blue gleam, although so closely shaven it seemed almost artificial. She distrusted him instantly.

"Yes," she said, ignoring the hand he held out. "What do you want?"

"Could we talk privately?"

She examined him without speaking, from the slick-shiny hair, past a faintly stained, home-washed tie and spiffy slacks, to his gleaming shoes, and wordlessly led the way into her office, where she deposited her handbag in the bottom drawer of her desk and ostentatiously turned the key in the lock.

He handed her a card. "A private detective?" she asked, wondering if this were someone Clarice had turned up, and if so under which damp log.

"Formerly with the FBI," he added, as did his card.

She bit her tongue to keep from asking why he'd been kicked out. "Yes?"

The man closed the door and drew the client's chair around to the side of the desk. "I'm working for an attorney in Duluth," he said.

Phew! Miss Peck thought. *Not Clarice's!* "And who is that?" she asked.

"Er—Michael Goodenough." The detective pulled a pack of cigarettes out of his shirt pocket and crossed his legs.

"I don't permit smoking," Miss Peck said.

"Oh." He sat up, like a ten-year-old caught doodling during arithmetic period, and put the cigarettes away. "Oh, sure, I get it, you get a break on the insurance, right? Every little bit helps, I always say."

Miss Peck blinked. She said nothing.

"I—uh—this attorney—Mr. Goodenough is looking for a woman called Alexa Frazier, twenty-four years old, who stands to inherit a chunk of money if she can be found by November four. Now, I have reason to believe that your employee, Celia Lewis, is actually Alexa Frazier."

Long practiced at self-discipline, Miss Peck merely said, "Indeed?"

"So, where is she?" The man displayed several nicotine-stained teeth in what Miss Peck supposed was meant to be a smile. "I know she's not out there," he continued, jerking his head toward her door. "The nigger's a nigger, and the other one's got those big brown eyes."

"I don't employ any niggers," Miss Peck said coldly. "And I can't tell you where Celie is." *The man is not worth anger,* she decided, feeling distant from her own body.

"No?" His left eyebrow rose. "Now, don't get all offended and do something you haven't thought out, you know?" He groped for the cigarettes, caught her stern eye, stopped. "There might be a little something in it for you if you help me find her, you know? Reward-type stuff, know what I mean?"

"Yes?"

He responded to the word and not the tone. "Uh, I don't want to get your hopes too high, but it might be like a couple of hundred, you know? Something like that. If you tell me where she is."

"I don't know where she is."

"Aw, come on . . . Ethel, is it?"

"Miss Peck," she corrected, with as much frost as she could muster. "Why do you need her now? You've got six weeks."

"Well, like I say, she gets a lot of money if she turns up in time."

Not what I asked, Miss Peck thought. "And if she doesn't?"

124

"Then she doesn't get the money."

"Who does?"

The detective twitched slightly. "I don't know if I'm allowed to say who gets it if she doesn't."

"I see." Miss Peck stood up. "I'm sorry," she said. "I'm afraid I can't help you."

The man remained sprawled in the chair. "This Celia, is she a good typist?"

Miss Peck remained standing. "She is the fastest typist I have ever employed," she said, acutely uncomfortable without quite knowing why.

He grinned. "And you won't tell me where she is."

"I can't."

Finally he got to his feet. "Maybe five hundred," he said. "That's as high as I can go."

"I have already told you that I don't know where she is," Miss Peck pointed out.

"Well, that's too bad. You've got my card," the man said, with an odious wink. "So if you think it over and you happen to remember where she is, you just give me a little call and I'll see if I can, you know, help you out a little. In cash."

"Thank you. That won't be necessary." Miss Peck crossed to her door and held it open. "You're a detective," she said. "I suggest you go somewhere and detect." Under her stare, the man passed through the outer office and out the door. Miss Peck marched after him and shut the door softly. *Not worth anger,* she reminded herself, totally unaware that she had just been invited to cheat on her income tax.

"Is that the same man who was here yesterday?" she asked Barbra.

"Oh, no. That guy was blond, and he was real sweet."

"A lot of people seem to be interested in Celie, don't they?" Miss Peck mused. "Well, this one's easy to check."

She went back to her desk, found the area code for

Duluth, called information, and two minutes later was talking to Betty Shannon.

"That can't be our detective," Miss Shannon said. "That's not his name, and ours has blond hair. He wouldn't have any reason to disguise himself, would he?"

"I don't think he was in disguise," Miss Peck said.

"Oh, dear. I wish Mr. Goodenough were here. Celia Lewis, you said? I don't know . . . I don't think he's found a name, yet . . . see, Mr. Goodenough isn't acting as an attorney in this case, he's acting as executor of the will, so I don't know much about it. I can tell you about the Frazier will, though, if that would help."

"Yes, it might." Miss Peck felt a sudden qualm. "That is, it wouldn't be any, er, breach of confidence?"

"Oh, heavens, no. A will's a public document, once it's been filed with the clerk of court. Anybody at all can get a copy. That's how it got into the newspapers, I expect. The local papers had a story about it last spring, pictures and everything, and there was almost a whole column about it in the *Star and Tribune* last Saturday. Didn't you see it?"

"No, I missed that."

"Someone sent a copy to Mr. Goodenough. No pictures, but still quite a long story. But if you didn't see it, I'd better explain. Little Alexa was kidnapped by her mother years and years ago, when she was only three. The Fraziers were divorced, you see? And her father had custody."

In those days, a bad reflection on the mother's character, to say the least, Miss Peck thought.

". . . So, if she can be found by November something, I forget the exact date, but it's early—"

"November fourth," Miss Peck supplied.

"Yes, that's right. She'll inherit most of the estate. Otherwise, if she can't be found, Devin gets it all. Devin's her half brother. And I'll tell you, just between us, I hope they do find Alexa. I don't like Devin, and I know it upsets

Mr. Goodenough to deal with him. I hope he doesn't get a penny. Other than the ten thousand, of course."

Miss Peck blinked. She was beginning to feel as if she had had one too many glasses of Clarice's sherry. "Ten thousand?"

"That he gets if they do find Alexa. In that case she gets the rest."

Miss Peck had the odd sensation that her head was no longer operable. She seized upon the last sentence and asked, "What will the rest be?"

Miss Shannon hesitated. "I don't really know. A lot, I imagine. The house is on the market for six hundred thousand, and it ought to be free and clear; Mr. Frazier owned it fifty years or more."

Miss Peck swallowed, too surprised to say anything. Imagine Celie with half a million dollars or more! What on earth would the poor kid do?

"And he's got a lot of other holdings, too," Miss Shannon added. "It was all in the papers, last spring, when he died."

Other holdings! Miss Peck retreated to the beginning of the conversation. "You don't think this was your detective?" she asked.

"No, I'm sure not." Miss Shannon hesitated a moment. Her next words held the worried, nerve-building rush of someone plunging into waters perhaps more murky than she knew. "But I'll tell you what I'm afraid of, Miss Peck, is it? I'm afraid he's Devin's. Maybe I shouldn't say it, but Devin can be, well, ruthless. You tell Celia Lewis to be very, very careful."

"I see."

"I'll tell Mr. Goodenough you called," Miss Shannon said. The familiar words seemed to restore her professional voice. "I know he's very concerned about Alexa, from things he's said. He'll be glad to know you didn't answer that man's questions. Could I have your phone number? I'm sure he'll want to talk to you."

Miss Peck gave both of her telephone numbers and scribbled a note to herself to remember to set up the answering machine to take any replies to her ads. "Miss Shannon?" she asked, on a sudden hunch, "could you tell me what Devin Frazier looks like?"

"Oh, he's sort of skinny and dark. Maybe just under six feet. Reminds me of a snake, sometimes."

"Brown hair, brown eyes?" Miss Peck inquired.

"That's right."

"Thank you, Miss Shannon," she said, shaken. "I think I may just have seen him." She hung up, her mouth as pursed as if she had just bitten into a very green persimmon.

17 September 16

EXHAUST HUNG IN the air as the school bus picked up a shouting, surging group of passengers. Miss Peck rolled up her car window and waited for the lights to stop flashing. Beside her on the passenger seat lay the folded morning paper containing the two personal ads she had placed; she glanced at it a couple of times while tapping her foot on the accelerator. When the children had finally been absorbed by the bus, Miss Peck almost peeled rubber as she turned the other way.

A haziness near the horizon promised more warm weather. Miss Peck congratulated herself on having had the foresight to wear a short-sleeved dress as she almost ran from the parking ramp to her office building. The elevator was too slow; she huffed up the stairs, ending up as breathless as Clarice had been the day before, and let herself into her suite.

But the answering machine held no messages at all. Well, what did she expect? It would be the people with some leisure, reading the paper over a second or third cup of coffee, who might have seen the white Lincoln.

A chapter of Clarice's new novel lay on her desk next to the typewriter. Miss Peck frowned at it. Why wasn't it in the file with the original? And where was the original?

For a moment, she could only stand next to the desk, supporting herself on her fingertips, as the enormity of the possible loss struck her. She distinctly remembered snapping a rubber band around those untidy yellow pages *and* the typescript, with the typescript *in a box!*

Much to her relief, she found Clarice's abused-looking

manuscript just where it should be—except that it was in the box she thought she had put the typescript in! "Where was my head yesterday afternoon?" she asked herself aloud, taking out the original of the typed chapter to check against Sharmille's work.

The morning sun came through her window, spreading out each of the imperfections of the window glass across the wall of the room that was really a series of doors over shelves. A long, dark stripe ran down the wall near the right-hand end: one of the doors stood slightly open.

Why should that be? Hardly any of the boxes in the old storage room had been recovered: Miss Peck was quite sure that section of shelves was empty. She crossed the room to check: yes. She pushed at the panel; it clicked softly into place and became part of a panelled wall. She pushed it again: the touch latch let go and the door sprang open exactly as far as before. She closed it and turned away; her elbow brushed the panel, and it opened again with the faintest of clicks. That must be it. She had brushed against it yesterday, and it had come open, or the maintenance person had backed into it last night while vacuuming.

The outer office door opened. She took a sharp breath and spun around.

"Hi, Miss Peck!"

"Hi, Sharmille," she called. "Want to proof this chapter?"

"Oh, let me type a couple more, so I don't break up the work so much," Sharmille said, appearing briefly at Miss Peck's door before she headed for her desk.

"Fine." At her own desk, Miss Peck set Clarice's newest masterpiece aside and pulled out the insurance forms she would have to complete to collect damages for the explosion. *Odd,* she thought. *I'm sure I locked that drawer.*

"Miss Peck?" Sharmille stood at the door. "Somebody been messing with my desk," she said. "The lock's broke. Broken."

130

"Yes." Miss Peck observed detachedly that the hair along her arms was rising. "I was just deciding that my office has been searched."

"By that guy in the red car, you think?" Sharmille asked with a troubled frown. "How would he find us?"

"By paying two dollars to match up my name with the plate number on my car. Just as I did with him yesterday."

"You did?"

"Only the car wasn't registered to him. It was still in the name of the girl he bought it from, and she's moved to the West Coast."

Sharmille sighed. "Figures."

"I meant to tell you about it yesterday, but when I got back that detective was here," Miss Peck apologized. "Is anything missing?"

"I'll check."

The man in the red car? Would he have noticed her car following his? And how would he find her office? The car was registered to her at home.

Unlikely. Then who?

That detective. If he was a detective, and not Devin Frazier passing himself off as a detective. Somebody who wanted very badly to know where Celie was. Belatedly, Miss Peck saw that her answers yesterday could be construed as concealing knowledge instead of the honest ignorance she had claimed. And that could lead to curiosity. . . .

"Nothing missing from my desk," Sharmille reported. "But somebody been into Barb's desk, too, and Celie's. I don't know what Celie kept in her desk, but it's empty now."

A small, electriclike shock flickered through Miss Peck's abdomen in the instant before the explanation occurred to her. "The movers probably dumped everything into a box, and it got put away somewhere."

"Maybe. How come not mine, then?"

"You were there to defend it."

Miss Peck began searching through her purse for the former FBI man's card. She found it and dialed the phone number, only to find that she was not the only person in the city of Minneapolis who owned an answering machine. Unable to think of a protest suitable for lodging with a piece of recording tape, she hung up.

Mid-morning, the first call came. Miss Peck, scarcely able to breathe, received with some misgivings the news that a fancy white car that "might have been a Lincoln" had stopped in Sherrill, Iowa, to ask directions to Dubuque, "which anybody knows where it's at."

Miss Peck wasn't too sure, herself. On the river? Or was that Des Moines?

"So can I come over now and get the money? Because I happen to be in the bus terminal."

"Why don't you tell me first when this took place?" Miss Peck suggested.

"Oh, sometime last week. Thursday or maybe Wednesday."

"Then that's no good to me."

"Now, look, lady," the voice began, but she reached out and hung up while it was still expostulating. Sharmille had come to stand in the doorway.

"It's going to be a long day," Miss Peck predicted.

"Not the right stuff?"

"Not the right stuff."

Three different women claimed to be Celia Lewis. For all Miss Peck knew, they were. Just not the right Celia Lewis.

Clarice called to bubble over the "gorgeous" ads and "incidentally" to see if there had been any replies.

"See, I'd been hitching," the voice, young, male, doubtful, said. "And I was a little nervous about these guys, I

132

couldn't see why they would just drive up to a rest area and sit there. I mean, why not get out and walk around or go to the john, you know? Big guys. And I—I'm kind of small, you know? So you got to be careful when you look, uh, like me, you know? Sometimes . . . well. Anyhow, I was hanging real far back in the picnic area, where they couldn't see me, waiting to see what they did, you know? And this white car, it could have been a Lincoln, came through the rest area real slow, and two of the guys got out of the car and jumped into the white one, and it took off."

"That sounds interesting," Miss Peck said. "Did you see who was in the white car?"

"No. It was too far away, and down the hill. But both of these guys got in back, see, so I bet there were two people up front."

"What about the other car?"

"The guy who was left drove it away a couple minutes later."

The first car, alas, had been dark blue. Miss Peck elicited a description of the white car. Yes, it matched the Lincoln, but the boy hadn't noticed the license plate number. "And this was on 35, going north, just south of Rush City, is that correct?"

"Uh-huh."

"What did you do then?"

"Oh, when the noontime crowd came I caught a ride into Duluth, and my folks came and got me. I live in Cloquet, see, and I've been working in St. Paul, only I got laid off."

Simple words, with the barest hint of a tremor. Unemployment on the Minnesota iron range was nearly a quarter of the work force, had been for two years. "Are you calling from Cloquet, then?"

"That's right."

"Well, I don't know yet if this is the reward information, but give me your name and address and I'll send you the cost of the phone call, at least."

"Oh, you don't need t'do that," the young voice said, and the line clicked in Miss Peck's ear.

Clarice Klenk phoned to see if there had been any calls, and Miss Peck surprised herself by saying no.

A pious, elderly, female voice assured Miss Peck that Celia Lewis had entered heaven many years ago. Miss Peck expressed her profound satisfaction at learning of Celia's blameless life of good works, explained that she was looking for someone who had been alive no later than the day before yesterday, and hung up.

Sharmille finished typing two chapters of *Amor Español* and Barbra one, not quite as uneven an accomplishment as it might sound. Miss Peck assigned Barbra to typing page numbers on what was finished and served as copyholder for Sharmille as they checked what needed proofing. A suspicious Lincoln was reported from Eau Claire, Wisconsin. Doing what?

"Oh, I dunno, it was just suspicious, going along, like. I saw a UFO last June, you wanna hear about that?"

Miss Peck declined the opportunity, referred the caller to a local organization that investigated such objects and, with a sigh, picked up a new page to read to Sharmille. "Clarice will think we're slighting her," she remarked. "She always expects us to have these things done the day before she brings them in."

"Seven hundred pages?"

Miss Peck shrugged and straightened the scrawled copy. " 'Catalina'—oh, I do wish Clarice had chosen a different name for her heroine, I keep thinking of bathing suits— 'Catalina tiptoed down the marble steps pressing her skirts against her hot thighs to keep them from rustling so loudly'—the skirts, I trust, not the thighs . . ."

"No comma after 'steps'?"

"No."

"Damn." Sharmille uncorked the bottle of correction fluid and grimaced in disgust as the little brush stayed behind in the bottle. "It's one of those days," she sighed, getting up to fetch a fresh supply.

An enterprising young man called to say that if it was information Miss Peck wanted, she couldn't do better than to buy this encyclopedia that he just happened to be selling. Then, a few minutes after Clarice had come by to pick up the day's finished typescript—and complain about having the encyclopedia salesman passed on to her—another young man called.

". . . Drinking beer with a couple of the guys, but I wasn't drunk, no, ma'am. I mean, there's not much else to do, is there?"

Miss Peck, no authority on what there is to do in a rural gas station other than pump gas and maintain automobiles, murmured something noncommital.

"I mean, that was some car, and I know that's the scenic route, but it was funny, I thought, the guy driving was all dressed up and the girl didn't look too bad, but those dudes in the back were just ordinary slobs, you know?"

Dudes in the back! "What was the girl wearing?" Miss Peck asked.

"Oh, I dunno. Some kind of dress. Dark. Maybe blue."

For the second time that day, Miss Peck brushed her right hand along the rising hair of her left forearm. "Did you notice anything else about her?" she asked.

The voice took on an embarrassed overtone. "Well, she was—she was just a girl, I mean, uh—nothing special about her. And I was looking at the car."

"It was an unusual car."

"Oh, yeah, it was a beauty." Reverence deepened the boy's voice. "But see, I saw the two ads with the same phone number, and one was looking for a girl, and the other one was looking for a car like this one, and I thought, uh, maybe somebody kidnapped the girl?"

Miss Peck made some sort of noise.

"I mean, the guys all told me I was out of my gourd," the boy said plaintively. "But we all remembered that car, and the girl in the front seat."

"I don't think you're crazy," Miss Peck said. This time she got a name and address. She sat looking at her notes for several seconds after she hung up. Route 23, headed toward Duluth. And Duluth was where that man Frazier had died, the direction that other boy had been going.

"Sharmille?" she called. "I need two things, if you'd be good enough to get them for me. A Minnesota road map, you'll find one in the pocket on the back of the passenger seat of my car, and a copy of last Saturday's paper. You can get that at the back issues desk of the paper, over on Portland. Take my car."

Sharmille reached under the right-hand front corner of her typewriter and switched it off, almost, Miss Peck suspected, with relief.

18 September 16

CELIE LIFTED HER eyes from the page and listened, her head turned toward the door behind her back. She was sure she'd heard gravel shifting under someone's step, but the approach to what the men called the playhouse was too stealthy to be one of them. Or was it?

Her tongue flicked over her lower lip, swollen where Baker had kissed her when he collected the dinner tray. Baker was the reason she shoved the mattress up against the inward-opening door and sat on it with her pile of twice-read magazines, the reason she slept pressed as close to the door as she could get. Longdel was distantly businesslike, Morrison even seemed to like her. Baker had left bruises and threats behind with every visit, even this evening, when Longdel had been with him. The men had left arguing, an argument Celie tried not to think about.

A breeze washed through the aspens near the tiny building. Celie clenched her teeth against the watery sigh of their leaves; it drowned out every other small sound and left her with her ear pressed against the rough planks of the playhouse door, taut with doubt.

Another footstep, close to the door. Another wave of wind through the damned trees.

The door shifted inward a fraction of an inch. "Shit, it's stuck," said a girl's voice.

"No, it ain't." A boy. "It's got a padlock on it. We'll have to go someplace else."

"Help," Celie called, not too loud, hoping her voice wouldn't carry to her captors.

"Split, somebody's in there," said the boy. She heard footsteps moving away.

"No, please," she called, a little louder. She clicked off the lamp and rolled off the mattress to pull it away from the door, calling, "Help me, help me, please."

Steps came back, just when she had decided they were gone for good. "What's the matter?" the girl asked through the door.

"I've been kidnapped," Celie said. "They've been keeping me here all week. Call the police, will you?"

A long silence, while Celie waited, kneeling at the door.

"Ah . . . I don't know about cops," the girl said, after a year, ten years, a moment.

"Wait, wait, here's a note." Celie pulled the worn, sweat-softened deposit slip out of her bra and tried to pass it under the door, but even folded it was too floppy to push through the crack.

"Come *on,* Jennifer," said the boy, in such a low voice that Celie thought he must also have returned. For a moment, she wondered if it were the same boy. Must be.

She tore a cover from one of the *Reader's Digests* and folded it over the note, to stiffen it, and pushed it again under the door. "Can you see it?" she pleaded.

The note wriggled and slipped from her fingers under the edge of the door. "Oh, thank you," Celie said aloud.

"Hey!" shouted one of the men, from a distance. Morrison? Celie knelt on the mattress, her heart thumping in her ears. "You kids! Get away from there."

She heard the footsteps thudding away from her. The girl squealed, and Celie heard scuffling noises on the path. She backed off the mattress, pushed it tight against the door, and sat against the rough panel.

"Get him," the girl yelled, out in the garden. Celie heard a thump, a groan, and the footsteps running again, the change in tone as they gained the lawn near the house, and then they faded away. One of the other men started shouting.

Brisk steps grated on the gravel. Someone knocked on the playhouse door. Celie kept quiet. The knock changed to a pounding, and Celie, putting as much sleepiness into her voice as she could, said, "Yes? What's the matter?"

"You all right in there?" It *was* only Morrison, thank heaven!

"Of course I'm all right," Celie said, faking a yawn to sound both sleepy and indignant, the way she had years ago, when her mother had caught her still reading at two in the morning. "Did you wake me up just to ask if I'm all right?"

"As you were." Morrison crunched away on the gravel path. Celie closed her eyes. Hot tears fell down her cheeks. She folded her arms across the knees she couldn't quite bring together against the relentless separation of the plaster that encased her ankles and rested her forehead on the cold skin of her forearms.

"What in hell are you doing, Baker?" Longdel demanded. Five kids, maybe thirteen, fourteen years old, faced him on the wide sweep of the drive, yellow-faced in the light of the porch lamps, uneasily watching the gun in Baker's hand.

"I caught them messing around the playhouse," Baker replied sullenly.

"So? You want me to call the cops or something?"

Morrison, coming out of the shadows at the corner of the house, picked up the hint. "Those were our trespassers?" he asked, sounding mildly incredulous.

"Nobody else back there, I take it," Longdel said. "No big booze party on for tonight?"

"Nope." Morrison caught on, thank God. "Want to call their parents?"

"Aw, come on," said the oldest of the boys. Baker frowned from Longdel to Morrison and slowly holstered the gun.

"Okay, kids, scram," Longdel said. "You lucked out this

time; I'm too tired to bother getting on the phone. Go on, get." He waved at them as if they were a bunch of pigeons surrounding a park bench and he had run out of crumbs. "Go on, you want to get yourselves arrested?"

They began to walk down the drive, not as fast as he'd expected them to, glancing back at him from time to time. He stood on the top step with his hands on his hips, feeling chilled and silly in his pajamas, willing Baker to keep his mouth shut. Baker put his hand on flap of the holster and started after the kids. They ran.

"She was asleep." Morrison came up the steps yawning. "I about had to knock the house down to wake her up."

"Christ, this is dragging on," Longdel complained. "I wish Frazier would make up his mind."

"I'll pick up a Polaroid tomorrow and get those pictures he wants," Morrison said. "That'll move him."

"Yeah, if we've got that long." Longdel stepped into the house with a sour glance over his shoulder. "What happens if those kids call the cops, tell them we're up to something funny here?"

"They were up to something funny themselves," Morrison said, sounding amused. He held a six-pack of Budweiser up to the light. "A little pot, too, I bet, and some screwing around. I don't think any cops will be coming."

"Makes me nervous, all the same," Longdel said.

"Nothing like guilt for a gag," Morrison replied, dragging open the screen door with another yawn.

The five kids drifted along the street through leafy shadows, toward the blue streetlight a little further on. "That guy's still looking at us, Mike," the youngest boy reported.

"Stay mellow, baby."

"I mean, the one with the gun. He's just standing at the end of the driveway, looking at us."

Mike glanced back. The guy with the gun stood just

inside the gate, one of the two gaps the boy knew of in the tall iron fence that surrounded the old estate. "He ain't shooting," he said, and turned to the older girl. "What was that you picked up, back there at the little house?"

"She passed me a note."

"What's it say?"

"How should I know? You think I can read in the dark, with guys running around pulling guns on me?"

"Okay, okay. We'll find out." Mike rummaged in his shirt pocket for a loose cigarette, stopped for a minute to light it, hands curled around the flame of the match. He shook the match out and dropped it.

Moving with the sluggish, fit and start motion of leaves caught in a slow stream, they came to the streetlight. "That guy still there?" Mike asked.

"I don't see him."

Mike reached out, and Jennifer handed over the note with a shrug. "She's been kidnapped, she said. She wants us to call the cops."

"Kidding?" Mike unfolded the magazine cover and extracted the note, to read it with some difficulty; the letters were blurred and turning greenish.

"Where do you want to call from? MacDonald's?" the girl asked.

"We ain't calling no cops."

"But that lady—"

"We can't call the cops, airhead! First thing they'll want to know is, what was we doing back there? And then what do we say?" He fluttered his fingers and continued falsetto, "Oh, pardon me, officer, we was just passing our little joint and drinking up our nice six-pack."

"Where is the six-pack?" asked the younger girl.

"I dropped it back there," the nervous boy admitted.

"Oh, super. I musta hung around that liquor store for half an hour before I got anybody to buy it for me, and you drop it. Thanks a bunch, nerd."

"We don't have to tell the cops who we are," Jennifer pursued.

"Use your brain, if you can find it." Mike shoved Celie's note into his hip pocket. "What happens after they get the woman out of there? Every once in a while they'll be checking the place to see who's using it, and what if it's us?"

"Oh, Christ," the nervous boy said. "I see what you mean."

"And besides that, what if they've got one of those systems where the number you call from, you know, goes up on the computer? It's no good calling from a pay phone, they'd be there in two seconds."

The other four nodded.

"They musta rented that place," Mike mused, as they moved again toward his car, parked at the bottom of the hill. "But how come they wasn't there all summer, like summer people always are?" He kicked at the gravel beside the road. "They musta been saving it," he concluded. "They musta been planning this a long time."

"Who cares?" asked the youngest boy.

"Nobody." Mike reached into his jeans for the car keys. "I just like to keep things figured out, is all."

"We could go get a Big Mac anyway," said the nervous boy. "I'm starved."

"Whatja do, smoke all the stuff before we picked you up?" Jennifer teased.

They got into the car, slamming doors. Mike gunned the engine and jerked the wheel over.

"You know," Jennifer said, "I really don't want to leave that lady there with those guys."

"She's okay."

"They kept her a week already, Mike," Jennifer pointed out. "How'dja like to be stuck someplace with that guy with the gun?" She shivered. "I bet he rapes her for breakfast."

142

"No cops," Mike repeated doggedly, slowing for a red light just long enough to check for cross traffic.

"Take it easy," said the nervous boy. "We don't want to get picked up."

"You wanna drive?"

"I'm not old enough."

"Me, neither."

"I mean," said Jennifer. "We oughta do *some*thing."

"Jen, just get off my back." Mike sounded strained. She assessed him with narrowed eyes. *He doesn't like it any better than I do,* she concluded.

"Mike—"

"Look, my folks will be home by midnight and if they find the car gone, they'll skin me alive, so if we're gonna pick up a burger we'd better just do that."

They sat in one of the yellow booths, eating french fries. "Hey, I got an idea," Jennifer said. "That note? She put down there somebody she wants to know where she is, right? That Miss Peck. So why don't we just mail the note to her? Then she can take care of it and we're out."

"Jen, maybe you got it." Mike smiled for the first time since they'd entered the restaurant. "Anybody know the number of that house?"

"What house?"

Jennifer shot a look of total scorn at the nervous boy. "Where we were just at! God, what a doorknob."

"For what?" the boy persisted.

"So we can write it on that note," Jennifer explained. "Before we send it to that lady. Otherwise how will she know where to go? Anybody got a pencil?"

Nobody had a pencil.

"Screw it, then." Mike took the note out of his pocket and crumpled it in one hand; Jennifer caught his wrist as he started to lob it at the trash can.

"That lady needs help," she said, as she smoothed the

deposit slip out on the damp table. "What if it was me in there? What would you do then?"

The youngest boy giggled. "It's been you in there, Jen! All summer!"

"No, stupe. I mean, locked up in there."

"It's different?"

"Yeah, it's different." Jennifer brushed her hair back from her face and got up to borrow a pencil from the cashier.

"You'll be grounded the rest of your life," the cashier commented, when Jennifer asked if she knew the address of the place up on the hill, way back of town. But she didn't know the house number.

Jennifer wrote the name of the street on the slip of paper. "Big house on top of hill," she added. Now all she needed was an envelope and a stamp. Those she could swipe from her mother. She shoved Celie's note into the back pocket of her jeans and went back to her french fries.

"Hey, Jen?" called the cashier. "Isn't the number up in the gate? Like a part of it?"

Jennifer stared at her. "Yeah, right," she said. "Mike, the minute we're done eating, let's drive past that place and I'll get the number."

Mike exhaled a triangular cloud of smoke and looked at his watch. "Maybe," he said.

19 September 17

"I REALLY SHOULDN'T do this, should I?" Clarice stirred a second spoonful of sugar into her pale coffee. "But sweets to the sweet, I always say."

Miss Peck smiled as slightly as the antique jest deserved.

"You're really upset about this girl, aren't you?" Clarice continued. "That's your trouble, Ethel, you're too soft-hearted. Always were."

Miss Peck shook her head and reached for her own black coffee. She wished—what did she wish? That the world were still the orderly world of her childhood, where papers in storage gathered nothing but dust, and clumsy, earnest typists had nothing more exciting happen than to drop their copy and get it mixed up. On the other hand, she reflected, her friends' older brothers had been going off to Europe and the Pacific, to fight a war . . . but even that had been a war one could almost understand . . .

"Bored, that's it," Clarice diagnosed again, still stirring her coffee. "I don't know how you can keep doing that typing stuff—most of it must be boring as hell. Other than mine, of course."

"Some of it's all right," Miss Peck said, without bothering to point out that she seldom did much typing herself, anymore.

"I was reading over that Barbra's shoulder yesterday," Clarice continued cozily. "And do you know what I saw her type? '*Tris*-hydroxymethyl-carbolamide!' That's something you won't find in one of my manuscripts."

"Not likely, no," Miss Peck agreed.

"Boring."

"Perhaps not to a chemist."

"True, but you're not a chemist, are you?" Clarice pointed out with her usual devastating logic. "What's bothering you this afternoon, Ethel? Just the girl? Or have you had some sort of answer to your ads?"

"Well, yes, I have," Miss Peck admitted. She looked out the back window of her kitchen, a view of brightly-lit evergreens. Pink phlox had bloomed in a row in front of the arborvitae, glowing even now that most of its leaves were lost to powdery mildew and the blossoms had faded. She told Clarice about the two calls that seemed significant.

"Did you look at your map? Have you got it here? Can I see?"

"Sure, I think there's one in my desk. Hang on." Miss Peck retrieved the spare Minnesota map from her desk in the living room and spread it out on the kitchen table, tracing the route with one finger: "It looks to me as if they went up 35 as far as Askov, and then turned off on 23. Route 23 goes all the way to Duluth, which is where that man died, but I don't know if the car went that far."

"Died! What man died?"

Miss Peck realized with a start that Clarice hadn't heard about Celie's possible inheritance. "Celie's father," she said. "Or at least, possibly Celie's father. It's a long story. . . ."

"You don't mind if I write all this down, do you?" Clarice said when she'd finished.

Miss Peck grinned. "Should Sharmille type it, or Barbra?"

"Oh, stop." Clarice started to scribble. "What makes you think this child is Celie?"

"A man came to the office Thursday afternoon and suggested that she might be. I called the lawyer—"

"What lawyer?"

146

"The man—it was a private detective by the way, and for a minute I was afraid you'd sent him—"

"Would have served you right, after you sent me that jerk with the encyclopedia. As if an encyclopedia could give me enough information to write with! Really, Ethel."

"I said I was sorry, didn't I?" Miss Peck reminded her friend. "Anyway, this detective said he was working for an attorney in Duluth, who was handling the estate. But the attorney's secretary said no, they had a detective trying to find the girl—her name is Alexa Frazier—but he didn't match the description of the man who came to see me."

"This is the *Frazier* estate?" Clarice stopped writing as her jaw dropped. "Ethel, why didn't you say so right away? That's—that's enthralling!"

"You know about it?"

"I read about it in last Saturday's paper. I thought, how perfect, imagine the girl coming to that big old house on the North Shore, on one of those steel-grey days in fall with Lake Superior all storm-tossed, to claim her inheritance—yum!" Clarice wriggled with delight. "And the fall leaves, yellow and whatever and hectic red, sifting down through the rain-blacked branches of the trees . . . Think what Amelita could do with that! Ah!" With a slap on the table to mark the change of tone from delirious to conspiratorial: "Who do you think the man was?"

"I think it might have been the half brother. Devin, his name is."

"Devin!" Clarice crowed, writing again. "Oh, perfect, perfect, perfect! I couldn't have thought of a better name, myself."

Miss Peck briefly considered saying something about the name "Catalina," and decided it might be safer to leave that up to Clarice's editor.

"But if that was the half brother, who kidnapped her?"

"I don't know." Miss Peck reached for the coffeepot and

refilled her cup. "At first, I thought it must be someone working for this half brother. After all, he stands to inherit a lot of money if his sister isn't found, and nobody else seems to benefit. But in that case, he wouldn't have had to come around asking if I knew where she was, would he?"

"Marvelous," Clarice said, writing again.

"Clarice, this is my employee, not one of your heroines," Miss Peck pointed out. "A flesh-and-blood woman."

"Yes, yes, I know," Clarice said, still scribbling. "How do you plan to find her?"

"I don't know." Miss Peck swirled the coffee left in her cup, surprised by a wave of bewilderment and sadness.

"Why don't you call this lawyer again, see if he can help?" Clarice suggested.

"He called me, this morning. More coffee?"

Clarice looked up at her with blank hazel eyes. "Coffee?" she asked, as if she'd never heard of it. "Oh! Oh, yes, thanks. What did he say?"

"Nothing that wasn't in the newspaper," Miss Peck sighed. "Except to keep an eye out for her."

Clarice puffed out her lips in exasperation. "Men!" she exclaimed.

"He said his detective was trying to find her—not this man who came to my office, another one."

"Maybe that's all right, then," Clarice relented. "Did you tell him about your ads?"

Miss Peck stared into her half cup of coffee. "No," she said. "I felt a little silly about them, to tell you the truth."

"In that case, you'll have to be the one to follow them up, won't you?"

Miss Peck looked again at the moulting phlox outside her window and shrugged unhappily. "I don't know how, is the problem," she said. "I'm not sure what I was hoping for when I placed them . . . Celie to call, maybe, and let me know she was all right. . . . An expensive impulse, I'm afraid."

148

"What you need is a Lord Peter Wimsey," Clarice declared, for all the world as if she had made a practical suggestion.

Miss Peck laughed. "When I was in high school I thought he was—what's the word?—a frightful fop. And not knowing French, I used to get *so* annoyed when Sayers went on in French for half a page or so, without a single clue for translation. But I had a whopper of a crush on Bunter." She reached for the pot and warmed up her coffee.

"On Bunter! You never told me that. You always were a mite peculiar, Ethel, if you'll forgive me," remarked her friend. "Where would I be if everybody went around having their crushes on the likes of Bunter?"

"Writing about panting young women having affairs with highly competent gentlemen's gentlemen, I suppose." Miss Peck sighed. "Still, if Bunter walked in the door this minute, he'd be welcome, and I got over that crush a long time ago."

Both women fell silent, in the companionable warmth of the kitchen, until Clarice wondered aloud, "How would one get from Alexa Frazier to Celia Lewis? I thought people usually kept the same initials, at least." She paused, several M-shaped furrows disturbing her usually smooth forehead. "Although now that nobody monograms anything but sweaters, I guess that's not much of a consideration."

"Do you know," Miss Peck said, stopping with the coffeepot again in her hand, "Celie has a ring with a monogram."

"Really!" Clarice's large face became meltingly wistful. "I wish I could see it."

"As a matter of fact, you can." Miss Peck put down the coffeepot and went up to her bedroom for her purse. The ring was still in the pocket she had zipped it into—only Tuesday morning? She took it out and returned to the kitchen.

"She's always leaving it on the shelf in the ladies' room," Miss Peck explained. She held the ring out. "I picked it up on Monday after work and was keeping it for her."

"Pretty thing," Clarice commented, taking the mother-of-pearl ring. "An antique, by the look of it, don't you think? The gold's got that yellowy color."

"Yes, I suppose it could be."

"A.F.C. That's A.C.F., I imagine, with the F that big. Funny that they made it vertical, they could just have turned the ring sideways and they wouldn't have had to squish it like that."

"The birthdate is Celie's," Miss Peck said.

"A Pisces. No wonder she reads the Tarot," Clarice remarked. "But I think the birthdate was put on after the initials, don't you? It looks a little squeezed, like an afterthought."

Miss Peck took the ring to look inside. Yes, now that Clarice had pointed it out, it did look as if the date had been added later. The script wasn't quite the same, and while the initials looked a little worn, the numerals were still perfectly crisp.

"I'd guess the C is for Celia," Clarice continued. "She might have been named for someone, and the ring given to her—doesn't that seem likely?"

"Now that you mention it," Miss Peck said doubtfully.

"Why don't you run it up to Duluth and show it to this attorney?" Clarice suggested. "Don't let him keep it, though, just in case."

"In case?"

"In case he's on the half brother's side! Honestly, Ethel, do you still have to have everything spelled out for you? You'd think we were back in high school."

Miss Peck, enjoying a clear shaft of delight that she would never again have to suffer high school, put the ring into her pocket and sat down. "I might do that," she said. "I could drive up tomorrow and see if I could find any other signs of Celie on the way. I can get the building super to let the girls in on Monday morning. Sharmille can take charge."

"That's my girl," Clarice approved. "Bunter would be proud of you. Now," she demanded, hunched and smiling, snapping the notebook shut and walking her elbows onto the table, "Tell me true, what do you think of the new book? So far."

20 September 17

"Look," Morrison said patiently. "I won't hurt you. I just want to take some pictures of the back of your right shoulder, that's all." The girl had recoiled into the chair when he'd first asked her to take down the top of her dress, and she stayed there, almost like she was spring-loaded.

"Why?" she asked.

"Because of the birthmark."

Celie clenched her fists and pressed her back against the fusty chair. "What makes you think I've got a birthmark on my shoulder?"

"Let's just say, I have a strong suspicion. And a deep hope."

It must be a way to identify me, she thought. But how could he know about it? And why the pictures? "Hope?"

Hope. Restored, now that, listening through the night in shifts to the police band radio, they'd heard no indication that anyone had the slightest interest in them. "Because if you don't have that birthmark," he said, "we've gone to a lot of trouble for nothing, and some of us, including me, are going to be very disappointed."

"What would you do then?"

"Then?" Morrison, cross-legged on the dusty floor with the camera in his hands, stared past her head at the bare boards of the playhouse wall. *One of them would kill her.* Baker.

That was Baker's role in the team Longdel had put together out of the former residents of Cellblock B, Stillwater State Prison, just as his own had been to talk her into coming along. That explained Baker. That also explained why Baker was so rough with her, why he sneered at the dark little house they kept her in, why he guffawed at the chemical toilet like a nine-year-old, snickered at the cold meals, at her stink. He had to keep her distant, subhuman, just in case.

No just in case about it. Baker would kill her, no matter what she had on her shoulder; Morrison understood that for the first time. None of them could risk letting her go. Morrision swallowed. He'd deluded himself, trusting Longdel's promises—ironic, that, the con-man conned—expected her to be let go when the time was up, expected to vanish himself into another life as he had already done several times, no one much the worse for wear (except financially), and his share of the half-million in his hot little hands.

He'd hung onto Longdel's insistence that she not be harmed. Now he let himself see that she couldn't be harmed simply because she was a bargaining chip only as long as she was alive: if she were alive they could threaten to release her, to take her to the lawyer who was handling old man Frazier's estate, and then the son would lose most of his money. But if she were dead, if they couldn't show the kid that she was still alive, then there wouldn't be any money. Simple as that.

So that was why Longdel had jumped at the idea of taking pictures, when Frazier had wanted a look at the girl before he agreed to anything. To keep Frazier from finding out where she was, so that he couldn't come and kill her himself. Morrison turned the camera in his hands, pretending to be figuring out how it worked.

And he should have known. The heater didn't exist that would keep her warm in an uninsulated playhouse in a North Shore cold spell, blankets or no blankets. Already, the nights were chilly, the leaves had changed color in just the few days they had held her here, the neglected garden between the big house and the little one had turned russet and brown.

"Well?" she demanded.

"We'll play that one by ear," he said shakily, looking at her again. She stared at him. She, too, understood. She looked down at the plaster imprisoning her ankles, and then she reached up and unbuttoned the top button of her dress slowly, glanced at him, and hurriedly finished unbuttoning the dress to her waist.

"Atta girl," Morrison said. Mindless.

"Help me up."

He scrambled to his feet and held out a hand for her to pull herself out of the chair, her other hand clutching the edges of the dress together. She turned and dropped the bodice back from her shoulders. There was the birthmark, a rosy-red arrowhead over an inch long. Her bra strap covered the center of it. Morrison realized that he had been holding his breath, and not only because her body odor had long passed the phase of evoking a mild titillation. "I, uh, have to uncover it," he said.

She reached up and pulled the strap aside herself. Morrison heard himself sigh. He focused and pressed the shutter release. The flash left an after-image of the birthmark behind his closed lids. "One more," he said.

She waited meekly while he took the second picture and the photo developed itself. Good shots, both of them. He held them over her shoulder, to show her. She nodded and ran her thumb under the grimy bra strap to adjust it, shrugged the dress up and quickly buttoned it.

"He wants some of your face."

Celie nodded. "I look like my mother."

"I guess that's it."

She faced him for the first shot, turned sideways for the second. Close-ups. Mug shots. Like all mug shots, they made her look almost ugly. Morrison gave her a look at them and she grimaced.

"You're really better-looking than that," he said. "When

154

you get out of here, get yourself a good haircut and straighten up a little when you walk, and you could really be pretty."

She cast him an incredulous, frightened glance and covered the finger-bruises on her arms with her hands. *She thinks I'm another Baker,* Morrison thought with disgust, and decided not to add that she had a decent figure, nice legs, although both were true.

"One more," he said, and handed her the newspaper Longdel had sent Baker out for that morning. "Hold that up so I can see the headlines."

She nodded and held the paper up beside her face, and he backed off so that he could get the whole thing in. "Smile a little, can't you?" he asked, without result. *Snap-flash. Whine.* The picture slowly became clear and dense: frightened face, placid headlines, dark background because he'd been careful to keep her away from the walls. Like Longdel told him. Longdel, who had located this house with the playhouse in back, way last spring. Longdel, who thought of everything. Good old Longdel, who had probably thought of a thing or two neither he nor Baker would like.

"Thanks for the pics," he said. She didn't answer, just sank back into the old chair. He went out into the clean, sun-warmed air of the garden and padlocked the door behind him, leafing through the pictures as he walked toward the big house along the weedy gravel path. In the brighter light he saw that the edges of the studs of the playhouse walls made a pattern of dim stripes in the background of the picture with the newspaper, and that the diamond panes of one of the blocked windows gleamed faintly to one side. *Well, maybe it won't matter,* he told himself, by now almost as frightened as the girl looked, with her no-color eyes widened in the flash.

Fifteen miles away, Michael Goodenough had foregone the chance to get in a round of golf on a warm September afternoon. Jack Carrera had left his office half an hour before, and now Goodenough spread out a large scale map of the North Shore on his desk and ticked off the number of airports in the area with considerable surprise. The big one out Route 53 he had known about, of course, and the one across the bridge in Superior, but not that one just southwest of town, or those private, grass-runway landing spots . . .

No doubt about it. He had handled this entire affair very badly, very badly indeed. How could he still, after most of his life in this profession, be such an innocent in such a calculating world?

Like Mary Lewis. How sophisticated he had thought himself!

Frazier's business phone, Carrera had said, had a line only in the old man's downstairs office. The bedside phone, from which he sometimes did business, was an extension of the private (Carrera had said "family") line.

Oh, yes, Carrera had remembered that call! How could he forget? Colin had yelled to him over the intercom to answer it—the old man was upstairs, changing for bed—and Carrera had gone along the lower hall into the office and picked up the phone. A collect call for Colin from Devin, in Cleveland, the operator had said. Carrera had accepted the charges.

And then? "I don't like to talk to the young mister," Carrera admitted. "So when the operator said to go ahead, I just said, 'One moment, sir, and I'll get your father for you.' And I put the phone down and buzzed Mr. Frazier on the intercom."

"So you didn't actually hear Devin speak?"

"No, sir. Only the operator. And then Mr. Frazier came boiling out of his room without even stopping to put on his slippers, and he tripped and fell down the stairs as you know, sir."

"You saw this?"

"No, I was still in the office by the telephone. When I

heard him start to fall I dashed out, but he hit that stone floor before I could get to him." Carrera squeezed his eyes shut for a moment. "I'm not as fast on my feet as I once was."

"None of us is," Goodenough sighed. "Did you look up the staircase? Was anyone up there?"

Carrera's mouth sagged. "Up the stairs? I—no, I didn't look—Mr. Frazier wasn't conscious, I guess he'd bumped his head on the steps on the way down. I yelled for Mrs. Swanson to call an ambulance. . . ."

"I see." Goodenough could picture the scene. That big cold hall and the two old men, one dead or dying and the other frightened out of his wits, fat Mrs. Swanson coming to see for herself whether she should bother to scream and running shrieking back to her lair when it proved she should. Glad he hadn't been there, Goodenough felt shamed at his relief. "Would you have noticed someone upstairs, do you think?"

"I—I think so. If there'd been a noise, sure. But it was dark up there, Mr. Frazier hadn't stopped to turn on the lights, so I guess . . . you don't mean Mrs. Swanson, do you? I was talking to her in the kitchen when the phone went, and what with her legs and her asthma, she couldn't have run upstairs that fast. And she was the only other one in the house."

"Yes. More or less what I thought." Goodenough swung gently in his swivel chair. "What about the telephone call?"

"Why, with all the excitement, I forgot it, don't you know. And when I remembered, the young mister had hung up."

So. Now Goodenough folded his map and returned it to his desk drawer. No golf today. He was going to look at the unsold mansion that had been Colin Frazier's home. As he shut the door of his office behind him, Goodenough realized that he had chewed his lower lip bloody.

21 September 18

ETHEL PECK, IN a weekend outfit of plaid shirt, jogging shoes, and a garment she still tended to call 'dungarees' although it had a well-known name stitched over her rump, set her suitcase, her lunch, and her heavy handbag on the floor in the back of her car. *The cat should be all right overnight,* she thought, shaking the ignition key loose from the bunch. She didn't plan to be away beyond the next afternoon, and she had set out extra food and water for the animal. At the end of the alley she waited for a large dust-colored dog to mosey out of her way before she turned east, heading for 35W.

Haze and the closeness of the car despite the wide-open window, on the rim of which Miss Peck rested her left elbow, threatened a hot day. *I could use some fall crispness in the weather,* she thought testily, using the humidity as an excuse to feel nettled about letting Clarice talk her into making this trip. What, after all, did she expect to accomplish? She could almost hear her mother saying, "Ethel, dear, you don't have to do something just because Clarice thinks it might be fun."

The downtown buildings shimmered as she approached them on the highway. A little bubble of glee rose in her: Clarice was right, she was bored; to be honest, half the reason for changing offices had been that she couldn't stand to look up and see her name backwards on the blurry glass of the door in the old place one more time. Today was one day she wouldn't have to go near a typewriter!

Miss Peck grinned as she headed north, although she

158

wished she had paid closer attention to the weather forecast. She had her folding umbrella and her emergency plastic raincoat in her bag, of course, but perhaps she should have brought along her sturdy cloth raincoat? Although the streaked and milky sky didn't seem all that threatening.

She reached the rest stop just short of Rush City a little before noon. Three other cars were parked in the lot, close to the brick lavatories. Miss Peck carried her lunch to one of the picnic tables. Yes, she could see where the boy who had called her might have waited. The car would have been downhill, there, and the men probably paying little attention to the picnic area. Miss Peck bit off a chunk of celery and frowned as she crunched on it. Why had such an odd meeting been necessary?

As she opened her thermos of cottage cheese, it occurred to her that she hadn't seen any other rest areas since leaving the Twin Cities. Perhaps the men had wanted to stay on main highways, keep moving to discourage Celie from perhaps jumping out of the car, and this was simply the first place they could safely meet. Miss Peck nodded. Celie wouldn't have gone with three strange men. One, well-dressed, with a nice car and a plausible story, maybe . . . although it seemed strange, even so. Celie, who jumped at unexpected noises? Who at first had insisted upon placing her desk so that her back was to the wall? Though, come to think of it, half a million dollars or more was a powerful motivator for a woman who earned $4.85 an hour for a thirty-seven and a half hour week.

Miss Peck finished her lunch and went down to the brick building to wash the thermos out. Her apple and most of the coffee in the other thermos she'd save for a second stop, later on, perhaps on Route 23. True, this wasn't a long trip, but she wasn't used to doing so much driving at once and to break it up seemed only sensible.

Two hours later, she was telling herself she'd been a fool to come. Might as well whistle jigs to a fencepost. She'd located the gas station the second caller had told her about, and had even had her tank filled, but without asking any questions: she'd found something unexpectedly intimidating about those huge young men lounging against the stacks of new tires, drinking out of cans. *Bunter,* now, would have had everything down to the serial number of the engine out of them. Ethel Peck didn't even know if they'd seen the car! Heading north again, she steeled herself to stop when she saw likely people and ask about the white Lincoln. Naturally, with her courage up, miles went by without her seeing anyone but a farmer on a distant tractor. She spotted a sign for a roadside rest.

May as well have my coffee. Miss Peck pulled into the lay-by and surveyed the "rest." Someone had raked recently, but a cloud of flies around the top of the trash barrel looked discouraging, and the green-painted table was littered with crumbs. A chipmunk, plump as something out of Disney, darted onto the table and stuffed crumbs into its cheeks. Even that didn't render the place appealing. Miss Peck put the car into gear and drove on.

She came to another gas station and entered the drive, avoiding the pump island. Here, mercifully, no crowd of young men passed the time. A worn-looking man of about her own age looked inquiringly out of the door without coming out.

Miss Peck got out of her car and crossed the gritty asphalt. She felt uncommonly silly. "This sounds funny, I know," she said to the man, "But I'm looking for a white Lincoln Towncar that I think passed this way last Tuesday. You didn't happen to see it, did you?"

The man studied her for a moment, then her car, then herself again. Wordlessly, he pointed to a sign.

Closed Tuesdays

Miss Peck crossed the yard, feeling his eyes on her back,

and got into her car. She stalled twice before she got away. "Damn you, Clarice, I should have made you come with me," she said through her teeth.

The afternoon ground on, hotter, stickier, dustier. Miss Peck began to feel as if she had spent her entire lifetime asking silly questions of strangers who looked at her as if she'd escaped from St. Peter's Security Hospital and who gave one-syllable, negative answers.

She rounded the long curve into Duluth in late afternoon, found a room in a motel on the edge of town, and showered the dust away. A few tears, half of frustration and half from the irritation of reflected sun and road dust, stung under her lids. The white Lincoln might as well have been swallowed up in a bog, for all the trace she'd found of it.

Clean, her hair towelled dry and rolled into its out-of-date style, Miss Peck put on a cool dress and went out to the motel's restaurant for dinner. Well. In the morning she would call Mr. Goodenough and arrange to talk to him and show him Celie's ring. That would provide a reasonable excuse, at least, for flying off like this.

She returned toward her room in the slanting red sunlight, with her dinner sitting heavily on her stomach. Parked next to the wing of the building that angled away from hers was a car that seemed familiar, a dusty green car she was certain she had seen before . . . but where? The curtain on the window of the unit where the car was parked twitched.

The feeling of eyes, that had come to her off and on all day, was with her as she opened her door and stepped into her room. Quite aware that they were useless, she put up the two chains the management provided, and supplemented them with a straight chair braced under the doorknob.

Settled in the one comfortable chair with a book, she remembered where she had seen the green car before: in the lot at the rest area, south of Rush City. "Now, you're as bad as Clarice," she murmured. Because it couldn't really be the same car, could it? Thousands just exactly like it must be traveling the roads of America. And even if it were the same car, it often happens on trips that one sees the same cars over and over.

Miss Peck read, not the mystery novels she had packed, but a fascinating book the librarian had recommended to her, all about information theory, until just before ten o'clock. Then she put the book aside and wavered over whether to watch the TV news.

As she reached for the control knob, she stopped and turned her head toward the door, holding her breath. Surely she had just heard someone step on the concrete path outside? And not move on?

22 September 19

THE PHONE BEGAN ringing just as the building superintendent turned the key in the lock for Sharmille. She flashed him her very best smile and snatched up the receiver, switched the answering machine off with her left hand and swapped hands on the receiver. "Peck's Typing Service," she said, the warmth of her smile lingering in her voice.

"Yes," said the caller. "About the ads you have in the paper?"

"Oh, yes. One moment." Sharmille set the phone down and shuffled through the papers on her desk for instructions. Finding none, she opened the door to Miss Peck's office and surveyed the bare surface of the new desk. *Damn. Now what?* Sharmille threw her hands up in disgust as she recrossed the room to the telephone. "Miss Peck is taking those calls," she said. "But she's not here at the moment. Could I take a message, or have her call you back?"

"Er," said the caller, followed by several seconds of silence. Sharmille began to think he might hang up, but he said, "I don't have any information for her. I was hoping she had some she'd share with me."

"Who is this?"

"I—my name wouldn't mean anything to her. I'm a private detective working for an attorney in Duluth, looking for Celia Lewis."

"Weren't you here Friday?"

"Friday?" The caller sounded confused. "No, not Friday. Why?"

"Somebody working for a lawyer in Duluth came in on Friday afternoon and asked Miss Peck a bunch of questions. That wasn't you?"

"No." Again, several seconds of silence. "I guess you're not the girl I talked to before. This other guy, did he leave a name?"

"Talked to before?" Sharmille asked, also confused.

"Thursday. Miss Peck was out. Did this other guy leave a name?"

"Just a moment, I'll check." Sharmille put the phone down again and went back to Miss Peck's desk. Locked, naturally, and Sharmille didn't have the key. She returned to her own desk for a paper knife and tried unsuccessfully to spring Miss Peck's lock. *Probably just as well,* she decided. "I can't find a name," she reported to the man on the telephone. "Can't you just explain what you want?"

"I just did." He sounded surprised. "Didn't I?"

Barb came in and gave Sharmille a curious glance; Sharmille realized she was sitting on Barb's desk and stood up, her hand cupped over her right ear, as Barb unslung her shoulder bag into her bottom desk drawer.

"I thought maybe somebody had told Miss Peck where Celia Lewis is," the man on the telephone said. His voice took on an anxious edge. "We've got to find her—an emergency, understand? She might be in real danger."

Sharmille stifled a snort of nervous laughter. "I'll tell Miss Peck when she comes in," she said. "That's the best I can do, I'm sorry. If you'll leave your name and number?"

"She wouldn't have it written down somewhere, there in the office?"

"I'm sure she doesn't have it in the office," Sharmille said. "That is, if she knows anything." *Finally* the dude coughed up his name and number, and Sharmille left a note on Miss Peck's desk.

"What's up?" Barb asked.

"Everybody's looking for Celie."

"She didn't turn up over the weekend?"

The telephone rang again. "I guess not," Sharmille said to Barb, and then said "Peck's Typing Service" into the telephone.

"It's me again," the detective said. "I forgot to ask you, what did this other guy look like? The one that came in on Friday afternoon?"

"Oh, six feet, dark hair, sort of skinny," Sharmille said.

"I was afraid of that," the man muttered and hung up.

"Some detective," Sharmille commented. That, of course, required some explanation for Barb, which Sharmille gave.

"I wonder if it was the same one that was in here on Thursday?" Barb said. "When you and Miss Peck were out chasing that guy with the car?"

"He says so. What did he want to know?" Sharmille asked.

"He said something about Celie maybe really being somebody else, she might get some money or something, only somebody else might get it instead. I don't know." Barbra grimaced and turned her eyes toward the ceiling. "It didn't make much sense to me."

"A lot of money?" Sharmille asked.

"I think so, but he didn't say. He was being cute."

"What did he look like?"

"Blond. Lots of teeth but no chin. Said he used to be with the FBI, but I thought they only took hunks."

"So did the other one," Sharmille remarked. "Say he used to be with the FBI, I mean. The FBI must be shedding agents like dandruff."

Barb pinched her lower lip. "I think I'll try giving Celie a call," she said, picking up the phone. "No answer," she reported, a full two minutes later.

"Did you think there would be?"

165

Barb slumped, her hand still on the phone, and turned a woeful face toward Sharmille. "I guess I just sort of hoped," she sighed. "Where's Miss Peck?"

"That's what I mean by everybody looking for Celie," Sharmille said. "She's in Duluth."

"Duluth! She thinks Celie's in Duluth?"

"*I* don't know what she thinks," Sharmille complained. "All I know is, she called up Saturday night and left a message with my mother that the super would let me in this morning, she was going to Duluth, up to us how to divide the work. So—" Sharmille tossed her hands open and let them fall. "You want to keep going on that novel?"

"Sure!" Barb brightened. "I want to see how it ends, don't you?"

"You can let me know." Sharmille picked the keys to Miss Peck's filing cabinet out of her desk and strolled into the inner office. "Anyway," she raised her voice to continue, "if my mother got it straight, Miss Peck's hot on the trail of that Lincoln, and she's going to talk to this lawyer whose detectives don't the one of them know what the other one's doing. She'll be back late today. Meantime, you and me is it, sister."

"You can have that chemist's stuff," Barb said sweetly.

Sharmille rolled her eyes. "I asked for it, I guess."

"Cheer up. At least it's not on Dictatape."

About the time Jim Clifford of the Minneapolis Police Department's bomb and arson squad learned that the dynamite used to blow up Miss Peck's storage room had been stolen from a construction site in Elyria, Ohio, Miss Peck returned to her motel room from a breakfast of watery scrambled eggs to place a call to Michael Goodenough.

"Oh, dear." Betty Shannon's distress came clearly over the line. "He's not here today. Could you possibly stay over until tomorrow? I know he wants to see you, but I can't reach him."

"I suppose I could," Miss Peck said unhappily.

"He just might come in late this afternoon. If you could call back around four?"

"Yes, I could do that," Miss Peck said. *Damn Clarice, anyway,* she thought. *And damn all crook books and Bunters, for tempting me into this.*

"I'm really very sorry, Miss Peck." Betty Shannon even sounded sorry. "I know he'll be sorry to miss you, but he had me cancel all today's appointments, so he could undertake an urgent investigation."

"I see."

"Since you're driving, why not go up the North Shore?" Miss Shannon suggested. "You'd have something to do, and it's really beautiful this time of year. And besides, it's cooler than the city, and this weather—I don't know, the summer has been something else, hasn't it?"

"It has indeed," Miss Peck agreed. "And thank you for the suggestion. I may just do that."

Sharmille and Barb had just started their mid-morning coffee break when Clarice Klenk poked her fluffy grey head around the edge of the outer door. "Who's typing my manuscript?" she inquired cheerfully.

"Me," Barbra admitted. She set down her cup with a regretful glance.

"Oh, finish your coffee, finish your coffee," Clarice told her. "We do want you alert!"

"What can we do for you, Miss Klenk?" Sharmille asked.

"It's what I can do for you," Clarice announced, grandly placing her left hand on her bosom and bowing. "I thought, since Ethel isn't here, I'd come by and help you with the proofreading."

"We could use some help," Sharmille agreed. Barbra cast her a look of agonized appeal, which Sharmille ignored.

"You haven't had any more answers to those ads, have you?" Clarice bustled across the room without waiting for a reply and stuck her head in at Miss Peck's door. "I'll just use Ethel's desk," she said. "She won't mind; I see she's cleared it off. Where's what you've got finished, Babs?"

Barbra knocked the dozen or so pages she had completed into a neat stack and took them to Miss Klenk, who had settled into Miss Peck's swivel chair with a delighted smirk. "She really got herself a beauty, didn't she?" she remarked, caressing the teak-grained Formica. "I bet it cost a young fortune."

"She got it used, from Podany's," Barbra said.

"Just like Ethel. I bet she got them to knock the price down ten percent, too. Where's my—oh, is that all?"

"You picked up what was done on Friday," Barbra pointed out. "And I've only been here an hour and a half."

"Yes, my handwriting is a little difficult to decipher," Clarice said kindly. The noted author grabbed the sheaf of pages with a carelessness that made the typist wince. "Well, it's better than nothing. You haven't had any answers to those ads, Babs, have you?"

Barbra glanced over her shoulder at Sharmille, who was typing very slowly on the chemist's paper. "Only somebody asking if we'd had any answers to those ads," she said.

"Who was that?"

"I don't know." Barbra grinned. "You'll have to talk to Sharmille, she took the call."

"Let's call that even," Sharmille said, without taking her eyes off the chemist's copy. Miss Klenk looked from one of the typists to the other with her eyebrows raised, but neither of them explained.

"Who was it who called, Sharmille?" Miss Klenk asked, after a moment in which Sharmille picked carefully at the typewriter, key by key.

Sharmille sighed, flipped off the typewriter, and swiveled her chair to face the inner office.

The green car in the parking lot at the Split Rock lighthouse was surely the same as the one at the motel? Miss Peck, again wearing jeans and joggers, turned on one heel to survey the area around her. No one who looked familiar, but had that flicker of motion at the edge of the lighthouse been someone ducking out of sight?

Her heart began to thump almost lazily. She started toward the building half-hoping her eyes were playing tricks on her. Because she was slow and cautious, by the time she had circled the lighthouse and come out to stand looking over the parking lot, the green car was just driving through the exit.

So it wasn't someone following her, after all. Just coincidence, the coincidence of two people touring the same points of interest. Certainly, she was not about to pursue the green car! A tour of the lighthouse was scheduled to begin in just ten minutes, and Miss Peck had never seen a Fresnel lens before.

The pack of letters the mailman put on the desk just after lunch was fatter than usual. Sharmille sorted through them. Bills, mostly, from the stationery store and the typewriter repair service, one for the new desk. Something from the insurance company. And a letter in a pink envelope with butterflies on it, addressed to Miss Peck in a round script with circles for the dots over the i's.

"I wonder what this is?" Sharmille held the letter up for Barbra to see. Barbra paused, her fingers resting on the keys.

"Who's it for?"

"Miss Peck. But it doesn't say Typing Service, so maybe I'd better let her open it herself when she gets here."

"What's that?" Clarice Klenk called from Miss Peck's office.

"Nothing. Letter for Miss Peck."

"What about?" Clarice stuck her pencil into the hair over her right ear and sauntered into the outer office.

"I don't know," Sharmille said. "It's personal."

"Who's it from?"

"I—" Sharmille snatched ineffectually at the letter as Clarice scooped it off the desk and pirouetted away.

"No return address," Clarice observed as she tore the upper left corner of the envelope off. "And postmarked Duluth. I think that's important, don't you?"

"Maybe," Sharmille said grudgingly.

Clarice already had her thumb in the envelope, ripping it open. "My goodness," she said, pulling the bedraggled deposit slip out. "This certainly has been through the wars!" She smoothed the paper out on the surface of Barbra's desk. "It's one of Celia Lewis's deposit slips!" she exclaimed, and turned it over. "And there's a note on it. Can one of you make out what it says?"

Sharmille took the note. "Looks like something got spilled on it," she said. "That must be 'please notify.' Yeah. 'Please notify Miss Ethel Peck.' Fine, but how can we? And what's this address? The one in pencil, I mean; the other one's ours."

Clarice took the deposit slip back. "It must be the place where whoever found this note found it," she decided. "Look, you can make out 'held here' up near the top. And the handwriting on the address is the same as on the envelope."

"And the rest is Celie's," Barb added.

"Does it say what city?" Sharmille asked.

"No. Most probably Duluth, wouldn't you think? I'd bet on it. Sharmille, where's your map of Duluth?"

"*My* map of Duluth?" Sharmille stared at her. "I've never been to Duluth in my life, why would I have a map?"

"Don't you? Oh well, maybe I've got one at home," Clarice said. "I've got a whole collection of the things, very useful. Ethel didn't say where she'd be staying, did she?"

"No, she didn't. She probably decided when she got there." Sharmille held her hand out, and Clarice reluctantly returned the note, which Sharmille restored to the remains of the envelope and stashed in her own desk.

"That address,' Barbra said. "That's where Celie's being held, I bet you anything."

"I agree, Babs. Should we call the police?" Clarice wondered aloud.

"Oh, they don't pay any attention," Barbra said disgustedly. "Miss Peck's called them dozens of times and gone over there and talked to them and everything, but they just send her away with what she calls a flea in her ear."

"Oh, really?" Clarice let her head sink, fingering the soft bulge of flesh below her chin. "Do you know, girls, I've just thought of something urgent I should be doing. You two can carry on without me, can't you?"

"I imagine so," Sharmille said, but if Clarice Klenk noticed the sarcasm Sharmille couldn't keep out of her voice, she gave no sign as she hurried out of the office, head still down.

"Thank God!" said Barbra. "If she'd called me 'Babs' one more time, I think I'd have crammed her damned novel right down her throat!"

Sharmille giggled. "Without even finding out how it ends?"

23 September 19

Miss Peck dawdled over a late lunch in Two Harbors. As she left the small restaurant, pleasantly filled with a clear mushroom soup touched with thyme and an egg salad sandwich in which she thought she had tasted cumin, she paused to watch the herring gulls wheeling and mewing over her head and saw that thunderheads had rolled up above the western horizon, their creamy sunlit tops choppily reflected in the endless blue of Lake Superior.

Back to the motel, then, she decided. Not that she minded driving in rain, but although the road was well marked, it was also unfamiliar, and she didn't want to get lost, not when she was so anxious to talk to this lawyer! She arrived at the motel just before three: early, but she dialed Michael Goodenough's number the moment she got into the room.

"Oh, yes, Miss Peck," Betty Shannon said, her voice very bright. Miss Peck's heart sank. "Mr. Goodenough won't be in this afternoon, after all—he's with the county attorney. He wanted me to apologize to you for not being in."

"Oh, dear." She'd been fist-tense; now Miss Peck felt herself deflate.

"I've put you down for one o'clock tomorrow afternoon," Miss Shannon continued. "Will that be all right?"

Miss Peck took a deep breath and closed her eyes. "I guess it will have to be," she said.

"Fine. Then we'll see you tomorrow at one," Miss Shannon said, with the sort of professional cheer that covers a sneaking guilt, and hung up.

Keenly disappointed, Miss Peck rubbed her hands over her face. Another thirty-five dollars gone, for the extra night at the motel. At least she had Sharmille, or she'd have had to close the office as well . . . although, if she hadn't had Sharmille to fall back on, she might have let her better sense keep her out of this whole affair. But she hadn't, and here she was, sleuthing on a warm September afternoon in the admittedly attractive city of Duluth. Sleuthing? More like chasing wild geese.

"Ridiculous, Ethel, geese don't fly north in the fall," she told herself with considerable asperity, and closed the door of the room behind her as she headed for the motel restaurant for a glass of iced tea. The sky drew a wary look as she crossed the parking lot. Thundery, yes, but not ominous. Not green, anyway.

She ordered her iced tea to go, and carried the tall Styrofoam cup with its leaky plastic lid back to the restaurant's glass door. The first fat drops of a thunderstorm splashed down. As she gazed doubtfully out at the weather, the green car she had noticed before drove up to the same room as it had the evening before. After a couple of minutes a man got out, dashed for the door of the room, opened it, and vanished behind it in one swift motion.

"Oh, no! It's the detective!" Miss Peck gasped. Behind her, the waitress who had served her the tea paused in her rhythmic swipes at the orange counter and looked up. *Who would have thought it, at that woman's age?* she remarked to herself. After a moment the sponge began to move again, and as Miss Peck pushed open the door someone called from the kitchen and the waitress forgot her.

The air outside tasted metallic, heavy with ozone. Miss Peck slunk back to her room along the sidewalk that bordered the parking lot instead of cutting across. She closed her door and leaned against it just as the first crash of thunder shook the thin panel. *How did he get here?* she wondered, only half-conscious of the downpour beginning. Only one possible answer (unless he'd kidnapped Clarice and tortured the information out of her, *au roman à sensation):* he'd followed her all the way from the Twin Cities, maybe hoping she'd lead him to Celie. She couldn't be mistaken about that car, olive-green with the cloudy surface of a failing paint job, that particular slope of the trunk. And she couldn't write it off to coincidence anymore. The same car in three places? Driven by that man?

Miss Peck drew her curtain back just enough to peer out with one eye. A similar, wider slot between the curtains of the room in the other wing of the motel greeted her. She opened her own a little more and stepped back from the window. Devin Frazier. The man had to be Devin Frazier, didn't he? She was playing cat and mouse, then, and the cat was Devin Frazier.

Cat!

"Oh, my word," Miss Peck murmured. She glanced at her watch, and with a sigh of relief moved the telephone out of the line of sight of the twin openings in the curtains and dialed the front desk. "I have to place a long distance call," she said. She'd made a tactical error, she realized. She should have moved in the other direction, so she could see the door of that other room. She picked up the telephone and rearranged herself while the front desk put the call through.

"Peck's Typing Service."

"Sharmille, I'm so glad I caught you! It's Miss Peck. I'm still in Duluth, unfortunately. I'll have to stay overnight to see that lawyer. How are things going?"

"Okay, I guess." Sharmille sounded dispirited. "You got a real funny letter today, Miss Peck. It was personal, so I wouldn't have opened it, but Miss Klenk was here and she ripped it open before I could stop her, because it was postmarked Duluth. I'm sorry."

"That's quite all right, Sharmille. I know Miss Klenk very well. I'm sure you couldn't have stopped her with anything short of an elephant gun. What was the letter?"

Sharmille relayed the messages written on Celie's deposit slip, which she'd deciphered more completely in the hours since Clarice's departure. "Miss Klenk thought the address must be the place where Celie is being kept," she added. "And that would fit with the mileage on that car."

"I guess it's just as well Clarice was there," Miss Peck remarked. She noticed that her heart was pounding and her hands had gone cold. A roll of thunder echoed a crackle in the telephone line. "Let me get a pencil, and then give me that address again. Why was Clarice there, did she say?"

"She *said* she came to proofread what we got typed of her manuscript."

"Very considerate of her. But?"

"But she seemed a lot more interested in answers to your ads in the paper."

Clarice snooping. The thought released her anxiety. Miss Peck chuckled. "Sounds like Clarice. Were there more answers?"

"Uh-*huh!* Somebody name of Hansen who said the car was rented and we'd never trace it without his help. He wanted a thousand bucks for his information, cash in advance."

"A thousand—! What did you tell him?"

"I said I'd have to consult with you when you came back to the office. You think I should call the cops?"

"I don't know, Sharmille," Miss Peck sighed. "They want so much corroboration—do what you think best." *Could it be the third man in that car at the rest stop?* she wondered, and discarded the idea instantly: why would he sell himself out? "Were there any others?"

"Not really. Couple of kooks, somebody who wanted to know if you had any info about Celie, since he's looking for her, too."

Miss Peck began to feel a little short of breath. Talk about imagining things! "The same man who was in on Friday?"

"No. The guy who came around and bugged Barb on Thursday."

"Oh." Perhaps she hadn't been imagining things after all.

She found pencil and notebook in her handbag; with the telephone clamped between her ear and her shoulder she thumbed through the notebook searching for a blank page. "Any others?"

"Oh, some jerk who wanted to let you know there's a Lincoln in Oregon," Sharmille said. "I told him there's one in Nebraska, too. You want that address again, now?"

"Yes, please. And then let me speak to Barbra."

She copied down the address and read it back and then Barbra came on the line.

"Barb, I need you to feed Melange," Miss Peck said, getting to the reason for her call at last. "Would you mind very much stopping by my house on your way home?"

"I guess not," Barbra said.

"There's a spare key to my back door in the file cabinet in my office, taped inside a folder marked Keyes, K-E-Y-E-S. Maybe you'd better go get it while I hang on, just to make sure it's still there." The clunk was the receiver being put down: Miss Peck had scant hope that Barbra would ever learn to use the hold button. She heard a distant bang as Barbra slammed the file drawer shut and a moment later the slide of her palm against the phone. "She wants me to go feed Celie's cat," she heard Barb say, and then into the phone, "Okay, I got it."

"Thanks a million, Barb. I'll probably see you late tomorrow."

"Are you going to call the cops?"

"I guess so," Miss Peck said. "Good-bye."

Am I going to call the cops? Miss Peck sat on the edge of her bed with her hands clasped between her knees. How long would it take to explain this crazy situation?

Forever. And then they'd probably check with the police in Minneapolis, and the police in Minneapolis would tell them she was a nice old lady with a bee in her bonnet, but harmless. And that would be that. She didn't even have the note to show them, and if she tried to explain why she had

176

tried to follow a car north a week after it had come—harebrained old lady! She smiled ruefully at her image. About as far from the urbane and knowledgeable Bunter as she could get.

And what if Clarice were wrong about the address? Could she be sued for calling the police?

She tried calling Betty Shannon for advice and got only an answering machine.

"Well," she said aloud. Maybe the best thing would be to go to the house and find out what the situation was before trying to get help. Because if she actually found Celie in danger and went to the police then, they'd have to listen, wouldn't they? Miss Peck glanced again at the other room's curtains, behind which the detective with the shoe-polish hair might or might not be hiding, and discovered that they were closed. She picked up her handbag.

Better travel lighter than that, Ethel. She dumped the bag out on the bed to see what resources she might have. The paperback mysteries she quickly, almost furtively, laid aside. The Swiss army knife went back into the bag, along with her wallet, the sewing kit, her notebook, the steel tape, the flashlight, the folding scissors, the package of tissues, and the roll of adhesive tape.

Then she unfolded her map of Duluth and vicinity.

There. That was the road she wanted. A long one, that traveled through the hills north of the city until it ended in a T against a road along the bluff above the lake. The map didn't show house numbers as her map of Minneapolis did. Perhaps the best thing would be to start at that intersection on the bluff and keep going north. . . . Miss Peck traced the route she would have to follow with her finger. Satisfied, she nodded.

She took her rainhat from its case and spread the accordian pleats over her hair; she tied the plastic ties under her chin with an earnest expression that would have amused her had she seen it. Laboriously, she picked at the plastic raincoat until it came unstuck from itself, shook it out, and put it on, wishing she had remembered to pack the plastic boots still hanging in their carry-bag on a hook in her hall closet. Quite a pile of stuff was left on the bed. *Really,* Miss Peck chided herself, *I ought to clean out my bag more often.*

Swathed in thin plastic, her lightened handbag on her arm, she turned out her light and peeked around the edge of the curtain. The other curtains were still closed, and the rain fell in straight silvery sheets that might afford some concealment if the man should decide to pull the curtains aside and look out. Miss Peck drew in a deep breath and slipped through her door, shutting it silently behind her.

Rain had filled the gutter; a gout of water thrown up by the racing stream as it hit her front tire wet her jeans against her ankle. She whipped open the car door, slid in, and waited.

Two minutes. No sign of alarm from that other room.

Feeling excessively clever, Miss Peck did not turn on her headlights as she backed out of her parking spot and made for the exit. She waited there a moment, too. No one came out of that room as she studied her rearview mirror. The rear window was beginning to fog over; Miss Peck gritted her teeth and hoped her asthmatic defroster could handle it. At the first break in traffic she made a hard right turn and drove another block before putting on her lights.

She called the map she had looked at to mind as she waited for a traffic light to change. She had no way of knowing that the door of the motel restaurant had opened as she bumped into her turn from the lot and a lean, dark-haired man had hurried across the lot with his shoulders drawn up against the rain, or that he had slipped into the green car and done exactly what she had done only moments before. Nor did she notice that his car was now only two behind her own at the traffic light.

The light turned green. Miss Peck crossed the intersection. Behind her, the second car, a dark blob in the still-foggy rear window had she looked, stuck close to the car between them, showing only its parking lights.

"Seven hundred fifty, huh?" Sharmille was saying to Hansen. "You want to leave a name and number? . . . Hey, I'm not worrying about when you were born, don't you, either. . . . Why don't you call back, say, Wednesday. . . . Okay, that's up to you." She hung up and left the already-darkened office, giving the super's key two full turns the way he'd said.

24 September 19

THE DOOR OPENED easily to Miss Peck's spare key. Barbra stepped into the kitchen with a voyeuristic tingle. She'd been here only twice; last week with the cat, and once when Miss Peck had given a little party to celebrate the publication of Miss Klenk's first book. On neither occasion had she had much opportunity to see how her employer lived.

Melange parked herself square in front of the door and miaowed loudly as Barbra shut it behind her. "Hi, cat," she said, reaching down to scratch Melange behind the ears. "Miss me?"

The cat purred and rubbed her head against Barbra's legs as she searched for cat food in Miss Peck's cupboards. "Miss Peck sure eats a lot of kidney beans and chick peas," she told the cat. "Here's a can of sardines; I'll give you that if I can't find anything else."

The cat went to sit beside her dish, still purring loudly, with an occasional questioning *prrrt*. "Miss Peck has dinner plates just like mine," Barbra remarked. "What do you think of that, Melange? Did she get them at the supermarket too, do you think?" Barbra glanced at the cat, still staring at her with intense attention. "But she's only got eight, I've got twelve."

What with investigating Miss Peck's tea towels, and her stainless steel flatware, and the old cups and pink glass dishes in the cabinet next to the refrigerator, and deciding to water the philodendron hanging in Miss Peck's east kitchen window, and making an inventory of Miss Peck's vitamin bottles—did she really take all those every day?—and Miss Peck's supply of Tupperware, including the lettuce crisper Barb was thinking of getting next time one of her friends had a party, and discovering that Miss Peck bought her coffee in the bean and ground it in an efficient-looking little grinder that sat next to the stove, it took Barbra nearly twenty minutes to find the cat food standing on the counter beside the sink.

Naturally, she would have to check the house, to make sure nothing was wrong. She left the cat with its nose in the dish of Cat Chow and ventured out of the kitchen.

She'd seen the dining room, with its built-in buffet, when she was here for the party, and had even half-examined the dishes that showed through the glassed doors. Limoges, that plate with the pretty pink flowers. Funny, she'd never seen the pattern in a department store, all that time she was picking out her own china. . . . Barbra put the plate back with its rim in the groove of the shelf, adjusted it to be equidistant from its neighbors, and shut the glass doors. She pulled out a couple of drawers and admired some linens embroidered in cross-stitch. And a lace tablecloth that looked hand-made, something like crochet but not crochet. The cat purred and crunched in the kitchen.

Barbra decided the African violets in a row on the windowsill could do without any attention until Miss Peck got home. Besides, she'd have to go back to the kitchen for water. A board squeaked over her head, for all the world like the noises she used to tease Celie about. . . . Was Miss Peck ever scared by her house? Barbra wondered. Probably not.

She went through the wide arch into the living room, opened the cabinet she had suspected of concealing a TV, and was disappointed to find only a bunch of records. Stuff her mother liked, Sinatra and Crosby and the Andrews Sisters and Patti Page, and, surprise, some early rock-and-roll, Haley and the Comets and a fat, heavy LP of Elvis.

The rest of the stuff was only classical. Barbra put it all back and stood up.

Miss Peck had a nice black-iron mantel clock, which Barbra had noticed before. It was still ticking. No need to hunt for its key, then, and wind it up, but Barbra looked around anyway, just in case it should suddenly stop. She did find the key, tucked behind the clock, but first she had to look into a wicker picnic hamper which proved full of magazines, and a drawer with a number of letters in it, some of which she read and found boring. Nor was the clock key in the closet in which hung three coats Barbra recognized: a blue poplin raincoat Miss Peck had been wearing to work half of forever, a winter tweed, and a light spring coat still in a bag from the dry cleaner.

Squeak again. God, what a noisy house! You'd think somebody as old as Miss Peck would move into one of those nice condos by Lake Calhoun, nothing to hear but your neighbors through the walls. . . .

Nothing seemed amiss downstairs, but who could tell? Someone might have gone straight upstairs and ransacked the bedroom for jewels. Barbra wasn't sure Miss Peck owned any jewels, but a burglar wouldn't know any more than she did herself, she reasoned; so, feeling highly responsible, she went up the stairs that wound to the second floor from the north end of the living room. The first door was only the bathroom, a tub *with feet* tucked under the slant of the roof and not even a shower, for heaven's sake! And no medicine cabinet over the sink, an old-fashioned john with a porcelain handle on the big tank, a shelf with bath powder that smelled like Miss Peck and a soap dish with a half-used bar of lavender-scented soap and a little pile of hand towels. Barbra almost laughed as she reached for the next doorknob: this must be Miss Peck's bedroom.

Right. The room stretched across the front of the tiny house, with Miss Peck's bed—a double! (What did she need a double for?)—facing her from beneath three narrow windows. Drawers and closets had been worked in under the slant of the ceilings when the house was built. To her right a single window gave some light from a narrow dormer. Beside it, a closet door stood slightly open. Barbra headed for it eagerly.

A hand clapped over her mouth from behind. Barbra squealed. Something poked into her back.

"Stand still, or you're dead."

Barbra stood perfectly still.

"Kneel down on the floor. That's right. One little peep and I'll shoot you, clear?"

"Yes," Barbra gasped.

"Quiet!"

Something ripped. "Put your hands behind you," the man ordered. *His voice sounds familiar,* Barbra thought. She put her hands behind her. Something sticky wound around and around her wrists.

"What are you doing?" she demanded.

"Shut up."

The ripping noise again, and the sticky something— *adhesive tape, oh, no!*—pressed across her mouth. She raised her head, now, and saw the man reflected in the mirror on one of the closet doors. The blond detective.

"I don't know what you're doing here," he said. "But you shouldn't have been snooping. Believe me, snooping can get you into all kinds of trouble."

He should know, Barbra thought.

"If anybody ought to know that, it's me," he muttered. "Now, what am I going to do with you?" He surveyed her for a moment. "Stand up, we're going downstairs."

Barbra nodded. She stumbled ahead of him down the winding staircase, past the desk whose drawer she had left standing open—the blond man shut it with his hip as they passed—and into the living room. As she had feared, he opened the coat closet. As he glimpsed her face in the mirror inside the closet door, something in his expression changed. "Hold on," he said. "Aren't you the girl from the office?"

Barbra nodded. "You're the kid's old roommate, aren't you? Celia's?"

She nodded again.

"Do *you* know where she is?" Barbra shook her head. "Christ," the man muttered. "I hope she's still alive. Okay, in," he said, gesturing. He really did have a gun, right in his hand. Barbra wanted to run upstairs quick to the bathroom, but she couldn't say anything. She shook her head.

"Come on, come on." He pushed her, not at all roughly, into the closet. "Listen. I won't let on that you were poking around this house for nearly an hour if you don't tell anyone who I am."

"Mmp."

"You can imagine what your boss would think of you being found in her bedroom, right?" Barbra nodded. "So if they ask, and they will, just say I got you in the kitchen, and it wasn't anyone you knew. Deal?" Barbra nodded again, and the man shut the door. "Don't worry," came his voice through the heavy panels. A key turned. In the darkness, Barbra began to cry. She heard the man walk through the dining room, into the kitchen, and out the back door. The door shut and the latch clicked, horribly loud through the wall beside her head. Now she was all alone in Miss Peck's house, except for Melange, who was on the other side of the closet door and wouldn't really give a damn, anyway, not now that she'd been fed.

Barbra wanted to howl.

All she could do was moan through her nose.

A hundred and sixty miles to the north, Miss Peck drove slowly through the rain, her windshield wipers racing on high speed. Water boiled out of a storm drain at a corner and spewed across the road in a muddy stream. She eased across the mud, throwing up a dark spray. At the next

184

intersection she didn't see the same thing happening in time; she hit the mud going too fast, fishtailed wildly and winced as a dark shower splattered her windshield. Somehow she controlled the car and found plain wet blacktop under her wheels again. When the rain stopped, she'd have to get out and wipe off her lights. Meanwhile, slow down a bit and pray nobody hit her.

The section she was driving through now seemed new: comfortable houses on good-sized plots of land, where perhaps someone could keep a girl against her will. The road she wanted should be coming up soon. Alert for the turn, Miss Peck crested a small hill and saw the sign ahead of her. She ducked into the road where it made a T against the one she had been following, saw that the house numbers here were far too low, and sped up to round a curve. A nagging sense of urgency pressed her right foot down bit by bit. She was soon driving far faster than she considered safe, but the car responded accurately to her feather-touch on the wheel (no one drives through forty Minnesota winters without learning all about skids), and after a time that probably seemed longer than it was, an iron fence appeared to Miss Peck's right. Tall, spike-topped and forbidding, it climbed the hill to an ornamental gate into which the number of the house Miss Peck was looking for was worked. Miss Peck stopped with relief.

She wondered for a moment whether this could be Colin Frazier's house. A realtor had hung a board on the closed gate, saying that the house could be rented by the month or by the season—and hadn't Miss Shannon said the Frazier house was for sale? So this couldn't be it.

The house Miss Peck could see through the fir trees hugging the fence looked sturdy enough, in a brick, fake-Tudor way, but wasn't extraordinarily large. Four bedrooms, at a guess. And the grounds . . . Miss Peck put the car into gear and drove ahead a hundred yards or so. The iron fence made a smart right turn and marched away from the road. The grounds were large, but not enormous. Not $600,000 worth. She examined the shoulder of the road: yes, she decided, it would support the car without danger of getting mired in. Cautiously, she pulled off the road and rested her forearms against the steering wheel.

A fence like this was a challenge. And the house was rented out; at a guess, not nearly so well kept up as if a well-to-do family lived there. She would bet there was an illicit way through that fence, found or created by children, perhaps from this field of waist-high weeds creeping through the fence into the black line of firs.

She put the car into first gear, set the emergency brake, and got out into the rain.

Assessing the field as a world-class nuisance, she decided to try the gate first. Nothing like a silvery transparent plastic raincoat to make a woman feel conspicuous as she tries to stroll casually along a rusting iron fence in the tail end of a thunderstorm. Miss Peck walked up a slight grade to the gate and found it unlocked. She went a little way up the drive, saw lights on in the back of the house, and retired to the car to think for a few minutes.

She could come back in the morning and say that she wanted to look over the house with a view to renting it. But what if the people in it had rented it for several more months? She could try the agent. . . .

In the house, Longdel put down the telephone. "He doesn't answer."

"Where is he?" Baker demanded, with his mouth full of meatloaf sandwich. "He said he'd tell us today."

"I know what he said," Longdel replied irritably over the thump and shriek of Baker's radio. "But he doesn't answer his phone, so what can I do about it?"

"I want to get this over with."

"So do I. Can't you turn that goddamned thing down? I can't hear myself think!"

Baker reached out and twisted a knob, bringing the volume down to the point where Longdel no longer feared for his dental work. "There's more of Walt's meatloaf in the fridge. 'S pretty good." He ruminated over his sandwich for several more bites. "You think Frazier could have figured out where we are?"

"Jesus Christ, I hope not."

Morrison came into the kitchen. "Any luck?" The other two shook their heads.

"I'm taking the kid her supper," Morrison announced.

Better reconnoiter first, Miss Peck decided. Bringing down the local constabulary on the heads of innocent people was to be avoided. She returned to the gate and slipped through it. The drive stretched ahead of her in a black-top curve, not more than thirty yards to the front of the house, where a high porch with brick arches and iron lamps shielded a dark door. Steps, concrete and incongruous, led down to the drive, flanked by junipers whose gnarled, exposed branches had been flattened by snow winter after winter. No lights showed in the front of the house.

Miss Peck stepped off the drive into the unmown grass at the edge of the fir trees, thin threads mixed with spindly dandelion stalks that unloaded their water onto her pants legs. Closer to the fence, where the firs were densest, the grass was absent, and there was a path of sorts where lower branches had died of age and fallen, but Miss Peck could see no way to get close to the house by following the fence. She pushed on, concealing herself as best she could in the evergreen-scented shadows, worrying over the circle of silence that followed her as she frightened the singing crickets, until she was opposite the back corner of the house.

A door opened, shedding a yellow rectangle of light onto a wooden porch and releasing a blast of hard rock music, and a man stepped out. Miss Peck took an involuntary step backwards. A small animal darted out of the weeds near her feet. She clamped her mouth on a shaky breath that threatened to become an *oh!* Only a mouse, which sat up on its haunches with white forepaws poised for flight and examined her with opaque, polished eyes.

The man snapped open an umbrella and started down the steps, carrying a plate in his other hand. Miss Peck watched as he tramped past neglected patches of weeds that had once been a formal flower garden.

Her eyes anticipated his path, and she saw the playhouse at the back of the garden, cedar-shingled so that in this light, in the rain, it was almost invisible against the background of firs, marked off only by a small grove of aspens. The man stepped up onto a tiny porch and set the plate down at his feet and collapsed the umbrella. He knocked. Miss Peck remembered the folding opera glasses lying on the bed back at the motel. *Some sleuth!*

"Dinner," called the man. He reached into his pocket and did something to the door—unlocking it?—and the door opened a couple of inches, then a few inches more, and he picked up the plate and passed it to someone inside. The door closed again, blocking out the feeble bit of lamplight that had shone on the man's face for a moment. He relocked the door and started back toward the house with a snap of the umbrella.

Cold water trickled down the back of Miss Peck's neck. She almost stuffed her hands into her mouth to keep from crying out. The man was the one she and Sharmille had followed in Minneapolis, first in his grey suit and then in his plaid shirt. Today he was wearing jeans and a torn sweatshirt, but she knew his face, knew his walk, and she was in no doubt whatsoever.

Back at the motel, the dark-haired detective admitted defeat. He sank onto the end of Miss Peck's bed. The woman had left a heap of junk in the middle of the bed, books all over the place, a suitcase wide open on the shelf the management provided, toothpaste and brush on the side of the sink, a dress hanging on the rod beside the sink and a bathrobe on the hook in the bathroom, and not one single clue to where she had been going in such a hurry when she gave him the slip.

Hunched with his elbows on his knees, he reviewed his bank account and once again decided it held no money for new tires for the damned car that had dumped him into the shallow ditch while the red tail lights of the car he'd been following faded into the distance. With a sigh, he got up, cracked the door open, and peered out. The sky to the west was brightening. The puddles in the parking lot gleamed placidly. Sighing again, even more deeply, he hurried back to his own room and tried to call Devin Frazier to report yet another near miss.

Nobody home.

25 September 19

MISS PECK WATCHED as Morrison stopped near the house to pluck a pale blossom, from which he shook the rain before climbing the steps. Someone had closed the back door. Miss Peck waited with her fists clenched in her pockets and her breath stopped against her lower teeth while Morrison knocked and was let in. The rectangle of light that spilled through the open door seemed dimmer than before. She glanced at the sky and realized that the storm was clearing; shreds of dark cloud swirled over gaps of bright lemon yellow as the cool front arrived. She was already quite chilled: the sopped denim against her legs seemed to suck at her vitality.

She could see one other man in what might be a kitchen, seated with his back to the window on a tilted-back chair. *Three of them,* she reminded herself, to judge from the hitchhiker's account. Perhaps also the fourth, who had retrieved the car that had met the Lincoln in the rest area. All of them might be here. She would have to tread very, very softly.

Miss Peck backed slowly to the fence. Other feet had worn a path here. Kids, she guessed. Small boys. She followed the narrow track, barely dampened by the recent rain, until she saw the pale trunks of the aspens near the playhouse and knew she was behind it.

She came up through the firs, forced to be slow by the clumps of dead needles that stuck to her wet shoes, keeping the playhouse between herself and the main building and hoping that they hadn't set a guard. She could see the formal garden better from this point. At the near end of each bed was the dark fountain of a peony, the leaves already streaked with crimson, and last spring's flowers metamorphosed into clusters of what looked like the carapaces of small, cooked crustaceans. A few asters also remained, only their colors showing that they hadn't begun as wildlings, and the tail end of some dirty magenta phlox still bloomed among the rusty plumes of goldenrod.

The windows of the playhouse had been boarded over with new plywood cut to size, each piece a little less than two feet across and roughly three feet high. Miss Peck reached up and put her palms flat on the mossy edge of the roof. Still, she wouldn't be able to climb up on it, even assuming that a reason to do so might develop.

She tapped softly on one of the window boards, poised to run. Inside, a peculiar clunking, scrambling noise began. After a couple of minutes it stopped, leaving a cautious-sounding silence. Miss Peck knocked again.

"Who is it?" The voice was very close to the wooden panel, subdued, frightened, hopeful. Celie.

"Celie? It's Miss Peck."

Celie stared at the blank panes. She pulled back the pins that held the sash in place and pulled it out, set it down with a thump, and put her fingers into the shallow depression of a knothole as if that might bring her closer to Miss Peck. Tears spurted. "Oh, Miss Peck!" she gasped. "Thank God, thank God!"

"Celie, now that I know where you are, I'm going to get the police," Miss Peck said. "It shouldn't take long. Okay?"

"No!" Celie almost wailed. "Oh, Miss Peck, please," she continued, still urgent but quietly again. "Get me out of here. I don't have much time left."

"What do you mean?"

"They're just waiting to get some money for me, and then they're going to kill me. Oh, I'm so scared!"

"When is this money coming?"

"Tonight. Any minute."

"I see." Miss Peck fell silent. She thought of the drive to someone's house, the time it might take to convince the people there to let her use the telephone, the further time it would take to convince some unknown policeman that she was a stable, mature woman in possession of her wits.

So it was to be up to her, after all. The dark firs crowded up behind the playhouse, suddenly more menacing than friendly. Tears stung Miss Peck's eyes, too. She had never felt more helpless in her life. She willed herself to assess the situation. The Swiss army knife could get no more than a bare start on pulling the plywood off the window; each round nail had been bashed in deep with an extra blow of the hammer. She didn't really have any other tool.

"Miss Peck? Are you still there?"

"Yes."

"Oh, good, I thought you were gone."

"Just thinking." An old property like this one, with such extensive gardens, must have a toolshed. Miss Peck closed her eyes against a sinking feeling. She could almost see her grandmother's house, with the garden tools kept in a little lean-to up against the house, beside the back door. That she couldn't handle.

"Oh, Miss Peck," Celie said, close to the plywood. "It's hopeless."

"Nonsense. We'll get you out somehow and make a run for it."

"I can't run," Celie said. Miss Peck could hear the tears in her voice. "I can't even walk. They've got my ankles stuck together with a plaster cast."

Miss Peck jumped. Never in her wildest dreams would she have thought of that! "Things aren't ever quite hopeless," she tried to assure herself as well as Celie. "Even mice have been known to gnaw their way out of snakes that had eaten them."

"Really?" Celie felt an odd glow at the grisly picture. Trust Miss Peck to know a thing like that, with all the odd books she read. Never again would she giggle with Barbra and Sharmille about the peculiar assortments! Assuming she got the chance.

"Really," came Miss Peck's voice. "Now you be quiet. I'm going to look for some tools."

But where would she find them? Celie's anxiety returned in a wave. She pressed her fist against her teeth. Outside, silence. Had Miss Peck really gone looking for tools, or was she still standing there, thinking again, not getting any ideas?

"Miss Peck?"

No answer. Strangely, that was also no comfort.

More rain began to fall as Miss Peck moved along the back of the playhouse and peered toward the big house. The man who had been sitting just inside the kitchen window was still there. Only a few yards to her right was another small building, with diamond-latticed windows and cedar shingles. That would be the toolshed.

Miss Peck took one step toward it and stopped. Where was the garage? She didn't want to expose herself to someone going for a car, to pick up this money. Another look at the house both reassured her and told her that the house wasn't as old as it had at first seemed: two wide, brown-painted garage doors broke the facade at ground level on the end she had not seen on her first examination. She could keep out of sight of them with no difficulty.

She made her way over the yielding carpet of fir needles, careful to keep well within the darkness of the trees. A broken branch snagged her raincoat sleeve and tore it. Miss Peck hoisted her handbag onto her shoulder more securely and resolved to be more cautious.

As she had suspected, the door to the small building faced the firs with no regard for the inconvenience to the gardener. What had once been a matter of aesthetics to the occupants of the house gave Miss Peck a far keener pleasure than any they had derived from that small architectural decision. She picked her way past a tangle of asparagus spangled with tiny, gleaming drops of water on every leaflet, between rotting, weed-choked cold frames and a hump of compost—twenty years old at least and nearly absorbed into the ground—to the door of the shed.

The door was closed with a hasp and a rusted padlock. Miss Peck unfolded the screwdriver blade of her knife and attacked the corroded screws that held the hasp in place. The heads twisted off the first two, leaving two tiny spots of bright metal. The third turned in place in the shrunken wood. Miss Peck pried on the hasp. It came loose with an eerie sound like the distant cry of a bird and dangled from the padlock. She stopped to listen. Nothing but the drip of water and a couple of damp sounding insect songs disturbed the garden. From the house, the muffled beat of a radio; from the street two hundred yards away the splash of a passing car. She eased the door open.

The house door opened. Three beats of hard rock, the last snipped short by a slam. Footsteps thudded down one of the weedy gravel paths. Miss Peck stood on one foot with nowhere to go. If she stepped into the shed, she might blunder into a dozen clanging hoes and rakes; to back up would make the glimmer of her raincoat visible from that path.

The steps stopped. Someone at the playhouse: Miss Peck heard the hollow sound of a step onto the small porch. Celie screamed.

She almost ran to help. Almost. Didn't, because the torn raincoat caught on the loose hasp and held her back for one decisive second, in which she heard someone say, "Calm down, will you? I came for your plate."

Miss Peck eased one step inside the open edge of the shed door, her mouth open in the primal response of a woman straining every sense. A padlock snapped open, over by the playhouse. "Oh, for pete's sake," the man said, his voice a little muted. "Haven't you eaten it yet? What's the matter? . . . You want me to leave it? . . . Why not?"

One more cautious step and she was safely inside the shed. She lifted up on the door and swung it closed behind her. The hinges complained, too slightly, she hoped, for the man to hear.

Well, she was out of sight. But now the rain falling on the roof of the shed kept her from hearing what was going on outside, and she was stuck. The two tiny cobwebbed windows let in scarcely any light, but made it impossible to use her flashlight until the man was back in the house. And, now that she couldn't hear him, how was she to know when that was? She crouched in the dark, listening.

After a few minutes she thought she heard the crunch of gravel under somebody's feet and decided to risk the light. She counted the seconds slowly as she felt through her handbag for the familiar blocky shape.

Two hundred. The small circle of her light on the dirt floor brought a scurry of many-legged creatures trying to hide from its rays. Miss Peck stifled a shudder and continued her search. The last gardener to use this shed had been a neat man. A coil of hose rested around a wooden spool, so sheeted in cobweb that she didn't at first know what it was. Tools, once oiled against winter and still not badly rusted, hung from a rack on the back wall of the shed.

Miss Peck chose a sturdy-looking hoe with a triangular blade only slightly pocked with rust, and a slightly less well-preserved pruning saw, and snapped off her flashlight.

A shout from the house.

"Nobody here," she heard a man call, only yards away.

After a moment Miss Peck opened her eyes and let her frozen breath escape through her nose. She willed her knees to stop shaking. She had been about to walk straight out into somebody's arms. Three, possibly four dangerous men. What on earth was she doing here, in this drenched and dying garden? Why hadn't she just run to her car, driven to one of those nice houses down the road, and called the police?

"Ah, he had to be bluffing," said the voice, a smooth baritone at odds with the words. "How the hell would Frazier figure out where we are?"

A gruff mumble Miss Peck couldn't make out replied.

"Forget it," the smooth voice said. "I checked around. Everything's fine, Baker."

Miss Peck thought of the policeman she had talked to back in Minneapolis. How politely he had eased her out the door without paying any attention to what she had to say. She might, even now, have been shouting at some pig-headed desk sergeant, while Celie . . . and they'd need a search warrant, there'd be a judge to find and convince, just as that officer back in Minneapolis had pointed out. Miss Peck took a tighter grip on the hoe. This little dark room with its cobwebs and centipedes might be the last shelter she'd ever have.

Stop that, she chided herself. *Just be patient.* The gravel creaked again; the dust-curtained glass of the narrow windows darkened for a moment. Miss Peck, huddled as far under the potting bench as she could get, put her watch to her ear and counted off five minutes, four ticks to the second. Then she boosted her handbag strap onto her shoulder, tucked the pruning saw under her arm, held the hoe at the ready, and gently pushed at the door of the shed.

26 September 19

THE SHED DOOR abruptly sagged outward, the top hinge gone. Miss Peck almost choked on her heart. Beyond the little clearing where the cold frames rotted, water dripped from the dark firs. A light mist of rain still fell.

The sagging door left a wide V of space between it and the shed. After a moment, when no one came running, Miss Peck stepped through the V, hugging her implements tightly. With the shed for a screen she made for the firs, wishing she could risk her flashlight. The faint glimmer of the worn wood of the cold frames helped her to get her bearings in the dimming light.

She reached the firs, stepped behind one of the thin, ragged-branched trunks, and looked back toward the house. The man who had tilted his chair was gone from the window. The light from the window seemed almost like heat on her face, though she knew that was just an illusion. She couldn't hear anyone moving in the garden, couldn't see any darker shadows, any white faces against the firs on the other side of the flowerbeds, fifty yards away. *But I don't know that all the men are white*, Miss Peck reminded herself. She'd only assumed so, because the hitchhiker hadn't said anything different. Should have gotten a better description. No help for it now. Old prejudices, old assumptions she'd thought she'd squelched years ago, coming back to trip her up.

Miss Peck took a slow, deep breath and began the trek to the playhouse. What looked like a crouched figure was only an enormous peony. What sounded like steps was only water dripping from the scented evergreens. What seemed like eternity was only two or three minutes, and then she was back among the aspens at the window she'd knocked at once before, knocking softly once again.

"Miss Peck?"

"Yes."

"Thank God! Morrison was here—"

"Quiet," Miss Peck said, not sure a *shh* would carry through the plywood. She got her flashlight out and held it close to the panel. Only half an inch thick, she saw. Maybe they hadn't used very long nails, after all. And the heads of the nails looked slightly rusty, not yellowish-brown, so with any luck the nails weren't coated with glue, stuck beyond pulling with her poor tools.

She put her handbag down at her feet and leaned the hoe and the pruning saw against the building. With the flashlight held very close to the plywood, she began to chip away at the wood around the nailhead in the lower right-hand corner of the panel with the blade of her knife, until she could get the screwdriver blade under it and pry—*Not too hard, Ethel, you'll break the knife.*

The nail moved outward, not more than a fingernail-thickness. She cut away some more wood.

"Miss Peck?"

"Be quiet."

Now she would have to work by touch. Flashlight in her pocket, she felt along the faintly visible edge of the plywood until she found the nail she had been working on. She rested the handle of the hoe on her shoulder and guided the edge of the blade under the top of the nailhead. Tongue jammed against her teeth, she rocked the handle of the hoe toward the wall, prying upward.

The nail grunted and yielded. Miss Peck felt her handiwork. Now she had about a quarter-inch between the nail and the surface of the board. Satisfied, she put the hoe down and drove the screwdriver blade under the corner of the plywood. She pried and felt it give. A sliver of light was her reward. She let the knife handle return and stifled a yelp as she pinched her fingers in the disappearing gap. "Celie," she said. "Turn out the light." She couldn't be sure, but she thought she heard a click after the scrambling noise had stopped.

Again she rested the handle of the hoe on her shoulder, letting the blade rest against the house. She pushed the screwdriver back under the wood and pried upward. Keeping pressure on the knife handle, she got the tip of the hoe blade into the gap and wriggled it through a couple of inches.

Now came the test. Everything else had been only a prelude. Miss Peck folded the knife and dropped it into her pocket, and leaned on the handle of the hoe. The low cry of the nails coming loose seemed terrifyingly loud in the dark.

Stop and listen. Only rain.

How was she doing? She took her flashlight out and checked the edge of the panel and nodded, satisfied. The corner nail had come out of its hole and was now holding the plywood away from the frame of the window. Miss Peck returned the flashlight to her pocket and moved the hoe upward, to pry again. A fetid odor, like the lair of some animal, came to her. Maybe released spores of dryrot, she thought. The panel was coming easily, the wood of the frame soft with age and exposure, but she heard herself beginning to pant and remembered those men in the house, maybe in the garden, listening.

She stopped again to listen for herself. Water dripped. The aspen leaves clattered. Something scurried behind her, something small, perhaps another of the mouse clan. That was all, not enough to bring on the shuddering twilight fear that sometimes gripped her. Not quite.

Again she applied the hoe to the board, with more leverage now because the space was bigger and she could slide the triangular blade against the shaft of each nail as she pried. Something wet struck her cheek and clung there. Miss Peck clutched the hoe, this time for support, and with a ragged inhalation reached up to feel her face.

Only an aspen leaf.

It's not too late, a little demon told her. She could drop the hoe, run back to her car, get in, and drive away. Call the police from safety. Her knees shook; for a moment she wondered if she would even be able to walk once she got this panel off.

With the bottom and sides loosened, she took hold of the bottom edge and levered the board up. *Working without gloves again, Ethel,* she could almost hear her mother say. Certainly she had a splinter in her left index finger.

The panel came loose. She set it aside.

"I can't climb out," Celie whispered. "I can't get my feet apart."

"Then I'll come in." Miss Peck prepared to climb into the dark opening. She stopped, shocked at the stench of the untended toilet. Poor Celie! Wrinkling her nose, she boosted herself through the window. "Where are you?"

"Here." Celie touched her shoulder. "I can see you against the window."

"Let's see this plaster." Miss Peck knelt beside Celie and flashed her light at the girl's ankles. The skin at the top of the cast looked badly chafed, despite the padding someone had put inside the plaster, and her feet, with shreds of nylon clinging to them, looked somewhat swollen. But there was a neck of plaster between the ankles. Miss Peck almost laughed with relief. "Hold on," she whispered.

She leaned back out the window and groped against the house for the pruning saw. "Do you have a chair?" she asked.

"Yes." Celie dropped to the floor and wormed her way over to the chair. "Over here."

Miss Peck followed her voice, found the chair by touch. "Sit in it," she ordered. "Now, hold still." Still working by touch, afraid that light would reflect on the trees behind the playhouse and attract the men, Miss Peck sawed at the plaster until it separated. "Can you move?" she asked.

"Oh, yes," Celie sighed, as if in luxury. She spread her feet as far apart as the chair would let them go. "It's heavy, but I can move."

"Good. Let's get going."

Both women heard the crunch of feet on gravel at the same moment. "Where's your lamp?" Miss Peck whispered.

"Right here."

For once, her snapshot memory proved to have a use. Miss Peck screwed up her eyes and recalled the line drawing in a book she'd read not long ago—"Put your feet together so the cast looks whole," she whispered hastily, "and *after* whoever that is comes into the room, turn on the lamp."

The steps turned hollow on the tiny porch. Miss Peck tiptoed, hands stretched before her, to the wall beside the door. The sound of a key being inserted into something came through the wood. Miss Peck ran her fingers down the edge of the door, found no hinges, and hastily took three steps to her left.

The door opened against her.

"Where are you?" asked the man.

"I'm here," Celie said.

"Turn the damn light on, can't you?" The man took a step toward the sound of Celie's voice. Miss Peck squeezed her eyes to slits and tensed.

The light went on.

Miss Peck pushed the door away and sprang for the man. She heard the soft *thuck* of the door shutting as she grabbed his shirt collar in both fists and rolled the fists forward, like the drawing in the judo book. The man clawed at his neck and sank to the foor gasping. In half a minute his eyes rolled up and his body went limp.

"My God, what did you do to him?"

"It's called a collar hold. I read about it a couple of weeks ago, and Clarice and I practiced grabbing each other." Miss Peck said to Celie. "I'm glad he was wearing a shirt. I never really used it before."

"Is he dead?"

"Oh, dear, I hope not." In fact, the man was already moving his hands. Miss Peck, still holding his shirt collar, rolled her fists forward again and the hands stopped moving. "We've got to tie him up—or no, first stuff something in his mouth."

"I wish I had some scissors." Celie sounded almost savage.

"In my pocket, my knife. It's got scissors in it."

Celie tottered across the small room and thrust her hand into the raincoat pocket for the red-handled knife. She found the scissors, pulled down her pantyhose, and snipped off the legs at the top of the cast. With two hard yanks she had the hose off.

"Hack off a leg, will you?"

Celie wordlessly jabbed the scissors into the pantyhose and ripped loose one of the legs. Miss Peck let go of the man's collar and snatched at the wadded nylon.

"No, put the panty part in," Celie said savagely, reaching to stuff it into the man's mouth herself. "He deserves it." Miss Peck tied the cut-off leg securely around the man's head to hold the gag in place. He was starting to stir again, his hands flopping.

"Help me roll him up in the blankets.'" As Celie scrambled on hands and knees to lay one of the blankets out straight, Miss Peck applied the collar hold once more, and the tensing body again went limp. "I hope I'm not doing any permanent damage," she worried.

"Kill him, for all I care," Celie said. "That's Baker, he's the worst one."

Miss Peck controlled her surprise. Dishwater Celie? "How many are there?" she asked.

"I've seen three."

Celie dragged on Baker's feet to line him up with the blanket as she spoke, and they rolled him up in it. He was glaring as they rolled him into the second blanket, trying to wriggle loose.

"Against the wall," Miss Peck panted. She heaved on the heavy, squirming body. Celie dropped to her knees beside her and shoved, and between them they got Baker wedged like a sack of grain against the wall. "Sit on him while I get the chair," Miss Peck gasped.

"Chair?"

"To keep him from unrolling."

Baker made an angry, inarticulate noise.

Celie giggled. Miss Peck hauled the overstuffed chair across the splintery floor and tilted it onto Baker as Celie scrambled out of the way. "I'd spit in your face," Celie told him. "But my spit's too clean for you."

Pleased, as if one of those problem students she had rooted for so long ago had finally turned in a perfect paper, Miss Peck retrieved her knife. "Let's get out of here," she said. "Turn off the light, and we'll go through the window."

Celie snapped the lamp off and headed for the lighter rectangle in the rear wall, exultant. With a boost from Miss Peck, she got her plaster-encased right ankle outside, balanced on the sill for a moment feeling for the ground, and with another boost for the other ankle found herself outdoors in the sweet, rain-washed air. Over her head the little stand of aspens provided applause, along with a shower that felt like cold, stinging needles on her back. She forgave the leaves every sound they had ever drowned out, every tap on the roof that had given her false hope, every minute they had kept her awake with their lachrymose sighing.

"That's only half of it." Miss Peck climbed out of the

window behind her. "Now we've got to get out of the grounds, and there's a fence all around them." She bent down and picked up a bulky object that had been resting against the little house; Celie recognized the handbag that had been the subject of so many office snickers and felt tears of nostalgia come into her eyes. "Oh, Miss Peck," she said.

Miss Peck misinterpreted. "Don't give up now," she said. "We've got to get through these trees and out the driveway, just as fast as we can."

Under the firs, even though the sky was again clearing, the shadows lay thick. Celie kept her hands ahead of her, wincing as she stepped on something sharp or hard with almost every move of her bare feet. Soon, not soon enough, she found herself against an iron fence of square rods set perhaps five inches apart, sharpened to spikes eight feet over her head where they were bound together with two horizontal bars. A decorative circle was set into each of the squares formed by the bars and two rods, but Celie could see no way to climb over, not even if she hadn't been weighted down as she was.

"That way," Miss Peck whispered, pointing to the left. Taking a chance, going over strange ground, but the distance was shorter and they'd avoid crossing the drive. Celie went first, walking painfully in the light that spilled from a field on the other side of the fence. Miss Peck wished again that she had brought the folding boots.

"I don't think they've missed us yet," Celie said over her shoulder. "Can we stop for a minute?"

"Shh. They will any second."

Celie stopped anyway. She pulled her half-slip down and ripped it in two and tied one half around each of her feet.

"Ah, good," Miss Peck approved. Celie continued with faster, still gingerly steps, grabbing for the fence from time to time. *Maybe it's lucky the man came,* Miss Peck thought. *Maybe that'll slow any pursuit—they won't think Celie, alone, could overpower a brute like that.* She wondered what he had done to earn such hatred. . . . She'd noticed bruises on Celie's arms, some green, some fresh, back there in the playhouse. Had he been responsible for those?

"Miss Peck. There's a space here."

One of the vertical bars had been bent aside. *Small boys,* Miss Peck thought again. The bar had been wrenched outward as well, so that a space nearly a foot wide and eighteen inches high had been made in the fence, with more space tapering above that to where the bar was still attached at the top. The broken stump stuck up wickedly from the bottom of the space, gleaming with lemon-yellow highlights in the light from the western sky, only an inch long but quite sharp. With a regretful sigh, she laid her handbag across the opening as a cushion. "Go on, be quick," she said.

Celie, despite the weight around her ankles, made a fast job of getting through the fence. Miss Peck followed, careful not to put her whole weight on the handbag, but as she had feared, the point pierced the leather. Well, better than her flesh, or Celie's, and perhaps it could be mended. She slung the bag over her shoulder and followed Celie along the fence.

"My car's just around the corner," she said, filled with a kind of astonishment that it should be so. Relief began to set in, making her tremble.

"Thistles," Celie said.

Miss Peck felt in the pocket of her jeans for the car keys and tightened her fist around them as a talisman. Ahead, beyond the end of the fence, the familiar nose of her old car glimmered as a streetlamp began to glow. It was all she could do to keep from running. She forged ahead through the wet, clinging weeds, making a path for Celie.

The last watery rays of the sun shed a golden, promising light across the field, hardly enough to cast a shadow, as she slogged toward safety.

In Minneapolis, Barbra, too, trembled with relief as she stared up at the man who had opened the closet door and saw his blue uniform.

"Well, what do you know," he said, as he squatted to rip the adhesive tape from her mouth. "One taped-up lady, exactly as advertised."

From the mantel, Miss Peck's clock slowly and sweetly chimed seven.

27 September 19

MISS PECK PULLED the keys out of her pocket and shook the ignition key loose from the bunch as they approached the car, almost laughing with relief. Never had she been so happy to have that key in her hand, not even on the day she had bought the car!

The streetlight came to full brightness as she unlocked the near side door for Celie, who half-fell into the seat and dragged her plaster after her with a joyous exclamation. Miss Peck slammed the door and rounded the front of the car as Celie leaned across the seat to pull the lock button up.

A dark figure crouching beside the car stood up, almost casually. Miss Peck stepped back. She glanced upward toward the man's face, but never got there, her glance arrested by the blue glint along the barrel of the gun in the man's right hand.

"Going somewhere, ladies?"

So, she had been seen in the garden, after all. And one of those three men had had the sense to go look for her car and crouch patiently beside it until she led Celie into his trap. But why? Why not just stop her with Celie still imprisoned? "When I saw the flashlight behind the playhouse, I knew it was only a matter of time," the man said easily. "I figured I'd let you get her out for me. Better than trying to take on those three apes."

Miss Peck recognized this type: full of himself. So pleased with his clever mischief that he never realized that the teacher was standing right behind him. Only this time, she wasn't standing right behind him, and this time, he had a gun. Her fist tightened over her keys.

"I didn't think it would be you, though," he commented.

The voice struck an echo somewhere in Miss Peck's mind. Something to do with Sharmille. And thinking of Sharmille, she suddenly matched this lean, dark man wearing an Irish tweed cap pulled low on his forehead with a snapshot in her mind. "It's Mr. Johnson, isn't it?" she said.

He grinned, the streetlight casting a sardonic shadow across his face as his cheeks lifted. "Not really. But you must have known that as soon as you saw that paper, right? One I resurrected from my junior year at the U. It got a C, as it happens."

"I'm not surprised."

"I bet that bomb surprised you, though, didn't it?"

"Somewhat," Miss Peck agreed. She felt sweat trickling down her sides, although she was still chilly. "Was that meant for me, or for Celie?"

"Celie? Oh, Alexa. No, it was meant for Alexa. I've been wondering what went wrong. It seemed foolproof to me, since she'd be the one working back there."

Miss Peck suppressed a fit of giggles. Johnson seemed to be playing a part in a late night movie, just as she was playing a part in a novel. It was there in his lounging stance, the pulled-down hat. *Absurd!* But what had he said? The bomb seemed foolproof . . . "Did it?" Miss Peck said. If she could keep him thinking about that, maybe his curiosity would keep him from shooting and she could come up with something . . . but the judo book hadn't dealt with armed opponents.

A large object hove into view above the crest of the hill behind Mr. Johnson, whatever his name really was. Miss Peck averted her eyes, not sure she believed what she thought she had seen.

"I guess I ought to be glad it didn't get the wrong person," continued Johnson, still in his Cagney role. "Es-

208

pecially since you're making things so easy for me now. Can't argue with fate." Johnson smirked—*no, Frazier, this must be Devin Frazier!* Then who was the other man, the one who had followed her to the North Shore? Really and simply a private eye, hired to find Celie?

The large object catfooted closer. Miss Peck closed her eyes. She did not believe this. She did not for one moment believe any of it. But when she opened her eyes, Frazier-Johnson still held the gun on her, the wind still moaned in the fir trees, the large object had her finger to her lips and her weapon at the ready, and in the car beside her Celie cringed.

"You can get in the car, now," Frazier said. He had the nonchalant manner and easy good looks of one of Clarice's heroes. One could almost see him doffing a broad feathered hat to a maiden who watched with palpitating heart. "We'll go up to the main house, and I'll get rid of those three," he said, bluntly dispelling the illusion, "and then you two—or maybe you two first, the noise will bring them out where I can get at them. Yes, that's better." He nodded. "That's what we'll do."

Miss Peck stood very still with her hand on the car door. The mound of tweed behind Frazier pushed her weapon into his back. "Drop it," barked Clarice.

Even in the blue light of the streetlight Miss Peck could see the color drain from Frazier's face. The gun clumped onto the dirt at his feet.

"Get the gun, Ethel," Clarice said. She pressed the ferrule of the walking stick into Frazier's back. Miss Peck approached cautiously.

"Have him back up a little, will you?"

"You heard her," Clarice said. She moved slightly backward. Miss Peck crouched and reached for the gun.

Frazier kicked wildly at her hand and whirled toward Clarice. A single syllable of laughter burst from him. Clarice thrust the walking stick between his legs at his first running step, and he sprawled onto the pavement. Miss Peck got the gun into her hand and shakily stood up. The thing was appallingly heavy; she wondered how all those people on television held their guns so steady.

A flash of a blonde woman holding a gun in both hands (how, exactly?) went through her mind. Miss Peck put her left hand out and covered her right with it, the gun aimed at the man on the ground.

"Dear me," Clarice said, chuckling. "That's not a very sensible place to lie down, young man. Suppose a car came over the hill? There'd hardly be time to stop before you were run over."

"Is that what you're going to do to me?" Frazier asked.

"Not me. I'm not the violent type. Why don't you get up? Slowly, of course."

Frazier got to his knees and looked from one woman to the other. Then he got up and poked at the mud on his trousers and put his hands in the air. "Oh, I remember," Clarice said. "Now's where you get him to put his hands on the roof of the car and feel him down for another weapon."

"Me?" Miss Peck squeaked.

"One of us. I will, if you like." Frazier looked again from one woman to the other and put his hands on the roof of the car.

"Where are your car keys?" Clarice asked.

"I must have dropped them." Sure enough, the keys lay in the dirt beside the car, where she had been standing when Clarice came over the hill.

"Oh, really, Ethel," Clarice said, as she had when they were small girls playing with sticks that floated in the gutter after a rain, and Ethel's ill-chosen "boat" capsized. She made a circle around Miss Peck and picked up the car keys. She continued the circle around the nose of the car, saw what she was about to do as Frazier tensed, and retraced her steps. "Don't let me get in your line of fire," she warned.

Miss Peck stepped sideways until she was behind the man and the gun pointed diagonally backward through the car. She couldn't see Celie. Nor could Frazier see her. Just as well. Her hands were shaking badly, and the gun showed it.

Clarice unlocked the trunk. "Climb in," she said to Frazier, much as she might have said, "More coffee?"

Frazier straightened up and started slowly toward the rear of the car, keeping a careful eye on Clarice. She raised the walking stick as he drew closer.

"There's a good boy," she said.

He whirled and ran. The walking stick flashed down on air. Before she had thought about it, Miss Peck's fists tightened around the swinging gun and the gun spat fire at the running man, a horrible burnt smell pained her nose and the gun spat flame straight up as she clutched it again and the man fell writhing on the road with a hoarse cry.

Only his leg. Thank God! It was only his leg.

This time Clarice held the gun, and Miss Peck put a pressure bandage on the wound with Frazier's torn-up shirt. She bound his wrists behind him with what was left of the adhesive tape from her handbag. She held the gun on him again while Clarice prodded him into the trunk of her car and slammed the lid. Somehow they got Celie unstuck from under the dashboard and, with Celie gulping and gasping with laughter, drove (Miss Peck still trembling, Clarice somewhat annoyed with Celie) to the nearest house and called the police.

This time they came, with sirens.

"Oh, no," Miss Peck cried. "I forgot those other three in the house!"

"They'll have to get out the way you did, if they're going," Clarice announced casually. "I chained the gate."

28 September 19

THE HOUSEHOLDER, WHO had heard enough of their excited chatter to figure the situation out, decided reinforcements were necessary. He put in a call and two more police cars intercepted the kidnappers just as Longdel finished sawing through Clarice's expensive bike lock.

"How on earth did you show up just then?" Miss Peck asked, an hour later.

"I drove up to Duluth as soon as Sharmille showed me that letter." Clarice sat back and looked around, as if she couldn't quite believe that she could be sitting here, waiting in a small room to tell her story to the authorities. "My word, was that only this afternoon? You can't imagine how hard you are to find, Ethel! I—" Clarice suddenly looked quite shy. "Well, I was afraid that this time I'd pushed you into something really dangerous, and I wanted to stop you if I could. I looked all over, and I never did find where you're staying, and I couldn't remember the name of the lawyer you've been talking to up here, and the girls were gone from your office before I thought of calling there. And do you know, after all this time, I don't know their last names?"

"What do you mean, *this time* you pushed me into something dangerous?"

Clarice flushed, a mottled red that surprised Miss Peck. "Well, you know, I don't think you'd have come running up here if I hadn't needled you about it, would you?"

"Oh, I don't know," Miss Peck said. "I might've."

"Well, I *thought* I might have had something to do with

it," Clarice continued, obviously nettled, "so I decided I'd take responsibility for it. And you can't deny that it's a good thing I did, after all these years of talking you into things I don't quite dare myself."

Celie came unsteadily into the room at that moment and sat down in one of the two empty chairs. "Hi," she said. Her ankles were red and scraped, but she bent over and scratched again, with both hands. "I don't think they'll ever stop itching," she replied to Miss Peck's glance. "Oh, but you can't imagine how good it feels to be able to scratch!"

Her feet were in the kind of paper slippers hospitals give their patients. She glanced down at them and tucked her feet under the chair. "I'm sorry I laughed at you," she said, her mouth twitching. "But if you could have seen it the way I did—Miss Klenk sneaking up like the mountain deciding to land on Mohammed after all, but so small in the mirror on the back of the sun visor—and the way she held that stick . . ." Celie stopped speaking. After a moment she shut her mouth tightly.

"Yes, I can imagine," Clarice said with a brief titter. She pressed her lips together and smiled oddly. "Well, but I was just telling Ethel *how* I happened to become the cavalry coming over the hill, or a murderous mountain, or whatever."

"Oh, please go on!" Celie gasped.

"Well. At any rate, I had the address of that house, thanks to the note. It took me a long time to find that, too, after I'd given up trying to find you, Ethel. I stopped at three different gas stations before I found one that knew the area. Person, of course, not a pump. And then, when I drove by, what did I see but your car, and that man parked behind it peering through the windows. *Oh-oh,* I said to myself. *What's this?* So when I got out of sight around the next curve I turned around in somebody's driveway and came back. I didn't think he'd seen me, you see, because it was just simply pouring down rain and he was so interested in your car."

"Mmm," Miss Peck said, somewhat ruefully.

"And what did I see when I got going back the other way? Houses are a little scarce along there, you know, it took me the devil of a time to *find* a driveway, and then I'm not too good at tight turns—I saw that man standing against the fence near your car, and his own car was gone!" Clarice's hazel eyes widened. "I couldn't imagine what he'd done with it!" She stopped and looked at each of them with exaggerated inquiry.

"What had he done with his car?" Miss Peck supplied, a little jealous of the ease with which Clarice had dropped back into her usual self when Celie appeared.

"He'd moved it."

"Well, of course," said Celie, not quite as practiced at listening to Clarice as was her friend. "But where?"

"Oh, just back down the road a couple of hundred yards. But it was hidden by the top of the hill, you see. The gate comes out almost at the crest of the hill, and then he was parked down near the bottom, and . . ."

"Yes, I think I see," Miss Peck said, taking a leaf from Celie's book and interrupting. "But how did you time your appearance so well?"

"Well, I waited." Clarice gave her friend an indulgent look, as if this were the part she had expected her to figure out for herself. "I parked my car behind his, and I went far enough up the hill that I could just see him, and I stood against the fence where those trees are and I just waited. Got good and wet, too, even with my nice cape," she added, rather indignantly.

Celie, who had been scratching her ankles with the edges of the paper slippers, went back to using her fingernails. "I can't wait to get a bath and clean clothes," she said.

"You could sound more impressed," Clarice complained. "I just saved your life."

"That's true," Celie said. "And I do thank you. But so did Miss Peck—she's the one who actually got me out of that awful place. And so did I, for that matter," she added, almost wonderingly. "I sent the note."

"How did you do that?" Clarice asked. "I've been thinking and thinking, ever since I saw that fence, and I can't imagine how you got a note out. A cleaning lady?"

Celie closed her eyes and shook her head, as if the thought were beyond bearing. *And perhaps it is,* Miss Peck mused. "Some kids came to the playhouse, I think it was Friday night, to do some dope," Celie explained. "I passed it under the door to them." She sighed and shuddered. "I had no idea whether they'd send it on, or call the cops, or just crumple it up and throw it away where one of *them* could get it. I've been scared ever since."

"Well," Miss Peck said. "They did pass it on, and I'm glad it's over."

"Ethel," Clarice said with an apologetic little simper. "You know, I've been wondering. Which of us do you suppose is Lord Peter, and which Bunter in this affair?" She raised her chin expectantly, clearly expecting to be nominated Lord Peter.

"Clarice, I'm sorry." Miss Peck closed her eyes, suddenly too weary to keep them open. "I'm afraid that one of us is Ethel, and the other Clarice."

"None of the Cockburn '96, then," Clarice remarked. "That's all right, I don't care for port anyway, and I always thought those two were a little, um, barmy on the subject."

"What on earth are you talking about?" asked Celie.

"Oh, just some mystery novels we've both read," Miss Peck explained.

"Oh." Celie hesitated. "Miss Peck, you know those men thought I was an heiress!"

"I know. They might be right. Oh, that reminds me." Miss Peck felt under her chair for her handbag, pulled it onto her lap and opened the zippered compartment.

"Here's your ring. You left it in the ladies' room again. Really, Celie, you ought to take better care of it."

"Lovely thing," Clarice put in.

Celie took the ring with an odd little laugh and put it on her finger. "It's loose," she said. "I must have lost some weight."

"Do you good," Clarice remarked as a policeman opened the door of the room and asked Miss Peck to step out.

29 September 20

"SO IT ISN'T A fortune, after all."

The girl looks pale and tired, Goodenough thought. Understandable. She'd been through quite an ordeal, an ordeal he could never have foreseen, and he was truly sorry that so much of Colin Frazier's estate had been offset by debts. It seemed unfair, especially since most of the loans had been taken out to bail Devin out of one scrape or another. The final irony was that the airplane Colin had bought for his son, the little Beechcraft that had figured so importantly in his death, was about to be repossessed.

"You'll want to have an accountant, or an attorney, go over all of these figures," Goodenough continued. "I'm sure they're accurate, but you do want to protect your own interests; in fact, the court will insist upon it."

"How much did you say, again?" the girl asked. If he looked, yes, he could see little Alexa in those features, thin as they were. She'd been baby-plump when he'd last seen her, and blonder.

Even more, he could see Mary: a little lightener in the hair, a little color in the cheeks, ten more pounds on her frame and other than the eyes, not Mary's lively, mischievous blue, Alexa would look very, very much like her mother . . . with perhaps a hint of her father's nose. He was pleased that she had found herself a skill, unwilling to inquire about the life he knew she must have led as a child. The detective's report was in his desk. He hadn't looked at it and didn't plan to.

How much, she'd asked. He stopped stroking his nose

with a jerk and said, "Er, roughly thirty-five thousand dollars."

"That sounds like a lot to me," Alexa—Celie, she called herself—said.

"It isn't, not in these days, but with careful investment . . ." Goodenough shook off his ingrained caution. "And there will probably be another ten thousand as well."

"How is that?" asked the older woman, the Miss Peck he'd spoken to last weekend. Remarkable lady. A sensible influence on the girl, he hoped.

"I shouldn't be saying this." Goodenough clasped his hands in front of them and looked at them. "Please don't let it go any further than this office, at least until official action is taken. I've found some evidence—in fact, the county attorney thinks enough evidence for a conviction—that young Devin murdered his father."

"Good heavens," Miss Peck remarked. Celie gasped.

"That's where I was yesterday afternoon, Miss Peck," the lawyer said. "Presenting what I'd found to the county attorney. He'd have sworn out a warrant for Devin's arrest even without, er, last evening's fracas."

"But where does the ten thousand come in?" Miss Peck wanted to know.

Goodenough smiled his approval. Businesslike. "The effect of homicide, under Minnesota law, is that the estate of the decedent is to be distributed as if the murderer had predeceased him. Since you, er, Celie, are the only other relative, and the residue of the estate was to come to you in any case, I believe you will get what was left to Devin. That's ten thousand dollars. Of course, he'll have to be convicted of the murder, first, and that may take some time."

"What sort of evidence did you find?" asked Miss Peck.

Goodenough matched the tips of his fingers and leaned back in his swivel chair. He stared out at the yellow elm leaves outside the window, unaware of the muscle jumping against his jaw. As he watched, a breeze fondled the slender branches and several of the leaves fell. He sighed. Well, Celie surely couldn't testify, and Miss Peck, living in Minneapolis, wouldn't be a venireman unless the trial was moved. . . .

"Again, please don't let this leave this office," he decided. "Can I trust you? Devin's a gambler, among many other things. He was badly in debt. His father had already paid many of his gambling debts and refused to pay more. Devin's connections were, er, unsavory, and he was in serious trouble. He owed that money to the wrong people."

"The Mafia?" Celie interrupted. Goodenough gazed at her. Did that perhaps show a strain of romanticism that might loosen her tongue? Well, he was committed, now.

"Let's just say, impatient people," he temporized. "I suspect he's only been able to put them off this long by lying about his inheritance. Or perhaps it never occurred to him that a man nearly ninety years old might be living off his capital. And I know he thought that if his father died, he would get virtually the entire estate . . . then, too, I don't think he realized that his father had made some bad investments, that the worth of his stocks in the mining industry had dropped so much, or that he had remortgaged the house in order to help pay his son's gambling debts and leave himself enough to keep his servants in employ."

Miss Peck's glance slid from his own face to Alexa's and back. Goodenough dropped his chin onto his fingers and lowered his eyes. "You were named for Colin Frazier's mother, did you know that?" he asked the girl. "That's her ring you're wearing. Her maiden name was Cecil. That's where the Cecilia comes from."

The girl examined the ring with a quick, enchanting smile like her mother's. "My grandmother's ring?"

"Alexandra Cecil Frazier's, yes." Goodenough pressed his lips tightly together and glanced at Miss Peck, but the woman was looking at the ring and nodding slightly. Alexa must have shown her the inscription; she must have wondered about it. Goodenough remembered the day Colin had given the ring to Mary, with her daughter's birthday engraved beside his mother's initials. He closed his eyes briefly and went on with his story.

"Devin called his father the afternoon before he died and told him he planned to have the old man declared incompetent and himself named as his guardian. Unfortunately, I wasn't in the office that day. Devin picked his time carefully. You see," he said in sudden appeal to Miss Peck, a woman close to his own age and possibly therefore able to understand, "that's what I've been forgetting all this time. All those years I was his father's lawyer—Devin knows me at least as well as I know him, maybe better. He knew I wouldn't miss the first Saturday of the fishing season, that I'd take that Friday off. And one—one tends to forget, when one's known someone since childhood, that they've grown up, especially when one hasn't seen very much of him. . . ."

Miss Peck, to his relief, nodded placidly.

"So, Colin couldn't get in touch with me. There's no phone at the cabin. He made a note to himself to ask me if such a thing were possible, when he was only a little forgetful, but I didn't find it among his papers until just a few days ago. And then, as he sometimes did when he was upset, he sent Jack Carrera, the man who lived with him, to get him some bourbon.

"Devin called again the next afternoon, to say he'd arranged to go to court. He'd done nothing of the kind. What he had arranged was for someone, I think the woman he lives with, to place a collect call to his father's office number on the night he was killed. The office was downstairs in the house, I should explain." Goodenough stopped and looked from one woman to the other. Both nodded.

"Go on," said the girl.

"Devin had been making similar calls, late at night after

his father was in bed, for several days. He could count on his father to be angry, especially after the call earlier that afternoon, and he hoped the old man would have been drinking. As he had been." Goodenough sighed. "The one sure thing was that Colin would come boiling down the stairs to the office to give him a piece of his mind.

"But Devin wasn't in Cleveland. He'd flown up here in that airplane his father bought him—the N number is on record at an airport near here as having landed that afternoon and taken off the next morning, and he actually filed a flight plan in Cleveland—and he went to the house and let himself in. Then he just waited for the call. When it came, he flipped off the upstairs hall lights and, as his father passed him in the dark, he hit his head with a pipe from behind and sent him flying down those stone stairs."

Goodenough stopped and gripped one hand with the other. How complex life was!

"The old man cracked his head on half the steps on his way down and on the flagging in the hall. And to finish him off, Devin waited until old Jack Carrera, the companion, ran into the kitchen for help. Then he slipped down the stairs and hit him again with the pipe. He's told us all about it, though he'll change his mind when he gets a good defense attorney. We found the pipe in the stables yesterday afternoon and showed it to him this morning. It's nice to know Devin's capable of making mistakes."

"Stables," the girl murmured.

"Then Devin just let himself out, went back to the airport, waited until just before dawn and took off—in a late snowstorm, by the way, quite illegally. He's not licensed to fly by instruments."

The girl, he couldn't help but think of her as Alexa, shuddered. "You can prove all this?" she asked.

"Pretty nearly. What evidence I haven't found, the prosecutor's office will. No way to check poor Colin's body, though. Devin insisted that it be cremated and the ashes scattered over Lake Superior." Goodenough smiled, a wry smile. "I thought he arranged that out of sentiment, because his father loved the lake. He puts on a good act, does Devin."

"And then he hired those three men to kidnap Celie?" Miss Peck asked.

"Oh, no. Devin didn't hire anyone, except a private detective, and he spun the poor man a tale about finding a sister he'd been separated from by adoption. As I understand it, those three enterprising gentlemen planned all that on their own. The papers had a big write-up on Colin Frazier's will last spring, and once it was probated they could check the terms themselves. They planned to use Alexa as a lever to pry some money out of Devin for keeping her until the time limit was up, and I'm afraid the detective they hired was more efficient about finding her than mine, or Devin's.

"Devin, of course, decided to string them along until he found out where they were holding her and then go kill her. The police found pictures of you—er, Celie—in the hotel room where he's been staying. They showed the walls of that place where you were kept. There was the edge of a covered window in one of them, a diamond-paned window. All he had to do was call realtors until he found one who had rented a house with outbuildings to several men." He shrugged sadly. "I'm afraid your half brother isn't a very pleasant man, my dear."

Her grey-blue eyes were steady. "I think I had that figured out for myself," she said.

"You know, he also set the bomb," Miss Peck said.

"Bomb?"

"That destroyed the storage room where Celie would have been working, if those men hadn't kidnapped her."

Goodenough pressed his palms to his desk. The jolting in his chest slowed and steadied. He drew a deep breath. "I hadn't realized the explosion was in your office!" he said.

"I thought, just in the building . . . but yes, I see. Devin worked for a construction company once, I know, and he'd know about explosives. But what a fortunate coincidence!"

"Not really," Miss Peck said. "I was moving the typing service to another building. Devin Frazier simply seized a chance that presented itself to him, and the other men had their timing advanced by the move, I think. I remember talking to someone who wanted to know an unusual amount of detail about the service before bringing us anything, just the day before. That might have been one of them."

"I suppose it will all come out in the trial," Goodenough said.

"What about the other detective?"

More solid ground here. "The dark-haired one was Devin's. I imagine he followed you here from the Twin Cities, hoping you'd lead him to Alexa. The blond one"— he sighed—"the blond one I have to admit was my own. He's done good work for me before, but this time he was out of his depth. A lot of the success of good investigation depends on having the right contacts, you know, and he took quite a while to develop them. And I understand that he went yesterday to your house to talk to you, and when he found you weren't home he decided to search the house. He pleads desperation, but it's inexcusable. He was surprised by an employee of yours when she arrived to feed the cat."

"Melange," Miss Peck said, inexplicably, to the girl.

"I must apologize. I never authorized such an intrusion, please believe me. The young woman is all right, however. He tied her up and called the police to free her once he had escaped the situation. Yesterday evening he called her at home and found she was safe."

"That must have been Barb," Celie said.

Miss Peck chuckled. "Yes."

"Figures. Nobody'd try to tie up Sharmille and get away with it."

Goodenough decided not to ask for clarification. "So, there we have it," he said. "My detective was slow, partially my own fault, I'm afraid. Or you would have been spared all this." He slapped the arms of his chair lightly, anxious to end this trying interview. "Anything more I can do for you before you go home? You'll be hearing from me of course, Alex—er, Celie. We have to compare the finger-prints we took this morning, and the photos of the birth-mark and your ears, and so on, but I'm satisfied. I don't think there will be any trouble there."

"One thing. Is this money mine to do what I want with?"

"Of course! After the taxes are paid, that is."

"Then I think part of it should buy a word processor for Miss Peck. She's—she's done so much for me, I want to do something for her."

Miss Peck blinked. "Good heavens, Celie, that's an expensive item," she said.

"Well, I am going to need to keep my job, and that looks to me like the way to do it," Celie replied.

"Very realistic of you," Goodenough approved, not quite comprehending what she meant. "Now, if you ladies will excuse me, I have a great deal of work to catch up on." He got up and extended his right hand to each of them across the desk, went around it, and held the door open for them with his face worked into a polite smile.

Miss Peck nodded as she passed through the door, a polite smile of her own on her lips and frank curiosity in her eyes. He averted her gaze. Alexa, whose grey linen dress, now that she stood up, seemed to have been made for Miss Peck rather than herself, echoed the smile with a little more warmth and took his hand again and squeezed it.

Goodenough watched her cross the outer office in the wake of her employer. The same soft wave to her hair as Mary had had, though the color was darker; the same tilt to her head; the same small sway in her step; the same mysterious, appealing sense that her thoughts weren't quite bounded by her skull, that she could somehow live in two realms at once—in Mary's case, he feared, a sign of diminished intelligence, but apparently not in her daughter's. A pretty girl. Almost, his palms remembered the silken feel of those hips under his stroke; almost, his mouth ached again with that long-ago hunger.

"She seems like a nice girl, doesn't she?" Betty Shannon remarked complacently. "I'm so glad."

"What? Oh, yes, she does." Goodenough turned and went back into his private office and shut the door and leaned against it with his eyes closed. He felt in his pocket for the vial of nitroglycerine tablets, sure that with his heart so squeezed and his eyes so tearless the pain must soon come.

It was, of course, still just barely possible, despite that nose and those familiar cloudy blue eyes, that Alexa really was Colin Frazier's daughter. But if she wasn't, well, he'd done his craven best to make it up to her.

If you have enjoyed this book and would like to receive details of other Walker mystery titles, please write to:

Mystery Editor
Walker and Company
720 Fifth Avenue
New York, NY 10019